Ridley's Revenge

A Purbeck Adventure

by
Raymond G Sampson

ISBN: 978-1-326-53100-3

PublishNation
www.publishnation.co.uk

I dedicate this book

to

my darling daughter Polly
who not only first suggested I should write a book
but also encouraged me regularly, read the drafts
and helped me with the mysteries of the computer
as well as putting up with me on a daily basis
enduring my highs and lows throughout.

CHAPTER 1

To Ridley, Ayala was the most beautiful woman he had ever seen, although she did not appear so now as he comforted her. His young Indian wife, having been violently seasick, was ashen faced and full of dread. The sickness seemed to have taken all her strength, leaving her limp in his arms. Now, looking down into her vulnerable eyes, he was overwhelmed by his love and a powerful protective instinct which led him to tighten his grip on her shoulder.

The couple were huddled together on a broad bunk in the little cabin they were sharing on this voyage from Egypt. Most of their luggage, some pieces of rather fine furniture and carpets purchased on their travels, were stored in the hold below decks. Their toiletries and changes of clothing were in a splendid military chest which, along with a small table, took up much of the remaining space in the cabin. That meant they were unable to do anything other than sit in these quarters, either on the bunk or on the chest, so that they had spent most of the voyage on deck, taking their meals at the captain's table.

Calm seas, glorious sunshine and balmy starlit evenings had accompanied them all the way, making it a memorable and romantic end to a journey that had started four months previously in India. Then they reached Biscay, where the weather deteriorated as the small, three-masted cargo ship battled its way from the Atlantic up into the English Channel.

Finally it became so bad that the captain ordered them to stay below decks until the storm abated. They had been cooped up for hours and the howling wind and shuddering of the ship told Ridley that the storm was far from over; if anything, it was getting worse.

'You'd be better off lying down,' Ridley said and, without waiting for a reply, he gently lifted Ayala's feet onto the bunk. She said nothing, simply acquiescing to his decision, and with a slight moan lay back and shut her eyes. There was vomit on the shoulder of her dress which he tried to wipe away with a handkerchief but it just seemed to spread the stain.

At that moment the ship lurched, falling away from a large wave, throwing Ridley across the cabin into the luggage chest which he grabbed for stability. With the next roll of the ship, he let go and allowed himself to be thrown back to the bunk. He pushed his hand down between the mattress and the bunk and hung on for a moment or two, before turning gingerly and lowering himself to sit by Ayala's feet.

What have I done? He thought in panic. Have I allowed my love to cloud my judgement? Have I brought her all this way for it to end this night – lost at sea?

They had sailed from India in a fine East Indiaman following Ridley's early retirement from his position as a Major in the company's private army. Had they stayed on that ship they would have been in Yorkshire by now, as indeed were most of their possessions which had remained aboard to be sent on to their new home to await their arrival. Instead they had chosen to disembark at Aden, sail up the Red Sea in a local sailing dhow as far as Djibouti and then travel with a succession of camel caravans up through Egypt to Alexandria. There they had resumed their journey home on this cargo ship – the *Golden Nile*.

It had been an eventful trip, full of pitfalls and delays, communicating with locals to explain their plans and organise their travel arrangements. Then there was the tortuous haggling over the price every time they changed transport. They found that they had to go through this exercise several times during the course of their journey. Their Arab guides having decided that the undertaking was more arduous, or more dangerous than they first supposed and argued at length to renegotiate the price.

When this happened, everything came to a halt. The guides erected a shelter and Ridley and the leading Arab sat down to barter. Sometimes all the luggage was unloaded, as if to impress the party that it was going no further until a new charge was agreed. After a while Ridley decided that this must be a national custom and ceased to be exasperated by it, simply resigning himself to the fact that the process had to be endured. Having served for some time in India, he was quite used to haggling over a price and soon got the measure of his opponents. He became quite astute in deciding how far he needed to go to get the company up and moving again.

Despite these travails, it had been a marvellous adventure and the magnificence of the country and its fabulous ancient monuments had made it the experience of a lifetime.

Now Ridley wondered if it had been such a good idea after all. What good was such an experience if this small cargo vessel were to fail and take them to the bottom of the sea? Then he found himself thinking of the magic of it all, the wonderful joy he had shared with Ayala and how every night they had settled down in their tent in each other's arms, almost hurting with love. A love that had intensified each day, although it seemed impossible it could do so.

No, he thought, I would not have missed that for anything. Nor can I believe it will end here. We will survive this storm, of that I am sure.

Having reached this conclusion he now felt restless, as if he must do something to make sure they would prevail. He turned to Ayala and said, 'I'm going on top to see if I can be of any help.'

Ayala opened her eyes and replied nervously in a faint whisper. 'All right, but be careful, Jack. You are no sailor.' Then she closed her eyes again.

Ridley reached under the bunk for a pair of black riding boots and, sitting on the bunk, he pulled them on. He was wearing a pair of dark-brown breeches, white stockings and an open neck white shirt. He put on a red army coat, now devoid of any insignia, which was lying on the bed. He stood up and, hanging on to the bunk, leant over and kissed his wife on the forehead. Timing the moment between rolls, he took down a canvas raincoat from a peg by the cabin door, put it on and made his way out of the cabin.

The door opened onto the starboard side of the main deck. Next to it was a wooden ladder leading up to the quarterdeck where Captain Erasmus Jenkins was standing behind a sailor who was struggling with the tiller.

Ridley looked down the ship but it was dark and thunderous and the rain was lashing down fiercely, so that he could make little sense of what he saw.

3

He discerned a couple of deckhands who were making their way forward, clutching on to any handhold they could find as they went, though why and where they were going he could not say. Then he saw another man pulling on some rope by the main mast. Ridley presumed this man was tightening one of the few sails the ship was wearing.

Coming out further onto the deck, he pulled the door shut then turned and grabbed hold of the ladder, which he proceeded to climb. The ship was pitching violently and he struggled to maintain his grip as he went up, but eventually he reached the quarterdeck and stood there at the top of the ladder, holding on to the railings that surrounded this deck.

As Ayala had said, Ridley was no sailor. He had no understanding of the *Golden Nile'*s condition, but he could feel the huge rollers as they roared in on the ship's port side. Each one caused her to roll, lift and pitch, while the gale force wind made her heel over to starboard. Just as it seemed she must roll over completely, she pulled back but never far enough to lean into the wind before the next roller and the wind took hold again.

A cacophony of sounds assaulted him as he stood there: the shrieking of the wind in the close-reefed top sails; the groaning of the woodwork as it reacted to the strains upon it, and the crashing of the waves as they pounded the ship before passing beneath her. Each time they did so, he felt the pressure of the deck on his feet pushing up through his knees as the ship first rose then fell. It took all his strength to hang on to the rail and remain upright.

Jenkins was of good Welsh stock and the epitome of a ship's captain. He was short and stocky, with greying hair and a full, close-cropped beard that had not begun to grey. It was, in fact, a strawberry-blond colour. He had a weather-beaten face and an easy-going but determined manner that would normally fill one with confidence as to his seagoing capabilities.

Now, however, Ridley saw that the captain had a very grave face and was clearly highly alarmed by the situation. Wearing a fawn, waterproof coat over his traditional captain's uniform, he was struggling to maintain his position by hanging on to a rope lifeline slung across the deck. He looked continually up at the rigging, muttering to himself before laying his head to one side as if to listen to every creaking sound the ship made.

At that moment the captain noticed Ridley and, not recognising him at first, shouted, 'What the blazes are you doing there, man? Get to your post. If you haven't got one, you should be helping with the pumps. We're shipping far too much water.'

'It's me – John Ridley,' was the shouted reply. 'Can I help?'

'Good God, man, you can't do anything here,' the exasperated captain said. 'This is a desperate situation and no place for a landsman. You'd be best employed below, comforting that wife of yours. If it comes to it, she'll need your help to get into the boats.'

Ridley was appalled; this must indeed be a desperate situation for the captain to talk of abandoning ship. My God, he thought. If it's this terrible in a three-masted ship, what on earth would it be like in a small rowing boat?

He started to navigate his way back down the ladder when a voice rang out through the storm. 'Light showing hard o' port.'

'Light to the port, you say?' Captain Jenkins yelled up into the rigging. 'What kind of light? Can you tell? How far off?'

'Seems to be flickering strongly, sir. I'd say it was a big fire, a beacon most likely.' This last was shouted with excitement. 'Hard to say how far, sir, but it's a good way off, I reckon.'

The captain, who was staring out to the port side, now called to the man at the tiller. 'I can't make anything out. Can you, Mr Isles?'

'No, sir,' the man replied. 'Though wait ... I think … yes, there sir, I see it.' He thrust out an arm, pointing slightly forward of amidships.

'Now I see it,' said Jenkins. 'Come around to it, Mr Isles.'

The man turned the tiller hard down and the ship seemed to shudder as it changed direction, then it went down into a trough before rearing up again.

Ridley, who had remained clutching the rail since the first shout, thought the ship had picked up pace with this change of direction but he didn't know if this was his imagination being driven by hope that had sprung from this unexpected light. He stared out hard into the dark but could see nothing.

Not so the captain, whose seaman's eyes were better used to such conditions. 'Yes,' he said, speaking to himself rather than anyone else. 'It's a beacon for sure. Though it's strange that it should be there. It must be the Star Point light, although we should have made that long before now. Perhaps they have a light on Portland Bill. It's got to be one or the other. We must have been making harder weather of it than I thought.'

Without stars, it was impossible for the captain to tell their exact position or what progress they had made. For all he knew, with the amount of sea they had shipped they could just be treading water.

'Now we've got that beacon to guide us, we can take her in nearer to the coast,' the captain called to the man on the tiller. 'If that is Star Point, as it must be, then we can pull into Start Bay. There should be protected waters there. We can hug the coast round to Lyme Bay and hold up there till the storm blows out. If it's Portland, we might find a bit of respite in Weymouth Bay. Set a course nor'-nor'-east, Mr Isles.'

'Nor'-nor'-east it is, Captain.'

So it was that, in the late summer of 1802, the *Golden Nile* ploughed forward towards the southwest coast of England, rising and falling in the malign sea but with hope of sanctuary ahead.

CHAPTER 2

Ayala had not changed position while Ridley was away but now, as he returned, she lifted herself into a sitting position and looked expectantly at her husband. 'How is it looking?' she asked. 'Is there any sign of this storm easing?'

'None, I'm afraid. But there is good news. The lookout has spotted a beacon and Captain Jenkins seems to know where we are. He reckons that by steering towards it we will find some protection and calmer waters. I don't know how long it will be before we feel the difference, though. So just stay there and don't worry.' Ridley decided not to say anything about the captain's concerns now that there was some hope but, as a precaution, he decided to get Ayala to put her coat on, in case they had to leave suddenly. 'You look pale, darling, and you're shivering. Let's get your coat around you to warm you up.'

At that moment, despite the noise of the raging storm, Ridley heard an anguished cry from above: 'White water ahead,' then, 'It's rocks, we're right upon them, rocks ... rocks...'

A great commotion started up and men could be heard running about and shouting commands. With that, the cabin door burst open and one of the crew staggered in. 'Captain says you're to come aloft at once. We must try to get into the boats. The ship is doomed!'

As he said this, the sailor grasped Ayala by the arm and pulled her roughly out of bed. With Ridley on her other side, the three struggled out of the cabin and made their way along the main deck. Some men were hauling on ropes, lifting one of the small ship's boats up and over the side.

'Hold it,' the man with Ridley shouted. 'Get the woman into the boat. She won't make any difference and it'll be easier for her than when it's in the water.' With that, he and Ridley bundled Ayala into the boat.

That was when the ship struck the rocks; there was a terrible crashing sound then a horrendous screeching as the rocks tore through the bottom of the craft.

7

The initial blow was tumultuous and threw Ridley and the sailors to the deck. The sailors who were hauling on the ropes of the ship's boat hung on to these to save themselves from the worst of it but Ridley, and the seaman who was helping him, had no such lifeline and they were sent tumbling and sliding. Ridley's fall came to a fearful end as he crashed into the wall of the cabin he had recently vacated. The seaman was not so lucky as he was thrown clear overboard.

Pandemonium broke out as the crew of the *Golden Nile* struggled in vain to recover from the impact. The ship had been driven up onto the rocks and was now at an angle pointing up to the sky, making it impossible for them to get to the second of the two small boats. Of the boat with Ayala, there was no sign and Ridley guessed that it had fallen into the sea.

Incredibly, the captain now appeared at Ridley's side and shouted at him, 'You must get over the side. The boat is in the water with your wife in it. We need to man it and move off from the wreck as fast as we can. Can you make it?'

'Yes,' said Ridley and hauled himself to his feet. He was just about to lurch forward when a huge wave broke over the ship, throwing him to the centre of the deck then washing him crazily back until he crashed into the side decking. This was accompanied by another great rendering as the ship was forced further onto the rocks and its bottom was gashed some more.

Ridley found himself entangled in a stray rope that had somehow come loose and he floundered around trying to rid himself of this encumbrance. No sooner had he succeeded than another wave broke over him. This time he hung on to the side decking to save himself from being thrown forward, which meant that he was engulfed in water. It seemed an age before the sea retreated and he could gasp for breath.

He knew that he had to get off the ship before the next wave arrived. The smallest mast had snapped, crashing to the deck and bringing a confusion of rigging and beams with it. With enormous resolve, Ridley hauled himself up by grabbing some ropes. He tried to assess the situation.

He recognised the rigging he was holding as belonging to the ship's mainstay. This was still attached to the main mast. The ship itself was not only pointing upwards but also seemed to be keeling over to one side. Little wonder that he was having so much difficulty keeping his feet.

Another wave roared in but, as Ridley was able to hang onto the rigging from the mainstay, it did him little harm other than knocking the breath out of him. That was when he realised that he had seen no more of the captain or any of the remaining crew. Had they all got off the ship, he wondered. Were they waiting for him in the boat?

He did not know the answers to these questions but knew that he had to get over the side and trust that the boat would still be there.

Clinging onto the ropes, he pulled himself up and round the mainstay. In normal circumstances, he would now be hanging outside of the ship over the water but, because of the angle of the wreck, he could see that below him the ship's side was sloping down into the raging sea where another wave was roaring in. He had no idea what was the right thing to do but resolved to hang on to the ropes until the wave passed him. He would then leap forward in the hope that the receding wave would pull him away from the wreck and the rocks.

This he did. He shot down deep into the cold, churning, malevolent sea where he thrashed about wildly, trying to return to the surface. Just when all seemed lost and his lungs felt as if they were about to give out, he broke through and gasped deep breaths – before descending again beneath the churning chaos.

The sea sucked him under several times. Each time he broke the surface he felt weaker and supposed the next descent would be his last. He struggled to remove his topcoat and his army jacket. When he was finally free of these encumbrances, he found the sea's pull was less powerful so that he was able to stay on top of the water.

The powerful current was sweeping Ridley eastwards along the English coast and the rocks on which they had foundered were soon left behind. At the same time, he was being swept forward by the massive waves, taking him nearer and nearer to the shore.

Ridley was unaware of any of this as, once he had surfaced from his final plunge into the abyss, all he could do was struggle to keep his head above water. Suddenly, his hand chanced upon some rigging.

Not knowing why, he pulled himself along it, passing hand over hand until he came at last to its source. It was part of a ship's beam that had been snapped off by the violence of the sea.

The beam, about eight feet long and some four inches in diameter, was draped in ropes and remnants of sail. Ridley threw his arms over it so that it nestled under his armpits and he found this served him well as a life preserver. He no longer had to fight to remain afloat, although he needed all his strength to maintain his grip on the slippery beam as the sea buffeted him. At least now he was able to assess his position.

Most of the time he could make out nothing but mountainous waves all around him, but occasionally he was swept to the crest of a wave and, for a few seconds, could glimpse what lay ahead. His vision was limited by the darkness of the night but the little he could ascertain gave him no comfort. There was no sign of the ship's boat or any of its survivors. All he could determine was an unbroken line of white foam ahead of him, roaring into the air as wave after wave churned into it. That must be land, he thought, and it must be very rocky for the waves to be breaking as they are. The next couple of glimpses told him a different story, however, as he realised there were some parts where the foam was breaking further in and with less violence.

Those must be beaches, Ridley thought. If I can steer myself towards them, there may yet be a chance! He began thrashing his legs in an attempt to drive himself towards where he thought the nearest gap in the turbulent surf lay. It was a wasted effort; another great wave surged over him, sending him where it pleased, so that he had no idea in which direction the beach lay. He let out an anguished cry of despair.

The next wave hurled him forward again, only this time it broke on the first outcrop of rocks against which Ridley and the beam were thrown with ferocious power. The beam hit the rocks end on so that Ridley, clutching on desperately, came to a jarring halt. That saved him from being smashed to death but also caused him to lose his hold. The next moment he felt himself being pulled back and under by the resurging swell. He was totally helpless and realised that death was only seconds away. In absolute panic and despair, he began to thrash his arms and legs. Somehow he came back to the surface, only to be hurtled forward by the next foaming wave. Miraculously he was thrown right over the outcrop of rocks which, in fact, were part of a reef that on a calm day projected only slightly from the sea.

He was suddenly becalmed in a pool of water protected by this reef. All around him the storm was raging but here, for a brief moment, was respite. He was all but done for, gasping for breath and trying to take in his present situation but in the darkness and through the lashing rain, he could see no further than a few feet. What he did see were the remains of the beam which had been broken against the rocks. Most of it had stuck in the rocks or been pulled back by the undertow to be thrown again and again at the rocks, until it was smashed to little more than tinder. But, like Ridley, one piece about a yard long had been thrown clear over and he snatched at it and hung on.

The respite was short lived as the tide slowly pushed him forward and the sea began to churn around him. Soon he was caught up again in the foam of breaking waves but they were not as powerful as those on the other side of the reef and he was able to maintain his grip on the beam. Then he was crashing into another rock and his right arm was crushed between the rock and the wood. He let out a dreadful yell of pain as he once again lost hold of his precious lifesaver. At that moment, an unexpectedly huge wave shot him forward past the rock on his right and up on to a beach of shingle which tore at his flesh.

The next wave thundered in on him, bringing the beam with it. This struck him violently on his back but the force of the water threw him further up the beach. He felt himself being dragged back by the retreating waters and tried desperately to halt the backward motion by digging his fingers into the shingle. Another wave crashed over him, hurling him forward again, then another and another. Each time he was forced further up the beach only to be dragged back by about half the distance, but he was making headway. Finally he was able to get a purchase with his toes in the shingle under his feet. With the last of his strength, he stumbled and crawled up the beach until he was clear of the sea before collapsing in total exhaustion.

CHAPTER 3

Ridley lay on the beach for some time before he felt able to move any part of his body. He slowly flexed his fingers, then his shoulders, before pushing himself upright and struggling to his feet. He hurt all over. His right arm was bleeding badly from a large gash and it felt as if all the bones in it must be broken. He had a searing pain down the left side of his chest. His body was terribly bruised and lacerated with cuts and his clothes hung in shreds – but he was alive. He slowly began to take in his surroundings.

He could sense rather than see clearly that there were high cliffs on either side of him that must run down as ragged rocks into the sea. He decided that he must be in a small cove and thought about waiting till dawn before attempting to find a way out but cold began to take over and he started shivering uncontrollably.

I must keep moving, he thought. Find some shelter, try to get warm. And so he stumbled on up the beach.

As he did so, he began to think about others from the ship. Had anyone else survived? What had happened to the boat in which he had put Ayala? He thought he had seen a glimpse of it out to the west of him, seconds before he threw himself from the deck of the breaking ship. If they had made it to land, they would be beyond the cliffs to his left – that's if he still had his bearings.

Ridley paused and then, giving up thoughts of shelter, he turned to his left and began to walk towards the cliffs. I must climb these and see if there are any more coves with survivors, he told himself. I must find Ayala.

The cliff loomed over him, a presence rather than a clear image, and beneath his feet the shingle turned first to stone and then to boulders as he neared its bottom. To his immense relief, he found the cliff was not sheer but rather a steep slope which he began to climb. Steadily the ground under his feet gave way to grass.

Exhausted as he was, the climb was still difficult and the wind and rain slowed his progress. He pressed on with his head bowed into the rain then, alarmingly, he crashed into a hedge. It was not a man-made hedge, he realised, just a natural hedgerow. He felt his face being torn by prickly bushes and his bared shins itched furiously from what he presumed must be nettle rash.

A few feet of hedgerow and he came to a dry-stone wall. There was more hedgerow on the other side but he scrambled over the wall and crashed through the bushes, receiving more scratches and cuts before he broke out again onto grassland.

He was beginning to lose his sense of direction, and he wondered if he was becoming delirious, but a sense of urgency made him hurry on.

Suddenly Ridley gave out a wild and despairing shriek as a huge beast stirred from the ground out of the dark and raised itself up in front of him. This new horror, combined with his fatigue and abject condition, turned Ridley into a gibbering mess and he sank to his knees in despair. The beast stood still for a moment and then let out a mournful low that made other beasts rise up in response to the heralding call. Ridley, on his knees with his shoulders slumped, stared and then, after a few seconds, he began to laugh – a hysterical laugh of relief rather than humour.

'Bloody cows,' he shouted. 'Bloody great cows.'

Despite all he had been through and the unhappiness of his situation, he was still chuckling, if somewhat dementedly, when he picked himself up. 'Cows. Pastureland!' he said to himself. 'That means a farm where I can get help and shelter – but where?' He had no idea; he could stumble around all night and not come across it. 'Better to go on and see if I can find the next beach and maybe other survivors' he decided.

He trudged on with the cows following him. After a short time he came to the other side of the field where there was more hedgerow. I'm not fighting through that again, he thought. There must be a gate somewhere, but which way? I'll start by heading back towards the sea, that means off to my left.

This he did and within seconds he found a five-bar gate. It was tied with rope, so he scrambled over it rather than wasting time undoing knots. If he had but known, the rope was simply looped over the gate to keep it shut and he could easily have opened it and walked through. As it was, it did not delay him long and he was off crossing the next field.

All this time the land had been climbing but now it began to level out. On reaching the next wall and another gate, directly in line with the previous one, Ridley sensed the land in front was dropping away. As he climbed over this second gate, he noticed a glow in the sky ahead of him but inland, off to his right. From the glow, he could just discern the outline of a small hillock that was blocking his view of the source of the light. Maybe it was a homestead. He did not want to climb the hillock so he decided to carry on straight until the light source came into view and, if it was a farm, he could make for it.

Sure enough, after a while the source of the glow emerged. It was a bonfire. Not a very big one now, but it looked like it had been much bigger for Ridley could make out a greater, darker shape around the central flames which was no longer burning but was still glowing in places.

That must have been the light the captain saw and mistook for a coastal beacon, which is why he thought he was further off-shore than he was. 'Oh God,' shouted Ridley. 'That bloody fire's what caused the captain to steer his ship straight on to the rocks instead of towards sheltered waters.'

Then Ridley wondered what idiot would light a bloody great fire at night and in weather like this? Unless it was indeed a beacon, not a coastal beacon but a warning beacon! Perhaps some other calamitous event was taking place at this very moment, an event so momentous that it totally overshadowed their disaster. He considered this for a moment. What events would you use land beacons for? An invasion?

These were troubled times. The French had had their revolution and then years of war with England. Although a peace treaty had been signed, relations between the two nations were still unsettled and their attitude towards Britain was certainly aggressive.

No, Ridley mused. The storm had been raging all day and night and surely not even the French would be stupid enough to attempt an invasion in a tempest. There had to be some other reason for the fire.

All the time since making out the beacon, Ridley had been walking towards it. Now, as he approached it, he felt its heat seeping into his aching body and smelled the dank steam rising from his sea-

and rain-sodden clothes. He got as close to the heat as he could and then stood there, luxuriating in the warmth and forgetting his unanswered questions.

After a while, his mind started working again. There was nobody in sight, no one attending the fire and no sign of habitation, as far as he could see. The fire was in the middle of nowhere and made no sense at all. Just then he realised that the flames were burning straight upwards; the wind had dropped and so had the rain. The storm had finally blown itself out.

That was when he heard it. From the distance, back towards the sea, there came a terrible shriek. It sounded like a fox screeching but it was shriller and too loud. 'Ayala!' he shouted, and set off running towards the sound. He did not really think it was Ayala who had screamed but she might be somewhere out there, being threatened by whatever creature had made that awful noise.

The ground was now falling away sharply and he felt himself losing control and hurtling downhill. His legs were pumping to keep him upright rather than to take him forward; inevitably he lost all control and went sprawling headfirst to the ground, where he continued to crash and roll head over heels down the hill. The next moment the ground disappeared and he was falling through the air. It was only a small drop and mercifully he landed on sand; even so he fell with a mighty crash that knocked the air out of him. The pain in his chest, which he had been trying to ignore, intensified so violently that he felt as if he had been run through with a heated bayonet.

As he lay there gasping for breath, he heard far-off voices. Above him the clouds were breaking up and moonlight was filtering through to give a ghostly atmosphere but this meant he could at last make out what lay ahead of him.

He stood up and groaned as the effort sent pains throughout his battered and bruised torso. His right arm was useless by now, hanging limply by his side. Straining his shoulders to ease the pain, he tried to see what was out there and where the voices were coming from.

He realised he was in another cove but this one was much larger than the one he had first landed on and the beach was sand, not shingle. About fifty yards ahead of him, midway up the beach, was a cluster of rocks standing some four to five feet high and beyond that, joy of all joys, he could just make out people moving about the beach.

He was about to alert them to his presence when one of them called out. 'No! No! Please no!' and there came a series of fearful screams.

Ridley ducked down and then, using the rocks ahead as cover, ran as quietly as he could towards them. On reaching them, he pressed himself flat against the rocks and slowly lifted his head to see what was happening on the other side.

The scene struck terror in his heart. Three men lay dead on the beach. Another was crawling on all fours but Ridley hardly had focussed on him when another man smashed the hapless fellow on the back with a stout wooden bludgeon. The defenceless man, who now cowered on his knees with his hands held tightly over his head, shrieked. A second blow across his back sent him sprawling. His adversary stepped forward and brought the bludgeon down violently on the man's head, clearly crushing his skull.

Ridley was powerless to do anything; not only was he too weak to tackle the killer who was a brute of a man, but he saw that there were five other men on the beach, all similarly armed. Three of these were surrounding another sailor, for Ridley had quickly realised that these unfortunate men were sailors from the wrecked ship. This last one was pleading for his life but to no avail. His assailants simultaneously struck out at him, knocking him to the floor, whereupon they bludgeoned him to death.

Looking away in horror, Ridley's eyes fell on a scene that to him was even more appalling. On the water's edge was a lifeboat in front of which lay the ship's boy with his head caved in. Worse still, was the sight of Ayala draped over the boat's side, her head hanging just above the water while the sea lapped at her dangling arms and hair.

A furious rage overtook Ridley. He leapt to his feet, intent on rushing these men and killing as many as he could before they got him. It was a futile piece of bravado; in his condition, with only one good arm and no weapons, they would crush him more easily than they had the forlorn sailors. Fortunately for Ridley, as he rose up he slipped on a mass of wet seaweed and his feet shot away from beneath him, sending him crashing down again. His head smacked against the rock, knocking him senseless. A further piece of good fortune was that the roar of the sea blanketed the noise of Ridley's fall so that his presence went unnoticed by the assassins.

CHAPTER 4

Although only twenty-four, Nathan Eldine was an important person in the community of Purbeck in Dorset. A tall, well-built man with flowing blond hair, he had an attractive appearance; he was not handsome but rugged, with a deep scar by the side of his left eye. He had gained this scar on the battlefield four years earlier, during the dismal Flanders Campaign in the recent war against France. Because of this and another minor wound, he had returned home to recuperate, only to discover that his father was terminally ill.

Within a few weeks, he had inherited the role of Squire of the parish of Holme Matravers. Despite having gone into soldiering at an early age, he was well-educated and quickly took on the duties that came with being the squire. He was now a local magistrate, a benefactor of many charitable activities in the area and employer of a good number of farm and quarry workers on his modest estate.

They had not been easy years. Nine years of war with France had taken its toll. Heavy taxation and extraordinarily high inflation brought many families to near starvation and crime had, at times, been rife. However, the Amiens treaty of March 1802 had bought much rejoicing at the return of peace and plenty. Rumours that the new emperor, Napoleon Bonaparte, had broken several of the terms of the treaty by reclaiming the Swiss cantons of Valais and Piedmont and was seemingly determined to overrun Switzerland, had done little to disturb this air of well-being. A long fine summer had added to the fresh hope and a warm feeling of tranquillity prevailed.

Smuggling was one of the crimes that flourished in the barren years and, despite the new affluence, it would be some time before those responsible lost their appetite for such adventures.

His youthful exuberance, his need for excitement and his military experience led Nathan to take up the task of combating this crime as an acting officer of His Majesty's Customs and Excise. This was at times a conflicting role for him as he sometimes found himself both accuser and judge, but he hoped that so far he had carried out these combined duties fairly and with true justice.

It was in this role that he now found himself, with a pistol in each hand, concealed behind a bush watching four men approach up a sandy path. He was acting on a tip-off that smuggled goods were to be landed in a cove at the foot of the path and he had hurried across country with a squad of six men from the local militia to apprehend the culprits. He had just returned from a local hunt when he received the tip-off and had not had time to change his outfit.

He wore a black riding jacket when hunting, having not taken up the red coat that was fast becoming so fashionable. This was fortunate as otherwise he might have had difficulty concealing himself.

When the smugglers had almost reached his bush, Nathan jumped out shouting, 'Halt, I am an officer of His Majesty's Customs and Excise and I am arresting you for the act of smuggling.'

The leading man of the four, far-from-desperate-looking bravadoes, whose way Nathan now blocked, replied, 'Hold up! Don't shoot sir, we are not armed and I'm afraid you've made a terrible mistake. We bain't smugglers, sir, just honest fishermen returning from a night's work.'

At this moment four soldiers, in their Dorset, dark green and white trimmed, uniforms emerged from their concealment behind a wall higher up the path. They were carrying rifles as they hurried down to surrounded the men, One of the soldiers, wearing a single stripe on his arm, quickly inspected the supposed criminals checking their waists and armpits with his free hand.

'He's right sir, they're not armed', the Corporal said, 'they don't appear to be carrying anything either, sir.' He added in a rather derisory tone. Nathan could see this for himself and had already realised that the men were not in possession of any illegal contraband. It must still be on the beach, perhaps in the boat that they had, presumably, used to get to the small cove, some four hundred yards down the pathway.

'Keep these men covered Corporal, while I check the beach. You, Sterne, come with me', he ordered and then accompanied by the selected soldier hurried off down the path.

The path meandered down a slight hill, between two steep and high grassy banks, before taking a sharp left turn whereupon it ran straight down into the small sandy cove. The cove was flanked by two headlands that both turned to the right as you looked out to sea and then ran parallel with each other. There they formed a narrow inlet, which ended some way beyond the line of vision from the sandy beach, giving the appearance of a pond rather than a cove. The sea beyond the outer headland was not visible from here and Nathan realised that this meant the cove would be equally indiscernible from the sea to anyone other than a local navigator. It also meant that the waters in the cove were protected from the wind and the, sometimes, heavy surfs of the English Channel, so that they would be as tranquil as they now were even in the heaviest of storms.

An ideal haven for smugglers and fishermen alike, as Nathan had to acknowledge.

There was a solitary boat dragged up onto the beach and it was typical of those used by fishermen all along the south coast of England. However, it was the only one and there were no signs of nets or the net repairing apparatus one usually finds where fishing boats are harboured.

While Nathan was standing on the edge of the beach taking in these facts, the soldier, Sterne, ran down to the boat, over which he gave a cursory glance.

'Nothing in this, sir, except some tarpaulin and a few old nets. They don't look like they would hold a determined sprat to me sir', he called back. 'They must have unloaded their cargo and hidden it somewhere'.

Nathan drew a fob watch from his waistcoat pocket and checked the time. It was six thirty on a fine autumn morning. A morning that gave no hint of the storm that had raged the previous night. 'If they did I doubt that they did it at night. Even experienced fishermen wouldn't have risked coming into that narrow passageway in a storm like we had last night and that didn't let up until the early hours.' he thought aloud.

Nathan was remembering the rain soaked journey he and his party had made the previous evening in order to be in position in time and the uncomfortable sodden night they had spent in wait.

'There was no moon last night and they had no lanterns with them, so they would most likely have had to wait till dawn before coming in.' Although Nathan was now speaking to Sterne, he was really just thinking aloud as he considered all the things that were wrong with this escapade.

He carried on in this manner as he walked down to the boat. 'That would be an hour ago at best, half an hour to navigate the cove, then they had to come up to our trap and the time that's lapsed since then, doesn't give them time to unload and conceal a cargo of any worth. And look! Their footprints are still plain, lots around the boat, even some indications that they were sitting in the sand by the side of the boat but their prints only lead straight off up to the path.'

Nathan climbed up into the boat and gathered up some of the water that lay in it. He put the water to his lips. 'This water's not very salty, it's more like rain water,' he said. 'If they had been out in that storm they would have shipped plenty of sea water, no I don't think they were at sea at all, neither fishing nor smuggling. We're on a fool's errand if you ask me, but why? That's the question.'

He climbed back out of the boat and then spoke directly to Sterne, who was occupying his time kicking sand.

'I'm going back up there to see if those beggars can shed any light on what's been going on. In the meantime, you look around and see if there are any caves or hiding places for smuggled goods. I'll send Guillam and Brownley down to help you but I very much doubt you'll find anything.' With that, Nathan set off back up the beach to the path as Sterne gave a disgruntled 'Aye, aye, sir'' and sloped off towards the nearest headland in search of caves.

When Nathan reached the fishermen they were sitting on the grass with the three remaining militia men standing over them, he sent the two privates down to assist Sterne, and then began his interrogation. 'What were you doing down on the beach on a night like that?'

The same man as before answered. 'You may well ask, sir. Me and my mates were in the inn last night, when this fellow approached us and offered us a shilling a man if we would sit with his boat through the night, he said he was afraid to leave it in such an isolated cove.

'Well we thought he was daft, no one around these parts would make off with someone's boat. We have too much respect for a man's livelihood to do such a thing. But for a shilling we weren't going to tell him that and we gladly agreed. Mind you we might not have been so willing had we realised what a foul night it were going to be. It were lucky we had that tarpaulin to cover us. We huddled under that all night so we did.'

The spokesman was round faced with a white beard. A jovial looking rustic, dressed in typical fisherman's garb, with a role neck jumper under a topcoat and knee high leather boots. Nathan recognised him as a simple but honest individual and had no doubt he was telling the truth. There were just a couple of last questions however. 'If you knew it to be unnecessary, why didn't you just take the shilling and not bother to stay all night? And why are you leaving the boat now, before your man has returned to relieve you?'

'In the first part, we gave him our word!' The fisherman spoke as if affronted that such a question should be asked. 'As for the second part, he said he only wanted us to guard it till daybreak, he thought it would be safe during the day and he would be back to it before the next evening. It all sounded jolly queer to us mind, but as I said a shilling's a shilling after all.' At which the rustic dried up and looked around at his pals as if to see if they had anything to add but they all stayed as quiet as they had since first apprehended.

'It's the same story he told us,' the Corporal said, unnecessarily.

Nathan asked about the man that had hired them but learnt little of any consequence and got a description that could fit a hundred folk in any township.

'All right, you've obviously been used the same as we have. You can go.' Nathan told the fishermen, who scrambled up and hurried off up the path. They had now found their tongues for they were all talking rapidly with each other about their adventure and laughing at the officer's obvious discountenance.

Nathan, grumpily, turned to the Corporal, 'Well Wallace, there's nothing more to be done here. We've been sent on a wild goose chase and our mysterious boat owner's not going to return - that's for sure.

'I suspect those fellows know more than they are letting on. I mean, having got their shilling, why would they all bother to watch the boat when one or, at the most, two would do? Still, I doubt they know anything of significance and we would just be wasting time questioning them further. Go and fetch Sterne and the others, then you can all return to barracks. I'm going off now to find out more about this tip-off.'

'Aye, aye sir,' the Corporal said with a slight grin as he contemplated an easy stroll home, away from this officer's command, and with the chance of a stop at an inn or two on the way.

Nathan made his way up the path until he came to two more soldiers standing by his horse and puffing on clay pipes. They came smartly to attention as he approached.

'We're all finished here,' Nathan said, giving no clue as to his irritation, 'I'm going on ahead, you should wait for the others. Then, make your way back to the barracks.'

'Yes sir!' they replied in unison with the same delight as their pal had shown earlier.

Having been the only member of his party on horseback Nathan now mounted his horse and set off to find Ned Stockwell, the man who had given him this false lead.

CHAPTER 5

How long he was unconscious, Ridley did not know but it must have been a while for the head wound, that he had incurred when falling, had totally dried up leaving his hair matted with blood and stuck to his forehead. His first thoughts as he lay there were to wonder where he was and how he came to be there and then he groaned as he recalled the hideous events that he had witnessed. Slowly he pulled himself up and peered over the rocks.

The first beginnings of morning gave a strange and unnatural light to the scene. It appeared as if a few candles lit parts of the bay. These areas were clearly discernible while other parts, shielded from the dawn, seemed dark and impenetrable but mostly the cove was bathed in an eerie half-light.

A calm and gentle sea washed the beach edge but of the previous night's terrible events, there was no sign. There were no bodies of broken sailors, no boat and no Ayala. What could it mean? Had he become delirious from fatigue and imagined the whole episode? Surely not, for here he was behind the rocks he had used as shelter and there was the cove, all as he remembered. So what had they done with the dead? That was when he saw the first of the sailors. He was a few metres from the shore lapping backwards and forwards in the sea. Ridley saw another further out to sea and then he saw the ship's boat floating upside down with its bows smashed in.

Beyond that, perhaps a mile or two away, he could see the wreck of the vessel that had brought him and Ayala here from Egypt. It was aground on a massive jagged outcrop of rocks a little way off shore, beneath the next large headland, west of this cove. The rocks were clearly part of a larger reef stretching out to sea, most of which was under the water but, even with this now gentle sea, the race of the tide over the reef was clearly visible by the white tops of foam. Now that the storm had abated the majority of the ship was high and dry, only its stern resting beneath the waves. It was clearly stuck fast as otherwise the damage to its hull would surely have caused it to sink.

Ridley was convinced that he, Ayala, the captain and crew of the *Golden Nile* were the victims of wreckers; those infamous men who it was rumoured had caused almost as many shipwrecks on England's shores as Mother Nature herself. He had thought that such practices belonged to history, with the criminals having been caught and imprisoned, banished or executed. Or else they had been forced into retirement by the efforts of the Customs and Excise men. Now, he was in no doubt that the practice had been revived on this stretch of the English coast.

Despair overwhelmed him and he sank back to his knees as he recalled the horrific scenes and saw again Ayala's forlorn body hanging lifeless over the boat's side. Where is she now, he wondered. Dragging himself up he rushed headlong into the sea, stumbling and thrashing about seeking everywhere around him for any sign of her shroud.

It was useless and finally, he gave up, just standing there, up to his waist in the water, his arms hanging loosely by his side, head bowed and gasping deep breaths. Eventually, with a huge sigh, Ridley turned and made his way back up the beach to the spot where he had lain overnight and he sat down with his back to the rocks and began to consider his position. Despair had now given way to anger and a determination to take his revenge. It was a cold calculated anger, which now gave clarity to his thoughts.

He had been incredibly lucky to survive, not just the shipwreck but also his folly when he had attempted to take on the wreckers and he reached down and picked up some of the now dry seaweed, shaking his head and silently thanking it and God for their part in his escape. He was alive and he determined there and then to bring these men to book. He suddenly realised that he was not out of danger yet, for soon they would return to their crime in order to reap their reward and if they found him in his current state they would obviously recognise him as a witness against them and Ridley had no doubts what that would mean.

He was sure they would return, because that was how wreckers were said to work. At night, the villains would light false beacons to lure the unsuspecting ship unto the rocks, and then they would wait for any survivors and bludgeon them to death before casting them back into the sea. They bludgeoned them so that it would appear as if the sea had crashed the unfortunate mariners onto the rocks.

There would be no slit throats or other clues as to how these poor souls really met their death. Having covered up any signs of their activities, the wreckers would then steal off home to await the morning when they would return, now in the guise of good ordinary folk happening innocently upon the wreck.

One of their number would be sent to inform the authorities but by the time any officials arrived the wreckers would have taken boats out to the wreck and be swarming all over it, making sure no one had stayed aboard and by some miracle survived. If anyone had, they would be quickly despatched. This precaution taken, the wreckers would set about helping themselves to the cargo and any other items of worth they may come across, which they would claim as theirs by rights of salvage and with no evidence or testament to tell otherwise, they would walk away from their evil crime, often with a very handsome profit.

Yes, they would return and soon, for they would not risk losing their prize should the coastguards or customs men, or indeed some truly innocent party, discover the wreck first.

With the wreck where it was, it seemed unlikely that they would return to this cove but there was always a chance they might, perhaps to see if any further survivors had washed up.

I must get away from here and fast and I must be careful not to run into any of the bastards, Ridley thought as he looked around for a path out of the cove. Behind him was the cliff face over which he had toppled in his desperate descent the previous night.

It was not a tall cliff face only standing about ten feet, which Ridley gratefully acknowledged. Any higher and the fall would probably have broken his back or neck, but it was too sheer to climb easily. He looked elsewhere and discovered an obvious track coming down off the land into the back of the cove.

He was about to head for this when he reasoned that this would most probably be the path the wreckers would take should they return to this cove. So he stopped and again looked around.

About thirty yards further down the beach were some fallen rocks nestling against the cliff face. The land here ran down in the form of a gulley and water, no doubt because of last night's storm, was draining off and falling onto the rocks below. The rocks looked easy enough to climb, although they might be wet and slippery and the top rocks were only a few feet below the cliff edge, so he decided on this route.

His injured arm meant that it was a more difficult climb than he had anticipated but eventually he was levering himself up onto the grassy cliff top. The gulley ran off in an almost straight line inland, rising as it went until it peaked, after which nothing could be seen from where Ridley stood. On either side of him the land rose sharply to some twenty or thirty feet and he realised that apart from the obvious path this was probably the only other way out of the cove as the land around him would be high above the beach and he had seen that the cliff faces were sheer.

The good news was that he could walk safely up this gulley, well concealed from anyone who might be out and about this early in the morning, unless they should come right up to the crest of the hills and there seemed no reason why anyone should do that.

He set off, quickly realising what an awful condition he was in, for although it was only a gentle climb, his muscles were soon aching and he had to stop every now and then to catch his breath. After what seemed an eternity he reached the top of the hill. Ahead of him lay field after field of stone walled grazing land. This rolled away to the horizon, which was formed by a high long straight ridge of land, running in a south easterly direction towards the sea.

This was Dorset in its full glory, with the day's morning light, like the very breath of life, awakening the idyllic scene. How could such a rugged and treacherous coastline suddenly transform into this blanket of perfection? Could these beautiful and tranquil farmlands truly be the source of such evil as Ridley had witnessed? How could such murderous villains be raised in homes nestling in this piece of heaven on earth?

It seemed so incongruous to Ridley that he almost felt as if the previous night's events had not happened at all, until he felt another sharp pain sear across his back as his body reminded him of his frailty.

He was beginning to see that this land was not as still and quiet as it had first appeared. He could hear birds singing. In several of the fields cows were grazing and in one, far off, a farmer's boy was gathering up the herd for milking. Some of the fields had deep holes in them, some grown over with the grass, while others looked raw with piles of white stone piled up around them. These were obviously the result of quarrying.

Ridley saw a donkey, or perhaps it was a mule, tethered near one of the fresh holes and he could just make out the wooden bar and winch, which would employ this beast to haul the rock up out of the pit. Then he saw two miners strolling along a path towards this very pit, lunch boxes in hand with picks over their shoulders. Although they were some way off Ridley still ducked down, uncertain as to his safety.

He would have to trust someone. The question was who? It was then that he noticed, some four fields ahead of him, a copse of trees with a farmhouse nestling just beyond. In front of the house, two children, about six or seven years of age, were playing a form of tag and now Ridley realised he could hear their laughter.

There, I'll try there, he decided, it seems normal enough.

The decision made, his tiredness swept over him again and he stumbled forward towards the house, falling down twice before eventually reaching a gate in the fence that surrounded the buildings. The gate squeaked as he opened it. The children stopped playing, turned to look at Ridley, then, without a sound, shot into the house. A moment later a portly ruddy faced woman wearing a white smock over a full flowing navy blue dress appeared on the doorstep.

She looked at Ridley for several seconds, showing no sign of any emotion, not shock, horror nor fear. Then, in a deep warm Dorset brogue, she said 'Lawd, look at thyself, what have thee been doing to get so? And all that blood, come on inside my lover, and let me have a look at thee, though tis a doctor thee needs not an old passle like me.'

Ridley had no idea what she was talking about but he was too tired to care and was immensely grateful to proceed inside and give himself up to her, whether she was a passle or not.

CHAPTER 6

It was just after one o'clock in the afternoon when Squire Nathan
Eldine arrived at the farm where he was surprised to see Stockwell
and Dr Palbrey, in conversation by the front porch. Dr Palbrey, who
had a practice in the village of Corfe Castle, was in his shirtsleeves
and there were bloodstains on his right cuff.He was an elderly man,
in his late fifties but had a full head of black unkempt, shoulder
length hair, which gave him a wild look. This, combined with the
fact that he always wore a black frock coat and black breeches with
white stockings, was why local people called him Dr Pallbearer,
though never to his face, for he was a man of ill temper and little
sense of humour.

'What's all this?' Nathan asked as he dismounted. 'Somebody
taken poorly, Ned?'

'None of mine, thanks Squire.' The big man replied. 'The Doctor's
here to see some poor fellow that turned up this morning in a terrible
state, seems he survived a shipwreck in the storm last night. It's
good you're here though, sir, for it's a rum do, there's no doubt,
according to what he said that is, but I'll let him tell you himself, if
he will. I would have sent for you but I knew you was off chasing
them smugglers. How did that go? Did you catch them?'

'A wild goose chase I'm afraid. I need to talk to you about that
but that can wait for now. Tell me what do you mean a rum do?'

Before Stockwell could answer, Dr Palbrey stepped forward.
'Considering what he says he has been through, the man is
surprisingly only superficially damaged,' he said. 'A cracked rib is
his worst injury, which will mend itself. I've bound him up, it's now a
matter of time and him taking it easy, otherwise he just has a number
of cuts and bruises. Some of these are quite severe and I will need to
check him out over the next few days, so I will be taking him back
with me in my trap.

'Stockwell here is apprehensive about his story but I can assure
you he is not delirious. Despite appearances, he is a gentleman, that's
for sure, so I see no reason for not believing him. I have given him

some laudanum for the pain, so he will probably be a little drowsy. I suggest you get the basic facts from him now but he needs rest and the sooner I get him to Corfe and into bed the better. I'll book him in at the Bankes' Arms and I suggest you leave your main questioning until tomorrow."

'Thank you, Doctor, I'm sure what you say is for the best but I still do not know what it is about this man's story that should concern me, other than the question as to where was this wreck and what has been done about seeking other survivors,' Nathan said.

Stockwell spoke up this time. 'When this man arrived here, Betsy took him in and started tending his wounds, he told her what had happened and she sent our Annie down to fetch me, I was down in the long field mending some fencing,' he explained. 'When I heard his story I got Archie and Tom, my farmhands, to go and muster some help from the farms and quarries. Once these had gathered I sent them off to check the bays out as our man didn't know exactly where he had come ashore.

'I sent Archie down to Swanwich to get some boats out and Tom took my horse to fetch the doc. Billy Fish, one of the helpers, came back a while ago, they've found the wreck. It's stuck fast on some rocks near the Kimmeridge Ledges. It seems it's a cargo ship called the *Golden Nile* and Josh White and his crew had already come across it when they were out checking their lobster pots. He and his men have boarded it. It was completely deserted but there were a number of bodies in the sea.

'They've found no survivors though they're still looking. Billy went back to help with bringing the bodies ashore. I would have gone too except I wanted to find out more about this man's story but he's not said much more. He seems nervous about talking of it.'

'Talking of what?' Nathan said sternly. He was looking very grim faced now. This had been sickening news. How many had died he wondered.

'He said something about it being a case of murder,' Stockwell replied. 'He said it were deliberate and there had been survivors. Then he clammed up and would only say there had been a shipwreck and that he had survived. He also said his wife was dead, murdered he said again. He were very distressed and rambling. I didn't know what to make of it.'

Stockwell was about to say something more when the doctor, who had gone back into the house, now reappeared with his coat over his arm and clutching his bag. 'For goodness sake Eldine,' he said, 'don't stand around doing nothing ask the man what questions you have. I need to be getting back; I'm a busy man; there may be other people needing my attention.'

Nathan did not bother to reply, though he was angry at the doctor's manner. The man had a very easy life. People in this part of the world were generally rather healthy and the doctor who had a private income from his family's estate was rarely hard pressed. He did have a strong liking for both food and alcohol and it was probably his desire for one or both of these that gave rise to his urgency.

Walking into the farmhouse, Nathan found his ill humour lift. He always enjoyed visiting the Stockwells because Betsy kept the place so delightfully homely. The parlour, which you entered straight from the front door, was warm and comfortably furnished and there was always a welcoming aroma: a combination of home baking and freshly laundered linen. The scent of cut flowers, which were abundant, added to the atmosphere to produce a quite intoxicating effect.

Then there was Betsy herself, the epitome of everyman's version of the perfect mother, or if they were of her age the perfect wife. A large and kindly lady with never a cross word or an ungenerous thought, she was blessed with an ample bosom, upon which one felt an overwhelming desire to rest one's head and let the cares of the world dissipate.

She stood now in the centre of the room, looming over a man in a large armchair who was using a spoon to eat hot soup from a bowl he held in his other hand. The man appeared to be naked apart from a blanket wrapped around him and, despite Betsy's administrations, was wearily hunched and ashen faced.

On hearing Nathan enter, Betsy turned to face him but the man did not look up.

'Good day to you Squire,' Betsy said. 'Am I glad to see you? Now we might have a bit of sensible thinking. The Pallbearer is insisting Mr Ridley here goes off with him to Corfe right away. But look at him he isn't fit for nothing at the moment especially not a bumpy ride in that old pony and trap.'

'I'm alright now I assure you, Mrs Stockwell,' the man finally looked up at Nathan as he spoke. 'You have done a fine job in restoring me and this broth not only tastes wonderful but is remarkably invigorating. If you could pass me my clothes, which must be dry by now, I will go with the Doctor and trouble you no more.'

'Trouble me! Sir, you have been no trouble at all, least a person could do for someone what has been through what you have. If you're determined to go then so be it, although you're welcome to stay as long as you wish. But those clothes of yours will not do. The under garments and the shirt are just about usable but the breeches are done for. I've put an old pair of Ned's out for you and a coat. They'll be too big for you, of course...'

'I have a few questions for you before you leave', Nathan cut in to this aimless conversation. 'My name is Nathan Eldine and amongst other things I'm the local excise man and from what Ned Stockwell has told me there are matters afoot that need my investigation. Tell me about yourself, who are you and what was your role on this ship that was wrecked, for you do not seem like a sailor to me?'

'No I'm no sailor, my name is John Ridley, formerly a Major with the East India Company and my wife and I were passengers on the *Golden Nile* sailing from Egypt.' Ridley began but before he could say more Nathan interrupted him.

'Your wife was on the ship with you! This is indeed grim news, for I have to tell you sir that at the moment they have found no other survivors.'

'Nor will they,' Ridley spoke fiercely now. 'Some did survive, my wife included but those butchers murdered them all and cast them back into the sea and I'm going to see them all hang for their foul deeds. Yes Captain Eldine, this is a case for you alright, the ship was wrecked on purpose and its crew slaughtered, I saw it all and could do nothing.' This last came out as an anguished wail.

'Calm yourself man, what you have been through is terrible indeed and have no fear, if what you say is true, these men will certainly hang. I promise you I will not rest until they are all brought to book.'

Ridley turned angrily on the young squire. 'What do you mean? If what I say is true? It's true alright, I tell you I saw it with my own eyes man.'

'Yes, yes of course. It's just that there has never been a case of wrecking in Dorset that I know of,' Nathan replied. 'You hear wild tales of such things having happened in Cornwall but even those are exaggerations of the truth. Luring ships onto rocks with false beacons just doesn't happen, for a start the weather conditions have to be such that the ship is in difficulty and how would the wreckers know when that was going to happen or that a ship was even out there. It doesn't make sense. It's too haphazard.

'Sometimes unsavoury villains have murdered survivors of shipwrecks to get their hands on the cargo but we came down on them with such wrath that the practice has been wiped out. It's hard, no terrible, to imagine that it might have started up again. Come tell me everything, begin with how you and your wife came to be on this ship.'

Betsy Stockwell, who had been interspersing the conversation with anguished comments, was crying now. 'You poor man - to see your wife killed,' she said between sobs, 'it's horrible, what's the world coming to. Ned has got some brandy out back; I think we could all do with a glass, before you make him tell you any more, Squire.' With that she hurried out of the room sniffing loudly as she tried to fight the tears.

At that moment, Stockwell and Palbrey came into the house. 'I think it's time to go, Mr Ridley if you don't mind. Perhaps you could get dressed now,' the doctor said.

'You won't be going for a while I'm afraid, Doctor,' Nathan turned on him, 'this is a very serious matter and I need to know all about it at once. Ned, your wife is fetching us some brandy perhaps you could get the doctor a glass as well.'

'Oh! Well if I must stay, a glass of brandy would not go amiss.' The pallbearer was easily placated.

When the Stockwells had retuned and dispensed the glasses, they all sat down on various chairs in the room while Ridley began his story.

'I met my wife while serving with the company in India, she is...' he hesitated for a moment, then 'she was, half Indian and it was some time before people accepted her into what they call society.

'Their attitude was such that I lost respect for them and found I was less and less happy in India. Anyway, I'd had my adventure, which is why I went there in the first place. I saw action in a number of skirmishes with local warlords but now things have quietened down. So, I resolved to come home and take over the running of our family farm in Yorkshire. I am the only living member of my family; I was looking forward to changing that, by producing some heirs of my own,' again he hesitated before adding quietly, 'that will not happen now.'

Ridley fell silent and nobody else spoke for a while. Just as the silence was beginning to feel uncomfortable, he took up his narrative again.

'When I went to India, I left the farm in the hands of some estate managers and they have done a fine job, the farm is very prosperous and they have built up a good bank balance for me even after their fees. So, I was looking forward to a very comfortable life. Ayala, my wife, wasn't so cheerful; she was worried that if the English found it hard to accept her in India what would it be like in England? I comforted her by saying that the colonial Englishman was not the same as the domestic Englishman. We would be among good honest Yorkshire folk and they would take her to their hearts.

'We didn't have a honeymoon when we got married so I decided we would have one on the way home. I thought it would be something for her to look forward to on the first half of the journey, rather than fretting all the way home about her welcome. So we stopped off in the Middle East and travelled across land, which is why we came to be returning home on the *Golden Nile*.'

As Ridley continued with his story of the voyage, the storm and the wrecking, Nathan studied the man carefully. He liked what he saw. Ridley was a strong healthy man of around thirty-five years with a lived in face; ruggedly handsome, he had long mouse coloured hair, which, Nathan presumed, he would normally tie with a bow at the nape of his neck in the current fashion.

A man's man yet, undoubtedly, he would also be very attractive to women. He was a man of action and if not deeply intellectual, he told his story clearly and fully, which was impressive considering what he had been through and that he had been administered laudanum for his pain. He was obviously a man of honour, with strong emotions, a clear sense of justice and a formidable determination to complete any task he set himself to the best of his ability.

Nathan thought he would not like to be on the wrong side of this man's wrath and that the perpetrators of this terrible crime had made themselves a formidable enemy who would never give up on his resolve for vengeance.

This man is going to need careful handling if things are not going to get out of hand, Nathan decided.

'That's when Mrs Stockwell took me in, Ridley ended his story. 'Then the Doctor came, I wanted to help with the search but Dr Palbrey would not let me.'

'I should say not,' Betsy Stockwell spoke up, 'as if you haven't suffered enough without having to deal with those poor souls and anyway I doubt you would have had the strength to even get back there.'

Nathan did not doubt that this man would have found the strength if he had to but that was not relevant now.

'Thank you, Major Ridley,' he said. 'That was a very clear account of what happened, it's a pity you do not think you could recognise these villains again but no doubt we will find some way to uncover them. It just might take a little longer that's all. Now I think you can get dressed and go with the Doctor. I for my part will get down to the wreck and see what more I can discover. I will need to question White and his crew; the fact that they were the first on the scene is significant.

'It makes them likely suspects, of course, but it isn't proof in itself and it could just be that they are innocent and that their early presence was purely coincidental. They might even have thwarted the ambitions of the real criminals.'

'Who is this man White?' Ridley demanded. 'I've been thinking about him since I heard he had discovered the wreck and I can see no reason why he would be at sea so early, given that the storm did not abate until the early hours. He would not have known that it would stop when it did, yet he must have had his crew assembled and ready to sail almost as soon as it did.'

'Joshua White is something of a rough diamond that's for sure and his crew are no better, I would not put it past them to commit a crime like this but the evidence is purely circumstantial at the moment so let's not get ahead of ourselves,' Nathan replied. 'I will come and see you tomorrow and let you know how my enquiry progresses but for now I will say good bye and trust that your journey will not be to arduous given your condition. Ned, you come with me. Good Day Betsy and thank you.'

'Doctor, Major Ridley.' Nathan nodded to each in turn as he said his farewells.

'As I'm no longer with the company I'm no longer a Major, so please call me Jack and may God aid you in catching these men,' Ridley said as the squire and Ned Stockwell made their way out of the cottage.

Stockwell's horse was still saddled from its earlier journey. He and Nathan mounted up and set off at a gentle trot towards the scene of the crime. As they went, Nathan turned his thoughts to his earlier adventures. 'Who told you the 'White Wigs' were going to be active last night, Ned?' he asked.

'Nobody told me, Captain,' Stockwell answered, automatically addressing the squire with his military rank, as everyone did when he was carrying out his role as a Customs and Excise officer.

'It was something I overheard,' the farmer continued. 'Tam Smith and that fellow Parkes were in the Ship Inn the other night and they'd had too much to drink. Thought they were whispering but it were easy to hear them close by, as I happened to be. They was talking about Isaac Gulliver and telling different stories about his career. Then Tam said, quite clearly, that Isaac's old gang were still active even if he wasn't.

'Parkes asked him how he knew and he said because he'd been asked to help with the disposal of a large quantity of spirits being smuggled in the day after next. Parkes was not impressed and told Tam he was just full of piss, if you'll excuse the language, sir.' Nathan did not bother to reply and waited for Ned to continue. 'Anyway, this annoyed Tam and he said it wasn't rubbish. He said he knew all about it from one of the smugglers and then he told Parkes the whole plan, just as I told you.'

'I see,' Nathan said, 'think about it Ned, could they have been acting drunk? Could it be that they wanted you to hear them, knowing that you would tell me and that I would go off on a pointless expedition, leaving the coast clear for this awful deed to be carried out?'

'Well it is possible, I suppose. When you think about it Tam was a bit precise about the plan, I mean he gave a time and place and everything.' Stockwell was somewhat abashed as he said this, realising he had clearly been duped.

'You realise what this means, don't you Ned?' Nathan did not wait for a reply but continued, 'If they knew you would report to me it means your cover is blown and that you won't be able to work for me anymore, leastways not as a secret informer.'

'Well, I can't say I'm sorry about that as I've never been comfortable with being an informer, but I don't know how they could have found out about me. I've always been very careful and I've never told nobody about it. Perhaps it was just coincidental,' Ned said, his voice trailing off.

'I didn't see you as an informer more an undercover agent,' Nathan tried to revive Stockwell's spirits. 'After all you didn't take money for the information you gave me. But I'm afraid I do not believe in coincidences, especially as trouble was taken to ensure that there were people on the beach where the smuggling was supposed to take place. This was done to keep me there as long as possible. They knew I would have to interrogate those people and carry out a search of the area, which I would not have done if there had been nobody there.

'No, I'm sure the two incidents are connected and that's more circumstantial evidence against Joshua White, because both Tam

Smith and Will Parkes have sailed with him in the past, although they haven't crewed for him recently.'

As Nathan finished speaking, he and Stockwell arrived at the beach below St. Aldhelm's Head, where they found the grisly sight of a line of bodies laid out on the beach. They were in a small bay known as Chapman's Pool on the westward side of the headland. The cliffs known as the Kimmeridge Ledges, where the wreck was, and the beach where most of the bodies had originally washed up were both to the West of here but this was the nearest bay with relatively easy access.

There were a number of men standing around and a horse and cart had been brought to the beach for the removal of the bodies, which task the men now set about. Nathan and Stockwell dismounted and Stockwell walked on down to assist in this unpleasant work.

One of the men came over to Nathan speaking as he walked. 'A bad business this Squire, we've found the captain's papers and there is a list of the crew. We think we have found all their bodies, but there is one strange thing, the log says there were two passengers, a man and his wife. That means we are two bodies short, we haven't found any sign of the woman and we cannot tell if these are all crew or if one of them is the passenger.'

Obviously, the men down here had not heard about the survivor. How many people were in the know? Nathan wondered. It might be best to keep it to as few as possible for the moment, he thought. So he said, 'Best to keep looking, but if we haven't found them by night fall we may have to give up. Perhaps they had already disembarked somewhere.'

'Maybe,' the man said doubtfully, 'but there is no mention of a port of call in the captain's log, which you would expect if they had done so.'

'Whatever the explanation perhaps we will never know. I will need to speak to Josh White to get his side of the story and to see whether he discovered anything when he first boarded the wreck. I assume he will be going back to Swanwich tonight so I will go there tomorrow to meet with him. Can you get word to him to that effect?' Nathan asked. The man simply nodded in reply. 'There are a few chores I was going to do tomorrow that I will now have to do tonight, can I leave you to carry on here?' Nathan added.

'Aye, I can do that Captain, we are going to take the bodies to the church at Worth Matravers, where they will be laid out till a burial can be arranged. The vicar has been down here already, now he's waiting for us there,' the man said before turning away and returning to his morbid task.

Nathan walked over to Stockwell, told him where he was going and gave him some instructions regarding the need, where possible, to record the names of the dead and their condition; he said to take particular note of the wounds to the bodies. He also told Stockwell to say nothing to these men of the survivor or his story of the wrecking as it might be as well to keep that secret for the time being.

The young squire was engaged to the very beautiful Madeleine Armitage, with whom he had planned to spend the evening. This he would not now be able to do, so his first chore would be to send one of his servants to her with a written apology. He and Madeleine had been friends since childhood but it was only after Nathan's return from the wars that their relationship had matured. Nathan was still coming to terms with this and even though she had agreed to marry him, he still felt unsure of himself and fretted over how she would react to his note.

This lack of confidence was a new sensation for him and was in part due to the attitude of Madeleine's father, Richard Armitage, the manager of a sizeable part of Lord Aldwin's estates in Purbeck.

As such Armitage probably ranked lower on the social scale than the young squire but the size of the estate and the fact that Lord Aldwin seldom visited this part of his domain raised Armitage's importance in the community. Lord Aldwin was a reasonable man who paid his workers relatively well so Armitage, who was in charge of the hiring of labour, was always treated with great respect by the populace.

He had aspirations of becoming the parliamentary representative for the area, which gave him an inflated sense of his own importance, causing him to question whether Nathan was of sufficient standing to court his daughter.

39

On the other hand there was a widely held theory that the similarity of the young squire's name to that of his Lordship was not a coincidence. Rumour had it that some many generations back a child was born on the wrong side of the sheets and although never formally recognised the child was given the surname of Eldine and bequeathed a small parish that it would inherit on maturity.

Nathan paid little heed to this gossip considering it nothing more than wishful thinking on the part of his ancestors, particularly one great uncle who had spread the rumour remorselessly in order to profit from the connection. However, it was true that his land was surrounded by the Aldwin Estate. Also, Nathan had a vague memory that when he was young there had been a very poor harvest and his father had encountered severe financial difficulties being quite beside himself with worry. Then miraculously the problem had disappeared and the family finances were restored. Whether there had been a mysterious benefactor or not, nobody knew. Some turned to the rumour, saying the family would always have a guardian angel, while others gossiped that Nathan's father had resolved his problems by indulging in a spot of smuggling.

Neither answer gave Nathan much comfort but the evidence and the persistence of the rumours certainly left Armitage in some doubt as to how he should treat this young man. When they met, Armitage would become overly pompous and treat Nathan as a subordinate but he was careful never to give offence and had only slightly hesitated over giving his approval to the engagement.

None of this was of much relevance to Nathan who cared little as to his future father-in-law's opinion, other than that he did not wish to upset Madeleine whom he loved deeply. It was, therefore, with some sadness that he wrote the letter before setting about his other chores including a complete report on his day's adventures.

CHAPTER 7

The Purbeck peninsular provides welcome cover for vessels entering the large bay that is the entrance to the natural harbour of Poole. Known as Studland Bay it is the largest of three easterly facing bays that form this protective headland. The small port of Swanwich sits in the middle bay formed by two headlands, which are the culmination of two long ridges running some five miles from the village of Corfe Castle in the West. The valley they form is about a mile wide and a plentiful supply of fresh water from numerous springs gives rise to many homesteads. Some clustered together to form villages while others stand imperiously alone as if challenging nature. A daunting prospect in these parts when ill weather rolls in off the sea. The beauty of these properties is that, whether majestic or humble, they are nearly all built from the attractive lime stone of the region.

A century ago Swanwich had been little more than a few fishermen's cottages on the mouth of a minor river nestling under the southerly headland. In recent years, however, it had grown. Purbeck men had been gathering stone from the surrounding hills, since time immemorial, bringing it to the river mouth for transportation by sea. The pits operated by individual families, known locally as quarrs, are mostly small, little more than deep holes where the miners cut away the clay on which the seams of stone rest and then drag the freed stone to the surface using a circular winch, often powered by a donkey.

At times the stone has come into great demand: when the Romans ruled and again with the great Norman development of castles, churches and cathedrals. These explosions of demand led to the formation of bigger operations and much larger quarries. Work here invariably fell off or ceased altogether when demand diminished forcing the masons to return to scratching a living from the family quarrs. Now once again stone was in great demand as towns and cities were developing and expanding in response to the industrial changes that were occurring throughout England.

41

Ball clay, the other commodity quarried here, was also enjoying a time of increased demand thanks to the nation's growing passion for tea and the subsequent production of fine china. Purbeck blue clay was ideal for this and thousands of tons were now being shipped to the Staffordshire potteries annually, so that Swanwich had grown into a small but busy port.

It was late in the morning, the day after the discovery of the wreck, when Nathan approached the harbour. He could see it bustled with activity. The whole place wore its recently acquired mantle of prosperity derived from these two industries but mostly from the stone, which it was shipping to all parts of the kingdom: London, the fast expanding capital, being the main recipient. The big stone quarries at nearby Durlston and Acton were again working flat out and landowners and master masons were reaping the rewards.

The noise, bustle and general air of prosperity delighted Nathan. It pleased him to see ordinary folk receiving a fair reward for their hard labour. However, his feeling of well being began to fade as he found himself pondering the disparity between the wages of the workers in the stone and clay industry and those of farm labourers. A quarry man's wage was not much but it far exceeded that of those who tilled the land. It seemed that in Purbeck more and more people were leaving the fields for those greater rewards.

From conversations with his prospective father-in-law and other people who moved in political circles, Nathan had learned that this was becoming a national problem. All over England, workers were converging on the fast expanding industrial towns to seek a better life. He had travelled through Lancashire the previous year and had seen first-hand the appalling conditions of the hovels where these workers lived and the foreboding mills where they worked. Yet it seemed even this existence of virtual slavery was preferable to that of farm labouring. Things were going to have to change. Britain acquired much of her supply of commodities from overseas, particularly from the colonies, but the country was still wholly dependent on its agricultural industry for its supplies of grain and fresh meat. That meant conditions had to improve if sufficient workers were to be enticed back to the land.

In Dorset, things were no better than elsewhere in the country. There were many rich landowners making highly acceptable profits from corn, dairy herds and the woollen industry. Entrepreneurs were enjoying rich pickings from quarrying stone and clay. The skills of artisans, such as stonemasons, smithies, millers and tanners were in high demand. On the other hand, much of the community was hardly able to make a living. Farm labourers, fishermen, quarry workers and those who worked for the tanners were paid a pittance and many could not even find work.

Nathan mused upon all of this as he watched the activity. It's little wonder so many turn to crime as footpads, smugglers and, God forbid, wreckers, when facing such deprivations and witnessing such inequalities, he thought.

Riding his horse slowly down the main street of the village, the young squire passed a cross roads, in the middle of which stood the village pump. The springs that supplied the pump were also the source of a mill pond nestling below the high road. A path ran sharply down towards this pond, beyond which stood the mill and an Anglican church. Keeping a course straight ahead, the road dropped down between a number of cottages. One, particularly well kept, was the home of Mary Burt. Nathan presumed her to be a distant cousin of William Burt, the constable at Corfe, whom he knew well but there were many Burts in Purbeck, especially amongst the stonemasons of Swanwich and how they were all related was anyone's guess.

Mary was popularly known as 'Mary who went for a walk' a name and notoriety she had acquired when, a few years back, she had become extremely agitated by the apparent ungodliness of her fellow villagers. One day, she decided that enough was enough and on an impulse, carrying her baby in her arms she set off, with two like-minded women, to walk to the head quarters of the South Wiltshire Methodist Society in Salisbury, nearly fifty miles away.

It was her intention to ask a preacher from the circuit operating there to come to Swanwich and knock some sense into her neighbours. To her absolute delight, she discovered that John Wesley himself was in Salisbury. Wesley was so impressed by her determination and piety that, with Mary in tow, he set off

43

immediately for Swanwich, stopping his carriage to preach at Corfe Castle and Langton Matravers on the way.

Nathan smiled to himself as he marvelled at this woman's resolve. That and Wesley's oratory skills appeared to have worked wonders for now all three centres had established meeting rooms for the Methodist Church although perhaps not with thriving congregations.

It was not just religion that these establishments were giving to their congregations, they were also educating them. The simple services, all in English, like their bible and song sheets and the Sunday schools run by the elders were all encouragements to their congregation to learn to read and write - and with literacy comes knowledge. Nathan welcomed this but knew there were many who were horrified by the idea, believing that an educated populace would only lead to civil unrest and might well undermine the very basis of society. They cited the French revolution as evidence, saying that the great terror could easily spread to England and that Wesley and his followers were a dreadful evil that could bring this about. Some even went as far as inciting violence against these reformers and hired thugs to break up their meetings.

With all the unrest being brought about by so much change, perhaps another war with France, would not be such a bad thing, Nathan thought. It might unite the people in adversity, and allow some of these changes to occur unnoticed, or at least, without too much disruption.

Nathan had now reached the Anchor Inn, a somewhat notorious establishment on the banks of the river mouth. He realised the Whites had returned to Swanwich as he could see their fishing boat, the *Mary Jane*, moored out in the estuary and he decided that the Anchor was as likely a place to find Joshua as anywhere. In this, he was wrong but he did find a motley collection of three men drinking together who were all well known to him and he wondered what could have brought them together.

The first was Roger Ridout, a notorious smuggler of yesteryear and former member of Isaac Gulliver's band. He was too old now to indulge in such deeds but as a younger man he had earned an infamous reputation for his acts of daring. Often at the expense of the unfortunate excise men who had pursued him in vain.

The second man was Thomas Hardy, a man of many parts, sometime stonemason but now prominent landowner north of Dorchester, popular myth had it that he was also a successful lander and distributor of smuggled goods. Nathan recognised him from cartoons he had seen in local gazettes, having paid them particular attention because of the man's reputation. Hardy had never come near to being arrested for such activities and Nathan certainly had no reason to investigate him. It could be that the only factor to stand against him was the gossip driven by envy of his fine wine cellar, which by all accounts was excellent. Finding him in this company added weight to the legend but nothing more.

Finally, there was Roger Bowles, a member of White's boat crew and a man who had been charged with smuggling in the past. Because his participation had been small he had got off lightly, serving just three months in jail. Even so the experience had been sufficiently unpleasant as to sour the man's disposition and he had an extreme hatred of all representatives of the law. Nathan approached him and introduced himself at which both Ridout and Hardy made excuses and got up and left. Bowles too started to get up saying he had things to do but Nathan put his hand on Bowles's shoulder and pushed him back down before moving to the chair opposite and sitting down himself.

Studying his man carefully before he spoke, Nathan saw a lean sour looking man, beardless but unshaven and although he was only in his late twenties, he was completely bald. Bowles was not dressed like a fisherman. Instead he wore a green velvet frock coat over an open neck frilly white shirt, with black breeches tucked into riding boots. He would pass for a gentleman if it were not for the fact that all these fine clothes had seen better days and Nathan assumed that he had acquired his clothes as seconds, as did many poor people at this time. Bowles avoided Nathan's eye by looking down at the table and fidgeting in his chair, clearly uncomfortable under this close inspection.

'Just what are you up to, eh Roger?' Nathan finally asked. 'Suspicious company you're keeping. Thick as thieves you looked.'

'We wasn't doing nothing wrong, just having a few drinks with my mates. Very nice it was too, until you showed up,' Bowles growled in response.

'Well there is no law against having a few drinks with your chums, but those chums are particularly disreputable so you can be sure I'll be keeping a close eye on you all,' Nathan warned him before going on to say, 'but that's not what I'm interested in at the moment. I'm actually looking for Josh White. Did you sail with him yesterday when he found the wreck?'

'What if I did? You got a law against fishing now?' Bowles remained as sour as ever.

'I was just wondering why you left so early in the morning, that's all,' Nathan pressed him.

'I couldn't say, I'm sure. Josh wanted to get away smart, that's all. If you want to know why, best ask him.'

This is getting me nowhere, Nathan decided. Then he said, 'I will, when I find him, I don't suppose you know where he might be, do you?'

To Nathan's surprise Bowles was quite forthcoming and told him White was with his brother down by the beach beyond the stone weighing pier. They were mending some lobster pots.

Leaving the Anchor, Nathan proceeded along the road that now swung round to the south following the line of the bay until it culminated in a stone jetty. Several two masted barges were at rest in the bay among the smaller fishing smacks, but only one, which was moored alongside the jetty, had any sail showing.

This part of the road was well made, built of stone it was in fact a very wide sea wall along which stone was carried in horse drawn carts to a weighing house before being taken further along the wall for loading onto the sea going vessels. The foreshore beneath this road was an area known as the 'bankers', where worked stone was stacked prior to shipment and in some places the stacked stone towered high above the road barring one's view of the sea. There were a series of derricks along the wall used for handling the stone and several of these were currently in use.

Despite the lateness of the year and the cool wind coming off the sea, most of the men handling the stone were stripped to the waist for this was hard work and steam could be seen rising from them.

The whole pier was astir but Nathan, uncharacteristically hardly noticed the hustle and bustle as he walked along. He was deep in thought. A smuggler, a lander and a possible receiver of smuggled goods all together in deep discussion, which broke up as soon as a representative of the law arrived on the scene. It must mean something, he thought. Bowles is a member of White's crew, so they may have been planning the disposal of the *Golden Nile*'s cargo. But why so secretive if the spoils are salvaged goods? That's not illegal, so what need have they of a villain like Rideout? Maybe they just want to use his carts as transport, he answered himself but was not satisfied with this explanation. If the goods have been obtained legitimately, why not use a local transporter? It would certainly be cheaper than bringing in an outsider. There's definitely something not quite right here, something I cannot fathom as yet.

Looking up, Nathan was surprised to find he had left the 'bankers' and the jetty behind and was now in front of a splendid Georgian mansion known as the 'Great House' This fine building consisted of an original magnificent three storey town house to which two enormous wings had recently been added. Overlooking a shingle beach, it dominated the section of the bay from the jetty to the point where it curved away to the promontory known as Peveril Point.

It was without doubt the grandest house in Swanwich, yet Nathan found it incongruous. While it enjoyed a beautiful sea view, it had little land attached to it. It had stables at the rear but its occupants and visitors would alight from their carriages at the front with no privacy from the townsfolk. It did not seem like a family home to Nathan who had no concept of a seaside retreat. He also thought the added wings were unsightly, sitting ill at ease with the architecture of the original building.

Nathan did not consider this now, however, for it was on the beach in front of the house that he found the White brothers, mending their pots. They were not alike. A stranger would never take them for brothers.

In close knit communities like Purbeck there is naturally much inter-marrying and it is not unusual for a number of prominent features to turn up regularly in the faces of the locals so that two people may look very similar even though they are totally unrelated. The link may have been forged many generations ago. It was strange therefore that these siblings were so very different in appearance.

At first, gossip had it that they did not share the same father but this rumour soon died when people realised that they were virtually identical in their mannerisms. When young they were particularly unruly, bullying their contemporaries. They soon became the leaders of a gang that was forever in trouble with officialdom. Maturity had not improved their dispositions and they remained a menace to the more genteel inhabitants of the town and a constant thorn in the side of the local constabulary. They were unusually close, even for brothers, rarely seen apart and intensely loyal to each other.

Joshua, the eldest and tallest, was now in his late thirties. He had fair hair and was clean shaven with boyish looks that would have made him seem quite endearing if it were not for a deep scar that ran from behind his left ear to his chin. He was not heavily built but had a muscular body from years of hard labour as a fisherman. Apart from smuggling, fishing was the only profession either of the brothers had known since they first went to sea with their father.

With the beginnings of a paunch and a bent back, Frank was altogether different in appearance. Although not short, he was several inches shorter than his brother. His head was covered by a mass of black unruly hair and he sported a full but cropped beard.

Three years the senior, Joshua adored his baby brother from the day he was born and despite the fact that he totally disapproved of the dissolute life the younger man led, Joshua had looked out for Frank devotedly ever since. When they were working, it was Joshua who would do the lion's share while Frank found reasons to avoid his duties wherever possible. Joshua never complained, he did not seem to notice and if anyone else remarked upon it he would be vicious in his defence of Frank, so that other crew members soon learned to leave well alone.

Drinking and womanising meant that Frank was forever getting involved in fights. Fights which his brother invariably ended for him. It was on one such occasion that Joshua had received his scar. Frank was immensely proud of his older brother and whenever the scar was mentioned, he would say, 'You should see what Josh did to the other fellow.'

As Nathan walked towards them he noticed that despite their disparity in appearance they were dressed almost identically in white woollen roll neck jumpers and black trousers with thigh length fisherman's boots rolled down to below their knees. The only difference in their outfits was that Frank sported a red bandana on his head, similar to those favoured by the French revolutionists.

They were sitting on upturned lobster pots with a number of other pots around them. Each man had a damaged pot between his knees and was holding a piece of wicker to repair it. Joshua was threading his through the pot but Frank was motionless just gazing out to sea. Both men were sucking on clay pipes but as he could discern no smoke, Nathan surmised that these were not lit.

'Good day to you, Joshua and to you Frank,' Nathan said cheerily as he approached them. Both men looked up and simultaneously removing the pipes from their mouths, they nodded their acknowledgement, without speaking. Then again almost in unison each man placed the clenched hand holding the pipe under his chin whilst leaning forward with his elbow resting on his knee.

'They tell us you want to talk to us,' Josh spoke first.

'About the shipwreck, no doubt,' Frank added.

'That's right, I need to know everything about it, so that I can make a full report,' Nathan told them.

'It's a terrible business that's for sure,' Josh White began his narrative. 'All them poor souls drowned and smashed by the rocks. It were lucky we were out there and came across them when we did for I fear they could have been smashed up even more before they were found.'

'Aye, it were lucky, that's true,' Frank interjected.

'There was nothing we could do, mind, they was all dead long before we got there,' Joshua added.

49

'Nothing at all,' Frank continued to express his agreement throughout Joshua's account, but as his comments were adding nothing to the story, Nathan ignored him.

'I can't think what the captain was up to sailing onto the rocks like that. The poor souls didn't stand a chance,' Joshua now said.

Given his suspicions, Nathan was angry at White's attitude, considering it hypocritical posturing but he was determined not to show this in his manner and almost carelessly asked. 'What were you doing there?'

'Gathering my lobster pots as is my custom,' White answered as if offended by the question.

'Yes but why so early?' Nathan pressed.

'Oh! Well I heard the storm in the night and realised it were a bad one so I gathered a crew and we made ready to sail as soon as it eased.' Joshua fell silent for a few seconds. Then, as if to add credence to his story, he added. 'You see, I wanted to recover as many pots as quickly as possible because I was afraid there might be lines that had frayed but not broken completely and they might go at any time. Anyway, soonest out soonest mended, is what I say.'

Nathan thought White's explanation for his early start sounded spurious but it was possible if unlikely. He decided to let that pass, instead, he asked, 'What happened when you got there?'

'Although it were a good way off, we saw the wreck as soon as we came round Durlston Head and we started towards it. As we got nearer, we saw a couple of bodies in the water so we pulled those in before mooring up to the wreck. Frank and Bowlesy went on board to see if there were any survivors. There were none on board. All the bodies had gone overboard, they had managed to get a ship's boat out but that had obviously been thrown against the rocks and upturned.

'No one was alive as far as we could tell but it wasn't till the shore party arrived that we could start collecting all the bodies and confirm this. They brought out small boats from the beach below St Aldhelm's Head, you see.

'I was just getting ready to sail back to Swanwich to report the wreck when they arrived. I was going to leave Frank on board, for the salvage claim you understand. Terrible business I know but it is my right, I found the wreck. No sense in letting someone else take the profit. Anyway, as I say, people arrived on the beach and then came out to us in one of the gigs so we placed the bodies we'd collected in the smaller boat and they took them back to the beach, a couple more gigs were putting out by then picking up the other bodies.

'It seems that Tom Joyce was in control of the shore party and he sent a boat out to us to collect the ship's papers, captain's log and that, said he wanted to check the body count against the crew list. Then we looked around, found a few bits and pieces worth immediate salvage, before checking out the cargo, wanted to see whether it was worth salvaging at all and how easy it could be done. After a while other boats started to arrive from Swanwich but there wasn't anything for them to do. We couldn't pull the wreck off the rocks, you see, because it was too severely holed. It would have just sunk.

'That's when I got the message that you wanted to speak with me and that you would be in Swanwich today so I decided there was nothing more I could do for the time being, anyway I was going to need extra ropes and stuff to transfer the cargo to my boat so I made my way back here. In the end, I left Matthew Trevellis on the wreck to protect our claim. I expect he's getting fed up by now, been there all night he has, so if you've finished with me, I'd like to sail as soon as possible. Anyway, I want to get back there and start unloading before another big sea arrives and she breaks up some more.'

'No need to worry yourself there, Josh,' Nathan said, 'you see there are some circumstances about this wreck that need looking into and until they are resolved I'm afraid I will have to impound the cargo. I will arrange to have it removed and stored in the old boathouse on Ned Stockwell's land. I don't suppose it will take too long to clear up these anomalies and then I will be happy to release the cargo to you.

'Actually, it occurs to me that as you have all the equipment necessary and because you have to relieve Trevellis anyway, perhaps you would be so kind as to undertake this operation for me.' Nathan was enjoying himself as he watched White puff with indignation. 'Oh! I'm afraid you will also have to put back anything you have already taken. Still, as I said it is only a matter of time. I expect this means you will have to make new arrangements now and won't be sailing until tomorrow, I hope Trevellis has some food and warm clothing!'

'What do you mean anomalies?' White was clearly unsettled by this and angry that he would have to wait for official recognition of his claim. 'There's nothing wrong with my claim, I found the wreck, there were no survivors, so I claimed salvage. What's there to be looked into?'

'Well there are some oddities that need explaining, for example, as you pointed out yourself, there is the question of what the ship was doing there in the first place, what induced the captain to sail in so close to the shore?' Nathan explained. 'Then there is the question of what happened to the passengers, their bodies have not been accounted for.'

'Passengers! What passengers? I know nothing of passengers!' Josh White was clearly discommoded now and was beginning to get very agitated running the palm of his hand across his brow to remove the sweat that was gathering there.

Nathan decided to unsettle him further. 'Why should you know of them? They are an ex-army type and his wife who boarded the ship in Egypt, according to the captain's log that is, but there is no mention of their disembarkation. Of course, it is possible that they left the ship in France or Spain and the captain simply had not got round to entering it in his log, although the original entry did say they were bound for Portsmouth.

'So, you see it will need looking into. Then there is the state of the crew and their wounds, which, from what I hear, are a little strange for bodies dashed on the rocks. Of course, it's all probably nothing to get excited about but I must work to the law and that means impounding the cargo. At least, until these questions are answered satisfactorily and all the paperwork is complete.' Quite intentionally, Nathan added this last with all the pomposity he could muster as befitting an officer of the law.

'Well I suppose you must do what you must do,' White conceded bitterly. 'But it all seems unnecessary to me, especially given the cargo. Just Egyptian bric-a-brac as far as I could see, it's hardly going to make anyone a fortune. I just hope I don't have to wait too long, that's all, I've got crew to pay you know.'

'You sailed to retrieve your pots not to claim salvage, so you would have to pay your crew anyway,' Nathan retorted sharply.

'Yes, that's true but now I've got to go back for Trevellis and then spend time getting the cargo ashore for you to impound. I'll probably have to employ another couple of hands to help with that.' White had clearly accepted the inevitable and was now considering the practicalities.

'Well, I will leave you to sort that out,' Nathan said. 'I'll tell Stockwell to make his boathouse available and I'll arrange to have the constable from Corfe meet you in Chapman's Cove tomorrow morning. He'll be responsible for the impounding of the cargo and its safe keeping, no doubt he will reimburse you for your costs. I take it that that is where you will bring the cargo ashore?'

'Chapman's Cove? Yes that's right,' White acknowledged, 'but we won't get there to start unloading until tomorrow afternoon.'

'Good, then I shall keep you no longer and I will go straight to Constable Burt to ensure he is there by the time you arrive.' With that, Nathan left the White brothers who set about tidying up their pots and equipment, all the while speaking animatedly.

In fact Nathan did not go straight to Corfe and the constable. Instead he went to see Ned Stockwell to acquire the use of Ned's boathouse as a warehouse for the *Golden Nile*'s cargo.

Nathan arrived there shortly after six o'clock that evening. As soon as Ned set eyes on his visitor he said, 'You look well done in, Captain. If you'll excuse me saying so. Best get back on that horse and get home. It'll be late enough by the time you get there and have some supper. Or you could have something to eat with us if you'd prefer it, that is.'

'No chance of that, Ned, when I've finished with you I have to go to Corfe to speak with the constable to give him instructions.'

'Hold on there, Squire,' it was Betsy who spoke. 'Ned's right you look done in. What time did you start out this morning? Don't suppose you've eaten either, have you? Before Nathan could answer these questions she continued, 'Can you write those instructions down for the constable, if so do that while I get you something to eat. Archie can take our horse and deliver the letter for you and when you've eaten you can get yourself off home.'

Nathan had to admit that he was feeling tired following the day's events but before he could say so Betsy assumed his answer to be in the affirmative and said, 'Ned find the Squire something to write with while I heat up that stew.'

So, as she bustled out, Nathan settled back in a comfortable armchair and breathed a deep sigh of contentment.

CHAPTER 8

Nathan arrived at Corfe Castle early the morning after his trip to Swanwich, and rode down the High Street towards the Greyhound Inn. This inn was the coaching station and dominated the small square at the end of the street. It was a long two-storey building with lots of small windows. It had a thatched roof and walls covered in white painted plaster. In its centre was a flat porch, supported by two impressive round columns. Another smaller, inn stood on the corner opposite the Greyhound. Called the Bankes' Arms, this also had an impressive portico. It gave the impression of being a sturdier structure than the Greyhound because it proudly displayed its strong light grey Dorset stone, rather than having it hidden behind plaster.

As he progressed down the street, Nathan passed between a number of small thatched cottages, also built from the pleasant Purbeck stone. He never lost his sense of pleasure on entering this picturesque little village snuggling beneath the ruins of what must have been an impressive and formidable castle

The castle stood on the top of a huge earthen mound in the centre of a gap between two high ridges, which stretched away as far as one could see. These were Nine Barrow Down and Kingston Down and the valley they formed ran all the way to Swanwich and the sea some five miles away.

The gap in the downs provided the only easy route into this valley and the castle dominating this gap must have given the residents of the valley a strong sense of security, until, that is, Cromwell's men destroyed it during the Civil War. The Bankes family, after whom one of the inns beneath the castle took its name, had played a major role in the defence of the castle, holding out for many months before an act of treachery had enabled the besiegers to gain access.

Nathan was thinking on these events, when the smell of fresh baked bread wafting out from one of the cottages assailed him. The cottage had been converted into a bakery. Two large bay windows either side of the front door having replaced its small cottage windows. These were each fitted out with three shelves on which the baker could display his wares. Looking in, Nathan saw the baker carrying a large tray, stacked high with loaves of different shapes and sizes that he was about to place alongside various buns and cakes already on the shelves. This was clearly a prosperous community if it could warrant breads made from both the household dough and the more expensive wheaten dough as well as a range of confectionery. Few towns throughout England could run to that. For the second time in two days Nathan was reminded of the evident disparity of wealth in Dorset.

The smell of the newly baked bread reminded him that he had set out early that morning not waiting for breakfast and although he did not expect his meeting with Ridley to take very long he determined to make use of the Greyhound's stables and indulge himself in some porter and a plate of mutton before the interview.

So on reaching the inn, he rode his horse round to the stables at the back and giving the stable lad a suitable tip told him, 'Remove the saddle and give her a rub down, then blanket her and give her some hay and water. I'll probably be no more than an hour or so but she might as well be pampered a little, she's had a couple of hard days, bless her.' Then he set off across the road to the Bankes' Arms and walked in through its porticoes.

The ground floor of the inn was divided into a number of small snug bars with tables and chairs or in some cases benches being the only furniture. Each room had its own serving area. The larger rooms had bars running along the length of an inside wall and would be crowded and very public later on, whereas the smaller rooms were for patrons seeking quiet and privacy and were generally served via a small hatchway. Nathan noticed a couple of travellers taking breakfast in one of these rooms, but preferring his own company he sought out an empty snug and waited at the hatchway for service. After a short while the landlord appeared at the end of a corridor leading away from the hatch and seeing Nathan, who he immediately recognised, called out, 'Good day to you Mr Eldine, what brings you to my door so early in the day? Not an official call I hope!'

'As a matter of fact it is,' Nathan replied, 'but nothing you need worry about, Samuel, I need to speak to one of your guests, that's all. But first I'm going to enjoy one of your renowned breakfasts.'

'Right you are Mr Eldine, you take a seat and I'll send Moll along to you directly.'

Nathan sauntered over to a table by the window and sat down. Looking out, he had a fine view of the small square, which formed the centre of the village and from which several streets ran in different directions. It was a growing community almost a town rather than a village really and containing some important buildings including a corn exchange, a bank, a courtroom and a gaol, it also had two churches and these buildings combined with the wealth of its inhabitants made it one of the most important centres in the area. It was already busier outside than it had been when Nathan first arrived. There were people milling about, servants mostly, visiting the bakers and the dairy down one of the side streets. Two men were mounting horses in front of the inn and an old horse drawn cart piled high with hay was making slow progress back up along the high street, to go out past yet another drinking establishment.

A foolish smile crept over Nathan's face; partly due to the pleasure he was getting from his simple and leisurely activities on what promised to be a glorious autumn day but mostly from his amusement at Sam Butler's obvious unease at this unexpected visit from an officer of the law.

Nathan was certain that Sam was a regular receiver of smuggled goods. He always had a good cellar of fine French cognacs as well as port and sherry from Portugal and Spain, respectively, and his wines, which seldom bore labels were the envy of many a connoisseur. Yet, previous searches of the premises had not uncovered stocks that could be traced back to any criminal activities nor had they revealed stocks of a quantity that would cause eyebrows to be raised. Nathan was not overly worried by this as, even if he could have found the evidence he needed, the Purbeck magistrates, being some of Sam's best customers, would have dealt very lightly with the accused.

It was commonly recognised that in cases of smuggling, unless violence and grievous bodily harm were involved, the best the revenue officers could hope for, in terms of punishment, was the impounding of the contraband, as most supposedly impartial juries would never condemn a smuggler. Indeed, Nathan himself was more than sympathetic to non-violent smugglers and often ignored minor offences. Even in the case of a sizeable operation, he would concentrate more on uncovering the goods than bringing the culprits to court.

His only reason for doing the job he did was that he well knew that smuggling had to be restricted otherwise it was quite capable of undermining the lives of honest traders and even the very fabric of society. When he spoke to others about this, he knew it sounded far-fetched, but only a few years previously smuggling along the coast and especially in the West Country had reached such heights that the effects on the economy were staggering and the value placed on goods sold legally was seriously strained.

'Morning sir, what can I get you?' Moll, who had arrived unnoticed by Nathan, broke into his reveries.

'Oh! Hello, you must be Moll," Nathan said somewhat startled. He was addressing a pretty young girl with strawberry blonde hair. She was slightly dumpy from the remains of puppy fat and Nathan judged her to be seventeen or maybe even eighteen years of age. She was wearing a puffy white blouse cut low enough to show a strong cleavage between her teenage breasts, beneath this she wore a rumpled black skirt that flounced out around her indicating that it covered a number of petticoats. A rather soiled, white pinafore protected all this.

'That's what they call me round here, but I prefer my real name. That's Mary,' she added defiantly.

Deciding not to get entangled further with this moody girl, Nathan quickly gave his order and watched her scuttle out of the room. In no time, she returned with his ale before hurrying back out of the room calling as she went, 'Food'll be with you directly, sir.'

Sure enough, he did not have long to wait and was soon tucking in to a delicious plate of mutton and potatoes with a side order of hot bread. He was nearing the end of the meal, mopping up the sauce with the last hunk of bread, when Sam Butler came into the room and sat down opposite him.

'I presume the man you want to see is that there Ridley fellow what arrived in such a state the other night. If the Doctor hadn't spoken for him I wouldn't have let him in. What's he been up to?

Whatever - it hasn't got anything to do with me,' said Sam, quickly distancing himself from any possible crime.

'He hasn't been up to anything, as you put it. He's a victim not a criminal, I just need to ask him a few questions, that's all, so you can breathe easy, Sam,' Nathan said jovially, before adding, 'what room is he in?'

'I put him in room two, just along the corridor; he didn't look like he could manage the stairs to my upper rooms. But you won't find him there,' Sam said. Obviously not impressed with his latest guest, Sam went on to say, 'He didn't stay in his room long. In no time he was back demanding a bottle of rum, said his body hurt too much to get to sleep. Then he took it off to the back snug and he's been there ever since, drinking rum and sleeping at the table, on his third bottle, at least, he is. So, I don't know that you'll get much sense out of him. I only hope the Doc's right about him; else who's going to pay me.'

'Oh Lord!' said Nathan. 'I thought this was too nice a day to last.' Then getting to his feet and draining the last of his ale from the pewter tankard, he said, 'I met him briefly the day before yesterday and from what I was able to gather, he's quite well placed, so I don't think you need worry about your money, Sam. Now, let's go and find him and see what can be done.'

On entering the back snug, they found Ridley slumped in a wooden chair at one of the tables; he was just staring into space with his hands hanging loosely in his lap. He had done nothing to improve his appearance since his arrival; in fact he looked worse than ever. He had discarded the coat the Stockwells had lent him so that his tattered and blood stained shirt was openly displayed. He had not washed or shaved for some time now and this, combined with the effects of the rum, gave him the appearance of a very rough diamond indeed. An empty bottle and a half pint glass mug containing a small amount of rum stood on the table in front of him while a second bottle of rum lay on its side but nothing was spilling out of it nor were there any signs that it had done so previously. This bottle was obviously also empty and, clearly, Ridley had consumed it.

'For Christ's sake,' Butler grumbled, 'are you sure this fellow is a gentleman?'

In response, Ridley turned his head and looked vaguely at the two men then he mumbled, 'It's my fault; I should never have let her get in the boat without me.'

'What's he saying?' said Butler, 'and what's this about a boat?'

'It's all right, Sam, I'll handle this. I'm sure you've got business to attend,' Nathan said ushering the proprietor out of the room. As he closed the door on the retreating Butler he added, 'And yes, I'm sure he's a gentleman.'

Nathan stood listening for a moment to Sam Butler grumbling his way down the corridor, then he turned and walked over to Ridley.

'For pity's sake man, what do you think this is going to achieve?' Nathan demanded. 'You've got nothing to reproach yourself for,' he said raising his voice 'there was nothing you could do.'

'I should have done something,' Ridley slurred back.

'What? Get yourself killed along with the others. At least this way you have the chance to bring these villains to account, although, with the little evidence we've got, I can't see how we are going to get them into a court.'

'What do you mean? I saw them, what more evidence do you need?' Ridley said somewhat alarmed.

'You saw them alright, but you didn't recognise them nor can you describe them. You told me yourself you wouldn't know them again.'

'There was the big man, he was huge he would stand out surely?' This time there was an element of pleading in Ridley's voice.

'This is Purbeck,' Nathan said. 'All the main forms of employment here involve heavy labour, so there are plenty of big strong fellows. No, we need you to remember something more than that. Are you sure there's nothing more you can tell me? I don't suppose there's much point in me asking you that just now, is there? Not after all the rum you've consumed.' Nathan was quiet for a moment. He decided that there was nothing to be gained by quizzing Ridley at this time. He was not even sure that the man would be able to tell him anything of use when sober.

Nathan had known loss - his father and more recently his mother had both passed on and he had grieved their loss but they had died natural deaths after a long life. Death is an appointment all men must keep but when it comes in such circumstances the pain of loss is bearable. Nathan had also seen young lives taken brutally on the battlefield, including the lives of friends of his, but again, despite the violence, the circumstances of war negated much of the initial sorrow. Only later did the horror come back and then the vastness of the deed made it hard to comprehend, turning it into a dream rather than reality. At first he suffered nightmares but these eased with time.

To witness the loss of a loved one in such brutal circumstances as Ridley had was something Nathan had never experienced and he could not begin to imagine the horror and pain this man must be suffering.

'Of course I cannot imagine how you are feeling, the dreadfulness of what you have witnessed is beyond comprehension, nothing I say or do will relieve you of your anguish and pain,' Nathan said, 'but you will not get solace from a bottle; that will only lead to worse nightmares.' He was quiet for a moment before adding, 'I promise you one thing, that is that I will do everything within my power to bring the perpetrators of this foul dead to book and they will surely hang for their crimes.'

Then he said, 'For the moment the best I can do is impound the cargo while I carry out an investigation. Even if I prove it to be a case of wrecking, I can't stop White and his chums from claiming the salvage unless I can actually show that they were the wreckers or were in cahoots with them. I also need a reason for the investigation; there have to be suspicious circumstances. Oh, I know I have you as a witness but if I declare that, then your life will be in danger, and I cannot risk losing you, so I need something else. Even if I find a reason, if the investigation does not turn something up, then they will get away with it. There is one thing though...' and he told Ridley of his fool's errand and the roles played by Parkes and Smith.

'Well that's it! You say they are cohorts of White and he fortuitously found the wreck, what more do you need?' Ridley was quite animated now.

'Proof is what I need, evidence of some kind. They will obviously deny all knowledge of any wrecking. As I said before, all that we know is circumstantial, and would not hold up in court against a good lawyer.'

Again Nathan thought for a moment before continuing, 'If they've got away with it once, then they'll probably try it again, and perhaps this will be our best chance of nabbing them. We must be on total alert and not let them know that we know this was a case of wrecking. That way they will be less careful. If we can catch them in the act ...'

By now, Nathan was speaking quietly, musing to himself rather than addressing Ridley whom he thought too sodden to think coherently. However, he was wrong; Ridley now looked up and said, 'That's too risky. They might wreck the ship before we get to them, with God knows how many more poor souls perishing; besides Stockwell knows I saw them butchering my wife and the others, so does his wife and the Doctor - then there are Stockwell's farm workers, I don't know how much he told them but they probably know there was a survivor. As you said, this is a small community everyone knows everybody's business, so if all these people know, everyone else will in no time. That'll put the wreckers on full alert and they won't take any chances. For all we know Stockwell could be one of them, he's a rum character, that's for sure and he's big.'

'No not Stockwell,' Nathan responded, perhaps a little too quickly. 'Rum character he may be but he's a good and honest man, I'd stake my life on it. I must go to him now, straight away, and make sure he lets his people know that they must tell no one about you.' He was amazed at how alert the man had become and his grasp of the situation given that he had seemed a total drunken wreck moments before.

'I'll also call on the Doctor on my way. Let's hope none of them have said anything as yet. Come on up with you,' Nathan said as he put his hand under Ridley's shoulder and pulled him to his feet. 'First we must get you sobered up and vigilant, if anyone does know you saw what you did, then your life is in danger and you are in no state to defend yourself.'

He took Ridley along to his room and laid him on his bed. 'You rest here for a while I'll set a few things in motion that will get you back on your feet then I'll be off to see Stockwell.' Then from under his coat Nathan drew out two pistols, which he laid on a small table beside the bed. 'You were a soldier you said, so I presume you know how to use these. They are all primed and ready to fire so be careful. I hope that you won't need them but just in case, eh!'

'Now, give me some details of your measurements, if you can, and we will see what we can do about getting you fitted out with some new clothes.' As he said this, Nathan took a pencil and a scrap of paper from his pocket and proceeded to make notes as Ridley detailed the necessary information.

With this done, Nathan left the room and went off in search of the girl called Moll.

CHAPTER 9

It was five days since Ridley had witnessed the massacre in the cove but there was no lessening of his determination to take his revenge on the culprits. If anything, his resolve had strengthened as his impatience to commence his self-imposed mission increased. The memory of that night haunted him, the picture of those hapless souls and, in particular, his beloved Ayala was constantly with him, tearing at his very soul so that he would almost cry out in horror. Unmercifully, his mind played tricks with him. Although it would hardly seem possible, the picture he now recalled was even gorier than the reality. He had visions of bodies strewn all over the beach, while the perpetrators of the crime appeared as fiends from the sea and worse of all, he saw Ayala being mauled and then cudgelled to death by those fiends.

His one doubt as to the justification of his intentions, was that he would make an enemy of the young squire. This troubled him, as the man had shown him nothing but kindness. It was due to Eldine and his support that Ridley was now decked out in a smart set of clothes and had sufficient funds to tie him over until some of his own monies could be obtained. As well as this, the squire was an intelligent and likeable man and under other circumstances, Ridley felt sure, they would have become good friends.

However, these misgivings were not sufficient to sway Ridley from his intended actions, so strong was his repulsion of the crime that had been committed against him, his wife and the crew of the *Golden Nile*.

Where and how to start? This question was always with him. Eldine had agreed that White and his crew were possible suspects but he had no evidence to back this up and apparently, his questioning of the White brothers had been fruitless. As incensed as he was, Ridley knew he could not wreak his havoc based on suspicions. He had to be certain he was going after the right people. He would not want to kill an innocent party and have Eldine hunting him before he had the chance to strike at the true culprits. The squire was a very capable young man, who would quickly link Ridley to the killings once they began.

He realised he might not get many chances to carry out his deeds and he had no idea how competent his foes might be. They might prove too good for him before he could take them all out, indeed, he might even fail at the first hurdle. He would have to tread carefully, overcome his rage and thirst for vengeance and become cold and dispassionate, planning his every move, yet he would have to move swiftly once he started.

After the first day at Corfe and the night of drinking, Ridley had pulled himself together. With the help of the barmaid Molly, acting on instructions from Nathan, he had cleaned himself up donned a new set of clothes, sorted his finances and armed himself with a fine sword.

Ridley had then spent the remainder of that day and the next engaging in conversations with the customers of the Bankes' Arms. He carefully made sure the conversations seemed innocent enough not to arouse any suspicions, saying little but encouraging his companion to gossip away about current events in the area. Drinking little himself, he was liberal in his buying of drinks; an arrangement that well suited those he spoke to and they invariably talked freely.

However, he learned little of use until well into the afternoon of the second day, when he fell into conversation with Robert Jones, a fisherman from Swanwich. At first Ridley thought he was wasting his time as Jones, who was a Welshman, seemed intent on telling his life story. It seems he and his brother Lemuel were once shipmates on one of His Majesty's ships having been press ganged in Cardiff during the recent war with France. With the coming of peace they had been paid off in Portsmouth and had travelled westwards, with the intention of returning to Wales. However, one thing had led to another and they had found themselves work as fishermen in Swanwich. They had fared well for a while working for different boat owners but then Lemuel had fallen in with a bad lot.

'He took up work with a fellow called White,' Jones recalled in his welsh accent, and Ridley was suddenly very alert, 'and some of that work had nothing to do with fishing, if you get my drift,' the man continued. 'No it was not the sort of thing I wanted any part of and I told Lemuel so, but he always had a wild streak and said I had no stomach for adventure. "Adventure! Is that what you call it?" I said, "more like crime to me." We argued and argued about it, so we did.

'Each time he did something for White, the more resentful he got of my criticism until it got too much for me and I packed my bags and left him. That's why I'm here now. I used to be a miner before the navy took me. I reckon there can't be a lot of difference between digging for coal and quarrying stone, only takes a bit of brawn. So I thought I would look for work here. I never did like fishing particularly.'

'Would you like another drink?' Ridley asked, as he considered how he could get this man to tell him some more about White.

'No thanks, I'm not a big drinker, see. Specially since I've seen what it's done to Lemuel. The crowd he is in with do nothing but drink it seems to me. There's a tavern in Langton called The Ship where they hang out. I went there with Lemuel once - the place was full of cutthroats. Even the landlord was a surly looking type. From what I could gather he helps the smugglers hide their stuff. They say there are hidden passages from there right down to the sea, but it's probably only an old wives tale. That was when I first tried to get Lemuel away from their company but he'd have nothing said against them. Told me I was imagining things but it's him that will end up badly, no doubt about it.'

'It sounds a terrible place - a place to be avoided that's for sure,' Ridley said but he was thinking, that is where I will start, I'll go and see these bastards in their lair and see what I can learn.

'A place to be avoided, indeed! Grim it is!' Jones said. Then getting up from the table he added, 'Well I must be off, thanks for the drink. Perhaps I'll be able to return the favour once I get some work.'

'No trouble, it was a pleasure talking with you, you tell a good yarn. By the way, where is this Langton? I want to be sure I avoid going there.' Ridley tried to sound only mildly interested.

'It's on the road between here and Swanwich, the high road that is, the one they call the Priest's Way, you know up the hill through Kingston. I'll see you around.' With that, the man left.

Ridley sat there a little longer working out how best to go about things and then, with a plan of action decided upon, he went to his room to prepare. He took a sheet from the bed, put his old boots and trousers on this and the coat the Stockwells had given him. Then he placed one of Eldine's pistols together with some spare powder and shot on the pile. Finally, he tied the whole lot up into a bundle. Next, he put a belt about his waist to which he fixed his new sword in its scabbard. He tucked the other pistol into his belt, before putting on his new bright blue coat. Pausing for a moment to ensure he had everything he needed, he then picked up the bundle and, inconspicuously as he could, he made his way out of the inn.

It was a long walk, especially as a large part was up a very steep winding road that ran from the outskirts of Corfe to the small village of Kingston, nestling near the top of the downs. Then a stretch eastwards along the crest of these hills to Langton Matravers. So it was early evening by the time his destination came into view. Autumn was advancing quickly and the nights were drawing in. A dank mist had formed up here, slowly drifting in from the sea that lay less than a mile to the south. All about him, the mist swirled a few feet of the ground, whilst off to the north it blanketed out the view of the valley below. It was the sort of cold sea mist that worked its way into every part of you, so that Ridley was grateful for his heavy coat, the collar of which he had turned up for extra protection. As he approached it, he was surprised to find Langton was bigger than he first supposed. Viewing it from a distance in the mist, he had underestimated the number of buildings in front of him.

It was obviously a mixed community. Many of the houses, although larger than usual for workmen's cottages, were run down and in a state of disrepair while others were well kept and freshly thatched. Several were newly built and Ridley was aware of a couple of very large Georgian houses a little removed from the others. Clearly, some of Langton's inhabitants were extremely wealthy, making it incongruous that the den of iniquity to which he was headed should be located in its midst.

The road now fell away steeply before rising again. The small trough did not appear to hold any buildings but near the top of the opposite slope there were a few cottages surrounding a church and on the crest, a large square stone building. This latter was The Ship Inn and it was a bleak looking place indeed. Beyond it, the land again fell away so that it appeared as if the inn was perched on the edge of the world - an eerie effect, exaggerated by the clawing mist.

It was a three-storey building with few windows, two on each of the upper stories at the front and none on the sidewall. To enhance the bleak effect, the windows were of the narrow sash variety made up of a number of small panes. Like the only door, also narrow and unwelcoming, the window frames were painted black and no light came from anywhere.

As he studied the place from a distance, Ridley recalled the Welshman's parting words "A place to be avoided, indeed. Grim it is." Grim does not do it justice, he thought, it's far worse than that.

Since reaching Langton he had been looking about him and had seen a rickety out-building by one of the earlier cottages. He went back to this. It was a small shed and judging by its state of disrepair, it probably had not been used for years. That looks right for my needs, he decided. He went over to it and checked that it really was not in use, a fact confirmed by the number of spiders' webs adorning it. Then he quickly removed his coat, the sword, the pistol, his new breeches and his shoes, opened the bundle and put on his old coat, trousers and boots. He placed all the discarded items into the bundle and then stowed this away in the shed. By the time he was done he was shivering but he was satisfied that his appearance had been transformed. In his fine new outfit and heavily armed he would have stood out like a sore thumb amidst The Ship's customers, which was the last thing he wanted. His intention was to be as unmemorable as he could, to go unnoticed if possible.

Ready at last, he finally made his way to the inn. As he approached, it became apparent that the main street went on beyond this building with a few more houses running down the hill.

Given the size of the village, Ridley was surprised to be the only person in view. Only a few of the buildings had any lights showing, implying that many of the residents would be early risers who had already retired for the night. The inn maintained its bleak appearance but as he drew nearer, he heard the sounds of revelry suggesting that, here at least, some life stirred.

The door had a thumb latch, which he depressed before pushing it open. Expecting to be dazzled by the light from within he was surprised to find it was hardly any brighter than the outside. He had entered one large room but this was divided into lots of small snugs either side of an aisle that ran down the room from the doorway. The snugs were formed by wooden panelling from floor to ceiling. Each snug contained a table and two benches, some were empty but there were varying sized groups of rough looking men huddled together in several of them and in each of these occupied areas a small stump of a candle had been set in the middle of the table.

The light emanating from the lit snugs provided a dim illumination to the aisle as Ridley walked down it. Eventually he came to an open area where half a dozen men were standing talking and drinking from tankards. Amongst them was a barmaid who had seen better days and paid no attention to the men, despite the fact that several groped at her as she passed. She was carrying a large jug of ale which she took to one of the snugs before returning to the bar located near the right hand wall of the open area. There was a man behind the bar on which two more candles flickered but again the amount of illumination was negligible.

A man could easily go unnoticed in this place, Ridley realised but he still took care not to approach the point of the bar where the candles were.

'What's your poison?' the barman said. Wearing a scruffy, collarless, white shirt he was a mean looking fellow and Ridley could feel the man's eyes studying him closely. He judged this to be the landlord of whom Jones had spoken.

'Beer,' Ridley said gruffly as he banged a penny on the bar before turning away from the man's inquisitive gaze.

'Beer's a hapenny a pot, and it's another half penny for a candle if you want a seat in a snug,' the barman said.

'Two pots, no candle, thanks.' Keeping his voice rough Ridley decided two pots was all he wanted for the night and this way he wouldn't have to return to the bar and the barman's scrutiny. When served he picked up both pots and moved away from the bar sipping on the first pot of ale. He slowly moved around the pub stopping near anyone engaged in conversation. As unobtrusively as possible, eavesdropping before moving on once he had determined that he could learn nothing useful. As the evening wore on he had pretty well covered all the customers and although he had heard many things, some amusing, and one or two villainous, he had heard nothing of import to him. He had almost finished his second pot of ale and was considering giving up for the night when one of two men sitting in a snug suddenly said, 'Whitey ain't going to show tonight, we're no nearer getting paid than ever and I can't afford any more beer.'

Ridley moved nearer, he had been listening to these men earlier, but they had not interested him, they were both drunk and their small talk had been mostly pointless or obscene. Now, with the mention of 'Whitey', he was alert to hear what more they said.

'Keep your voice down Tom Carter, we don't want everyone knowing what we done,' the other man answered in the loud whisper of a drunk.

'S'pose not, Parksie, but it ain't everyone what does what we done and gets away with it, is it?'

'Maybe not but a fat lot of good it's doing us.' Now the man dropped his voice lower but it was still loud enough for Ridley who had taken up a position in the snug next to them. With his ear close to the dividing panels he could hear quite plainly what the two men were saying whilst remaining out of their sight.

'All them killings and what have we got? Nothing!' Parksie answered himself. 'Not a word from Whitey, to say whether he collected the cargo on not, to say nothing of what it's worth.'

He went silent for a while and Ridley could sense rather than hear him downing his beer.

Then he spoke again, 'Go on Tom let's have another pot before we go I've still got enough for that.'

'Well that's real kind of you, Sam, if you're buying I won't say no,' the other man replied. Ridley heard the scraping of shoes as the man called Tom stood up. However, before he went to the bar he spoke again. 'If this works out as it should, we won't be worrying about the price of a pot for a while I can tell you. Mind you I don't trust the

Cornish man either, for all we know he could've grabbed the spoils from the *Golden Nile* and scarpered.'

Ridley almost jumped back from the panelling as he heard this. He had begun to suspect he had found his quarry as the men spoke but this last was proof beyond all doubt.

Tom Carter and Sam Parkes, he thought, two of the wreckers without any doubt and they have confirmed White's part in it. Then forgetting his resolve for careful planning as his thirst for revenge swelled, he decided, well, today will be their last day on this earth.

He nestled back in his snug to await their departure, when he would begin to take his vengeance on all or as many of the wreckers that he could. Not for one moment did he consider handing what he now knew over to the squire and letting the law take care of these miscreants. His revenge lust was far too great for him to think so rationally.

Some half an hour later Ridley found himself following the two men down Langton's main street keeping well behind them and slipping into doorways or alleyways, whenever he reached a point where a candle in a window illuminated the street. He would then wait until his quarry was well ahead before exposing himself and continuing his stalk. Once he was sufficiently clear of the main brightness he would increase his pace until he had them back in sight and then slow down to match their pace, always walking stealthily so as not to make any noise and making sure that they did not see him. At one point, Carter stopped and then began relieving himself in a doorway of much of the alcohol that he had consumed.

There was no obvious place for Ridley to dip into so he pressed himself up against the stone wall of the nearest building and prayed that the night was sufficiently dark enough for him to go unnoticed. Carter seemed to take an age with his ablutions and Ridley could hear the two men talking and laughing.

Suddenly and quite clearly Ridley heard Parkes say, 'Watching you has got me going now.' Parkes then joined in the process of defiling the doorway. Finally, Ridley heard Carter saying, 'Lawd, 'tis better out than in as they say, ashes to ashes and piss to piss.'

The two men laughed and started on their way again, along with their unseen shadow. As Ridley reached the spot where the two men had stopped, he was assailed by the stench of urine and creased his face in repulsion. He looked at the vandalised doorway where he noticed a brass plaque, which read 'Elias Small, Undertaker of the Bodies of the Souls of this Parish' and he realised the significance of Carter's cryptic comment.

After a while, they reached the outskirts of the village where the buildings began to thin out and the high street turned into a country lane with hedgerow on either side. It was near here that Ridley had stashed his bundle earlier so he left off following the men. He went to the shed and quickly retrieved his sword, one of the two pistols and the powder and shot which he put in his pocket. Then tying the belt around his waist he hurried to catch the men up. There were no more candle lit windows now. The mist still hung around and there was thick cloud cover, which meant little moonlight to help illuminate the men Ridley was following. In fact, it was becoming so dark that Ridley was having difficulty making out the road ahead and began to worry in case he should lose contact with his prey. He knew he had to get much closer to them, for if they turned off the road anywhere he would not be aware of it. On the other hand, in this darkness and with the road becoming less well kept than it was in the village, there was the danger that he may trip or stumble and if he was too close he might be heard.

Fortunately, the two men ahead of him were still talking quite volubly - no doubt because of the beer they had consumed - so for the time being he had their voices as a guide even if he could not see them.

Suddenly, out of the mist, only a few paces ahead of him, the outlines of Carter and Parkes loomed and Ridley stopped, frozen to the spot.

'It's a good job I know this road like the back of my hand, Tom Carter,' Parkes was saying, 'or you'd of had us both in the ditch, I've walked this route drunk and sober so many times that I reckon I could do it blindfold.'

'It's all right for you then ain't it, personally I haven't got a clue where we are and I can't see nought in this pitch,' Carter then muttered. 'Is it much further to the crossroads? I don't know how I'll manage from there - how far is Tam's cottage?'

'Don't worry, I'll get you to the crossroads, then you'll only have a few hundred yards to go and Tam knows you're coming, he'll have a light shining to guide you. Me on the other hand, I've got another two miles to go from there, past Downley's stone too. Some folk say he still haunts the place. I ain't never seen nothing but I still get a queer feeling every time I pass by there, even in the daylight. I ain't looking forward to that tonight I can tell you, not without no moon nor nothing.'

'Well sooner you than me,' was Carter's final comment as the two men started off again. Ridley let out an inaudible sigh. He could just make out that they were linked arm to arm and realised that neither of them was feeling particularly brave to be out on a night like this. Nor am I for that matter, he thought, as he once again took up his malevolent undertaking.

Moments later, the two men stopped again, 'Here we are then,' Parkes said, 'you go off down there. See there's the light in Tam's cottage. I'll go and see Whitey tomorrow, find out what we are to do with her and I'll be back here late afternoon.'

There followed a few drunken, muttered farewells before the men started in their different directions.

Ridley decided it would be too risky to engage Carter between here and the cottage as Parkes would still be near at hand and if he heard any commotion he might return to help his friend. Also Ridley had no idea who Tam was nor how many people may be in the cottage.

No, it would be better to follow Parkes, deal with him and then come back to the cottage to assess the situation. He knew Carter was going nowhere tomorrow, so he would wait for the right opportunity and then strike.

Instead, he waited a few moments to give sufficient distance between Carter and the crossroads, before setting off after his prey. The hedgerow had given way to a low dry-stone wall on the left and open down land on his right. The hard mud road had now turned into a well-trodden path running alongside the wall. This made it easy to follow the path and it didn't take him long to come within earshot of the shuffling Parkes, who was now breathing heavily. Ridley slowed his pace, stalking his man until he was confident that he was far enough away from the cottage. Any sounds would carry a long way on a still night like tonight and he wanted to be sure that they would not summons help for his intended victim.

Time had passed since that harrowing night on the beach but it had not dented Ridley's determination to avenge his wife's death. He felt no remorse, doubt or fear of what he was about to do - just a cold hatred for these men he was going to kill.

Now it would begin, he drew his sword and increased his pace.

Parkes, who had just drawn level with a tall standing stone, was muttering some sort of prayer beneath his breath. 'Well may you pray Samuel Parkes,' Ridley called out, 'for I know you and what you have done and I am here for vengeance.' Parkes said nothing he just turned around looking deadly pale and sank to his knees sobbing. Eventually, he did manage to say something, which seemed like gibberish to Ridley. 'I'm sorry Jack, it was the drink that did it, I never meant to harm you!'

This did nothing to appease Ridley, who put these ravings down to drunkenness - he simply raised his sword and brought it down with a thunderous blow angling into Parkes's shoulder and neck. It was the skilled blow of a professional soldier. Blood shot out from the deep gouge as Parkes crumpled and, without uttering a sound, he fell face down.

His body twitched for a few moments and then with a final shudder came to rest. Ridley wiped his sword on his victim's coat, sheathed it and, not giving a second glance at the corpse, he turned and set off back to the cottage.

On reaching the junction, he realised it was not a crossroad after all, the path had simply swung round down past the cottage, where the lit window was still evident. The other legs of the cross were the road from Langton, the pathway he had followed and a less well-walked path down which he could see nothing.

He took the road to the cottage and, on reaching it, crept up to the window and pressed his back to the wall listening for any sounds from inside.

It was a traditional stone cottage with a thatched roof and was in a state of disrepair. However, the heavy stone walls and the thick bevelled glass windows made for good sound proofing, so that all

Ridley could hear was a low murmur. He decided to take a chance and turned his head to peer into the window. The first thing he saw was four men sitting at a table. Each had a plate in front of him and a tankard and there were two jugs of beer on the table. They had obviously finished eating for the plates were empty apart from crumbs and leftovers. One of the men was drinking from his tankard while another was slumped on the table, his head on his crossed arms, and clutching his pot. The murmur was coming from the other two on the opposite side of the table who were deep in conversation. No one saw Ridley at the window, who having taken this in from a cursory glance before pulling back, decided he could afford a longer inspection.

This time he looked around the room. There was a large fireplace built into the opposite wall, where a log was burning on top of a deep pile of ashes. The fire had clearly been alight for some time. There were various pots hanging from hooks in the fireplace and a bread oven cut into the stone. An old leather armchair was drawn up to and facing the fire at an angle. It had obviously been a fine chair in days past but it was now scratched and torn with its stuffing protruding in places. Ridley could just make out that a woman was slumped in this, but could make nothing of her appearance other than her black unkempt hair, part of her arm, covered in white fabric, and the lower part of her legs, which were bare and scrawny. A pair of cheap ankle length boots lay by her feet where she had discarded them.

Looking up, Ridley saw that the room had no ceiling, with the beams of the cottage exposed. Half way along there was a dividing wall, which had two doors in it. This wall did not reach to the beams, instead it stood about ten feet high and there was a ladder leaning against it. Presumably, the area above and beyond the doors, would have a floor and would no doubt be sleeping quarters. This also had an exposed ceiling with the same black painted beams.

He returned his attention to the men at the table. The one who had been drinking now lowered his tankard and turned his head towards the two men opposite him and Ridley recognised him.

In an instant, Ridley was back on the beach and he had a clear recollection of the wreckers standing over their final victim, and this man was one of them. The memory was only a fleeting picture but, in his mind, there was no doubt that he had found another one of the villains.

He now looked at the other two men. One was Carter the other he did not know but he studied him carefully to make sure he would recognise him again. He could not make out any of the features of the unconscious man, so he pulled back from the window sensing that he had taken enough risks for now.

He shut his eyes and tried to concentrate on the image that had returned to him along with the other parts of that fatal night that he could remember. After a while, he opened his eyes. He was now satisfied that he had a complete recall of the events and was sure that there had been six wreckers on the beach. Parkes and Carter, he had already identified, now here was a third that he knew was involved. No doubt, this cottage was their lair and he could be fairly certain that the other two men in the room were party to the crime.

That meant he had identified five of his would-be victims, which left the big man, whom he had not seen in the room, and then there were the two White brothers to be taken into account. There were also two crew members on the boat when they discovered the wreck. Although there was no proof that these two were aware that the ship had been wrecked deliberately, Ridley's desire for revenge was such that he did not even consider this but simply decided that it would be easy enough to ascertain who they were and add them to the list. His only uncertainty now was the big man.

He began to plan his campaign. It was essential that he struck as quickly as possible taking out as many as he could before they realised they were being targeted.

No doubt, once they did, they would take measures to protect themselves. Most likely they would keep together to make themselves less vulnerable. Surprise was Ridley's main advantage and when he did strike, it would need to be fast and fatal, especially if he had to take on two or more in one attack.

There was nothing he could do for now, so he moved away from the house towards some outbuildings. He finally fixed on one appropriate to his needs, which he entered and found himself a dark corner for concealment but from where he had a good view of the front of the cottage. The night was so dark that he could only see the cottage because of the candle burning in the window and after a while this was extinguished.

As he could no longer make anything out, he settled down to await the morning, with an odd thought running through his head, Parkes called me Jack, how did he know my name?

This was indeed a puzzle for which Ridley could think of no answer.

CHAPTER 10

It was some time before Ridley was able to fall asleep. It was not that he was uncomfortable - in fact his place of concealment was both warm and snug - he was simply tense with anticipation of his acts of vengeance. He played out one drama after another in his mind as he considered different ways that he might set about killing these men. He knew this to be pointless. His ultimate strategy would depend on the actions of the men in the house but the uncertainty made him restless.

Eventually he did sleep but when dawn came, he was wide-awake and alert for any movement from the cottage. The morning passed slowly, with no sign of activity until, at last, the cottage door opened, and a young woman came out. He had caught a glimpse of this scrawny girl, sitting in the chair by the fire, the previous night. Carrying a jug, she made her way to a water pump by the side of the cottage, and set about filling it. She was not part of Ridley's plans, so he paid her little attention. Instead, he concentrated on watching the cottage but there were no further signs of activity. The girl returned to the cottage, went back inside and shut the door.

Midday came and went and Ridley, who would normally have eaten two meals by now, was feeling hungry and dispirited. What was happening? Why hadn't any of the men come out of the cottage? Perhaps they had done so while he slept and had long since left this place. It was a quandary, he wanted to go to the window and look inside but he could not risk exposing himself in daylight. He was on the point of giving up altogether and returning to Corfe, where he could get himself a fine meal, when the door opened again.

Two men came out one was carrying a basket for logs and the other an axe and they walked across the yard towards the building where Ridley waited. They got so close that Ridley began looking around for a place to hide. Then just before reaching the barn, they turned and left the yard, taking a path up-hill through a field. Ridley moved carefully to the front of the small barn and peered out.

The cottage door was closed so he felt safe enough to leave the barn's protection in order to get a view of where these men were going. They were a short distance up the hill heading for a large clump of trees and Ridley surmised that they were about to chop wood. The copse was sufficiently far from the cottage for his purposes. He could easily kill these two men in the copse without being detected. The question was could he sneak up on them before they saw him and this, he realised, depended on how far they went into the copse.

The fact that there were two of them on this mission probably meant they intended cutting more wood than just sufficient for their immediate needs so they should be up there for a good while. Having arrived at this conclusion, he decided to wait and let them move amongst the trees before sneaking up on them, if indeed they did.

To his great satisfaction the men did go into the copse and with such determination that they clearly intended entering well inside. Ridley, checked his pistol and then set off after them. On reaching the edge of the trees he stopped and listened. He could hear the men talking as well as the sound of the axe on wood. He crept in and edging his way forward as quietly as possible, he made his way towards the sounds. Eventually he reached a spot from which he could see a clearing where the men were standing. They were taking a break from their labours and the one who had been using the axe was facing Ridley. He was holding the axe at his side and showing no sign of having seen or heard anything untoward. The other, who Ridley recognised as Carter, was equally blissfully unaware of the menace lurking in the trees that was about to burst upon them.

With his left hand, Ridley pulled the pistol from his belt and quietly cocked it before drawing his sword. He edged forward until the men were only a few paces from him and it seemed as if they must spot him. Incredibly, they did not. He steeled himself then quickly walked out into the clearing. It was only then that the men looked up at him and it was too late. In one motion, as he strode forward, he brought the pistol up so that it was less than a yard from the face of the man with the axe and fired. At the same time, without checking his pace, he raised the sword above his head and slashed it down violently into Carter's neck. Neither man had moved and now they both crumpled to the floor, almost simultaneously, and it was all over.

Not bothering to inspect the bodies, Ridley turned and hurried back through the trees to the edge of the copse where he went down on one knee just inside the tree line. Calmly, he set about reloading the pistol whilst watching for signs of life from the cottage. He was not concerned about the men he had just assaulted. He knew from experience that they had both died instantly. His concern now was with the men still in the cottage.

He felt sure that they must have heard the shot and expected them to come rushing out to investigate. He did not realise that the occasional gunshot was not uncommon in these parts as the woods around were well stocked with pheasant and was, therefore, surprised when nothing happened.

He had expected this to be the hardest part of the day's work as the element of surprise was lost and he would now be the one being assailed. He waited and when he was satisfied that nothing was going to happen he considered his next move. Finally, he stood up sheathed his sword, tucked the pistol in his belt, closed his coat over them and started back down the hill.

When he had looked through the window the previous night, he had counted four men. He had disposed of two of these. The man he knew to be Carter and another whom he had not recognised. He presumed this to be the man that had been slumped across the table. Now he was making his way back to the cottage to attend to the remaining two men. He had recharged the pistol and felt confident enough in his abilities to be able to deal with both of them as quickly as he had Carter and his friend. He still had the element of surprise on his side and planned to use the window once again to place the men inside.

If they were together in the same room, he would employ the same approach as before by rushing in with his pistol in one hand and his sword in the other. He would shoot the nearest man and be on the other before he could react. If on the other hand, they were in separate rooms, he would have to employ a different line of attack. Probably he would use his sword to kill the first man and, with luck, there would not be too much noise to alert the other.

I'm getting ahead of myself, he thought, no point in planning my assault before I see the lie of the land.

The door of the cottage was now clearly in site. It opened and the man he had remembered from the cove stepped out. Ridley froze, quickly looking about for concealment. There was a dry-stone wall about ten paces ahead of him, with a gap in it of some five feet. The path he was on ran through this gap and there was a broken five bar gate leaning against the wall, which had clearly been there for a long time. Ridley considered running to the wall to gain cover but immediately discounted the idea. The man was not looking this way and had not seen Ridley but he might see or sense a rapid movement. As well as this, the path he was on was uneven, very broken up and stony, so that it would not be possible to run quietly.

Before he could decide what to do, Ridley heard the voice of another man from within the cottage who called out. 'Hold it a minute Tam, I've just got to get my boots on. What's the rush anyway?'

So that's Tam Smith, Ridley thought, as he stood rooted to the spot. Smith was in his late thirties and judging from his appearance was an old soldier. He still wore his military trench coat and a rather battered infantryman's peaked shako. Although all the insignia had been removed.

'The rush is that we've got to get to Swanwich and back. Parkes was supposed to be bringing us our money, remember!' Smith replied sarcastically. 'He was also supposed to bring us any news and to tell us what we should do about her. God knows where he's got to and I ain't staying cooped up here waiting to find out.' Smith started this by shouting but he lowered his voice as the other man came out of the cottage.

Younger than Smith, he too was wearing an ankle length coat, though not military. It was in fact of the type much favoured by pirates of yesteryear. It was buttoned to the waist where it flared open to show green corduroy trousers tucked into knee length leather boots. Made from brown leather, the coat had seen better days. The man was hatless and had a shock of black, curly, shoulder length hair but most noticeable were the deep pock marks that littered his young face. He saw Ridley immediately but before he could react, Ridley waved and called out, 'Hello there, I wonder if you can help me?'

Tam Smith swung around and the two men glared at Ridley as he sauntered over to them, trying to look as affable and friendly as he could. This was quite difficult given his rather disreputable appearance.

'I'm a stranger in these parts and I seem to have taken the wrong path,' Ridley continued, ignoring their hostile looks. 'I am supposed to be meeting an old acquaintance at some place called Langton Matravers. What strange names you give your villages in Dorset.'

Ridley knew he was taking a gamble in approaching these men openly but felt he had little choice as any other action would have looked very suspicious and he hoped his naive attitude would put them off guard. Tam Smith was a cautious man, however and had already noticed the sword at Ridley's side and the pistol tucked into his breeches.

'Stop there,' he said. 'That's near enough. Who are you meeting and why are you so heavily armed if your business is so innocent?'

Ridley hesitated only for a moment and then, with a flash of inspiration, he changed his manner into that of a felon and gruffly said, 'I don't mind telling you who I'm meeting, his name is Josh White but my business with him is none of your concern. As to my weapons, I consider a man would be foolish to take to the road in unknown country without protection. Have you never heard of footpads?'

Tam was clearly taken aback by this but he was also impressed for he too changed his attitude. 'Josh White eh! Well maybe your business is of interest to me for I happen to be an associate of Josh's and it's likely that your business with him will affect me.'

'That's as may be, but if so, then you will know not to expect me to discuss it with a stranger,' Ridley said sharply.

'Alright, alright!' Tam said. 'No need to get off your horse about it, but equally if what you say is true then you too will understand my position. We are wary of strangers around here, especially when they turn up in such a remote spot as this. Still if you're a friend of Whitey's then no doubt you are on the level but you certainly have gone adrift if you've been up that way.

'As it happens, you are lucky to have met up with us for we are on our way to see Josh. Although he won't be at Langton as you suppose. I don't know when you arranged this meeting but I happen to know he's in Swanwich at the moment. You best come with us.'

'Are you sure? He definitely told me Langton Matravers.'

'I know what I'm saying, he's in Swanwich. Anyway the road takes us through Langton so you can check for yourself but I'm telling you he won't be there.'

Marvellous, Ridley mused, his gamble had worked out perfectly. All I have to do is find the right moment to strike. I will go along with them, chat aimlessly, maybe give the impression that I am a fellow smuggler, until they are well and truly off their guard, then I will pounce.

'Is it far to this Swanwich place?' he asked casually.

'Far enough,' the other man spoke for the first time. He had a sour disposition and seemed less reassured by Ridley's remarks.

Best watch him - he is not so easily won over, Ridley thought

'It's about four miles and we have to be back by tonight so we better get going,' Tam said more amiably and the three men set off on their journey.

They walked for nearly half a mile without speaking. Throughout this time, the two men retained their caution, they walked either side of Ridley with the unknown man keeping a little behind.

This won't do, Ridley was thinking desperately. I must get them relaxed for I need to act soon if I'm to get back to Corfe tonight. Someone may find the bodies and there could be a hue and cry. I must not be found up here. I need to cover my tracks.

'So you're Tam Smith, are you, Josh has mentioned your name to me, not that he says much you understand. My name is Jack, by the way. I'm not a seaman like you, my activities are more land based, if you know what I mean.' Ridley tried to engage them in conversation but at first neither man spoke.

Then after they had walked another hundred yards or so, Tam suddenly spoke, 'Josh mentioned me did he? Well he must trust you, for he hardly ever talks of our arrangement with anyone. Yes I'm Tam and that there is Si - Simon Trevellis, that is. He's from

Falmouth, moved up this way cause things were getting a little too hot for him in Cornwall. That's right, ain't it, Si?'

'Aye, we had a good thing going for a while, we was bringing in brandy and wine and all sorts in a big way. You wouldn't believe how much we was shifting. I guess we over did it for the excise men got real busy and before we knew it they had half the gang locked up. Caught them red-handed; moving a cargo we'd had hidden for a while. Someone must have grassed on us for they were waiting in ambush. It didn't need us all to move it and I was one of the lucky ones that wasn't there.' Suddenly, Trevellis's mood had changed totally and he was confiding in Ridley as if he was an old friend.

It must be because Tam said Josh White trusts me, Ridley decided.

'Yes,' Trevellis continued, 'someone must have talked for they started rounding up other members of the gang even though they hadn't been there. That's when I skipped it. I have an uncle, here in Dorset, what does a bit for Whitey from time to time, and he gave me a berth and introduced me to the lads.'

Smith was chuckling and said something quietly to Trevellis who also started to laugh. Ridley did not know what they were saying for, while Si had been speaking, he had surreptitiously fallen back a pace or two. Now, as they shared this joke, Ridley drew the pistol from his belt, called to Tam and, as the man turned to face him, he fired. He chose to shoot Tam as he was the larger of the two men and as an old soldier he might have put up a hard fight. Ridley thought Trevellis would be the easier to take on with the sword.

Having fired the shot he threw the pistol down and drew the sword from its scabbard.

Tam fell to the ground, clutching at the wound in his chest crying, 'What the Hell!' before adding rather pointlessly, 'He shot me!'

In the seconds that it took for this to happen, Trevellis stunned Ridley by reacting with surprising agility. He spun round, jumped back two paces and swiftly drew a sword of his own. Because of the long coat, Ridley had been unaware that Trevellis carried a weapon. The two men circled each other cautiously, each waiting for the other to commit, while Tam continued to moan in pain at their feet.

Trevellis, although hampered by his heavy coat, was fast and nimble and Ridley realised he could not afford to take victory for granted. Again, they moved in a circle. Skilfully, the man back sliced at Ridley's side. Ridley jumped back, for he had been anticipating just such a move and the blade passed inches in front of him. Now it was Ridley's turn to strike and he drove his blade forward only to have it deflected as his adversary reacted quickly. Trevellis was getting confident now and as they again probed for an opening, he beckoned Ridley forward with his left hand, grinning menacingly. This did not alarm Ridley, however, as experience had shown him that over confidence in a fight was a weakness and he welcomed Trevellis's taunts. He made to move forward as if he were answering the invitation and, as he expected, Trevellis lunged his blade at Ridley's stomach but Ridley had not stepped forward as at first seemed. Instead he spun in a circle to his left. Holding his sword straight out, at chest level, he completed the spin and his blade sliced deeply into his opponent's sword arm. Trevellis's blade found nothing but air.

The fight was over. Trevellis still clutched his sword but the wound to his arm meant that he could hardly lift it to defend himself. All it needed now was for Ridley to deliver the coup de grace and he was about to do this when Tam, who was wounded badly but far from dead, grabbed him by the ankles in an attempt to trip him up. Seizing the opportunity, Trevellis moved his sword to his left hand and charged at Ridley. The result was farcical.

Tam's efforts caused Ridley to fall forward on to his knees and he only avoided going flat on his face by planting his left hand firmly on the ground. As he did so he pointed his blade up towards his oncoming assailant, who, inept in fighting left-handed, flailed his sword harmlessly at the point where Ridley had been standing and his momentum took him fatally straight on to the outstretched sword, which passed right through him. Trevellis gave out a fearful cry of agony and crashed forward forcing the blade from Ridley's grasp and landing sprawled across Tam, who in turn shrieked from the pain of the blow to his blooded chest.

Ridley kicked and pulled until his feet were free from Tam's grip, got to his feet and looked down on the scene of carnage. Lying across Tam, Trevellis was still twitching in his final death throes and blood was pumping from his wounds, much of which was pouring on to Tam who stared at Ridley in startled horror. Ridley's sword was beneath Trevellis and was clearly broken, so he stepped over the two bodies and picked up Trevellis's sword from where it had fallen and studied it. It was not of the quality of his own but it was certainly adequate for its purpose. Then he turned again and stood once more looking down at Tam who wore the face of a terrified man.

Eventually, Tam found his voice and shakily asked, 'Who are you? Why have you done this?'

'You might as well know why you are about to die. I'm the one you didn't kill.' Ridley said impassively. 'The night of the wrecking. You killed the captain, his crew and my wife but you didn't kill me and now I'm killing you.'

'I didn't kill your wife!' Tam gasped. 'Please, I beg you, don't kill me!'

'It doesn't matter who killed who, you were there and that makes you guilty of all the murders.' As he said this, Ridley put the sword point to Tam's chest.

Tam shrieked, 'No, no, you don't understand we didn't...' but before he could finish, Ridley placed both hands on the hilt of the sword and drove it down hard and straight through the man's heart. He then pulled the sword out and using his foot rolled Trevellis over. He, like Tam, was dead.

Ridley sighed, his shoulders now slumped as he felt the tautness leave him. Like any predator stalking its kill, he had been in a state of tense anticipation since the moment Carter and his friend had first exited the cottage to gather wood. Now he could relax slightly.

He still felt no shame or guilt for his acts, no compassion for his victims, just indifference. There was no weakening of his resolve. If anything, he was more determined than ever. He was slightly disappointed that he felt no joy either. Clearly, his thirst for revenge and justice, as he saw it, was not slated and he considered that this was because he still needed to find and kill the ringleaders, White and the big man, before his vengeance would be complete. Especially the big man! He shuddered at the gruesome memory of that man flailing the unfortunate sailor and, in his imagination, he saw Ayala in the place of the sailor and a terrible coldness swept over him.

Pulling himself together, he looked about. There was no one in sight in any direction but he did not want these bodies found too soon. He needed time to get back to the place outside of Langton where he had hidden his bundle.

He knew he must get back into his new clothes and return to Corfe as soon as possible. The road he was on was lined with dry stone walling and he set about manhandling the two bodies over this and then pressing them as close to the wall as possible. This meant that they were invisible from the road and the only way they would be found was when the farmer next visited this field, which hopefully was days or even weeks away.

By the time he had finished, he was in a more dishevelled state than ever, covered in blood and mud, so he picked up his pistol and the hilt of his broken sword, before making his way back to Langton very covertly, as he could not afford to be seen in this condition.

CHAPTER 11

Established as a Chapelry of Corfe Church, the village of Kingston dates back to Saxon times and sits on a high hill overlooking Corfe Castle. Removed from the more prosperous quarrying areas of Purbeck, a few of its inhabitants scraped their living as agricultural labourers but the majority worked in a local tanning factory. Factory was a grandiose name for what was little more than a cluster of buildings. Both tanning and farming were hard and demanding forms of employment, carried out by hand or with simple tools and the labourers were poorly paid. As a result, the majority of the homesteads, scattered around the small Saxon chapel were very basic thatched dwellings in run down condition. Nathan was again struck by the discrepancy of wealth that was so apparent in the county. He was aware of the unrest and resentment this created and felt sure that one day there would be a reckoning when the workers would turn on their masters. He did not know how this would happen but could only feel sympathy for those that might take up the gauntlet.

It must be particularly hard for the people of Kingston, he thought, as they looked down on the beautiful and obviously wealthy village of Corfe below them, a place where they were not particularly welcome, being considered inferior by the residents. However, this was not his problem today. He was here to meet constable Burt and find out what he could about the irregular death of Sam Parkes.

Nathan had begun the morning sorting out matters to do with his modest estate, when a note from the constable had been delivered. This advised him of the discovery of the body and its subsequent removal to the undertakers at Langton Matravers. He had hurriedly readied himself for the journey and proceeded to view the body. Mr Small the undertaker had then advised Nathan that the constable was to be found at the local inn at Kingston where he was making certain enquiries. So it was well into the afternoon when Nathan dismounted from his horse in the yard at the back of the inn. This establishment stood on the top of a steep winding road that was the only carriage route for travellers for destinations between Swanwich and the village of Corfe Castle.

After such a climb, especially if pulling a coach or a heavy laden cart, horses would need to be rested or even changed. As a consequence the inn was a large establishment for the size of the village, providing ample space for travellers and stabling in the rear. The view from the stable area was spectacular, allowing a panoramic outlook way beyond the village of Corfe Castle, across the rolling hills and valleys of Purbeck. A chalk ridge on the other side of the valley ran eastwards from Corfe, where Nathan could see sheep and cattle grazing with the occasional farmstead nestling along its lower slopes. It was a beautiful day with a cloud free sky giving an extensive prospect. A boy was on hand to attend to his horse and Nathan handed the reins over to him. Then he stood for a few moments taking in this tranquil rural scene while the boy led the horse away

The only drawback was that the air was constantly laden with the smell of urine emanating from the tannery. Used extensively in the tanning process urine was gathered from most of the nearby villages and brought here in barrels. Nathan could see a horse and cart, loaded with two such barrels climbing the hill from Corfe.

Having endured the smell long enough, he turned and entered the inn by the back door Although he did not have to, he stooped as he went through the door, because it opened into a narrow, low ceilinged corridor, which ran through the middle of the inn with a number of doors on each side. All the doors were shut, so that, despite the brightness outside, the hallway was dimly lit and the contrast made it seem even darker. Nathan moved cautiously down the corridor before entering the last door on the left. Again, the light changed, for this was a well-lit room with a large bay window through which sunlight was streaming, causing him to blink as his eyes adjusted to the brightness.

The bar was opposite the window and a man in a constable's jacket and trousers was standing here chatting with the barman. This was William Burt the constable from Corfe. As Nathan entered, Burt looked up, then picking up his stovepipe hat from the bar he nodded towards a table and chairs in the corner by the window. As he did so he said, 'Mr Eldine sir, let's sit over there, would you like a beer?' Before Nathan could answer the constable looked back over his shoulder to the barman and demanded, 'Bring the Squire a pint of porter will you?' The two men proceeded to the table and sat down.

Burt put his hat and the beer pot he was carrying on to the table then adjusted his position on the chair, shifting his bottom about as if he could not get comfortable. He was generally a slim man but with a potbelly so that his uniform was ill fitting being a couple of sizes too large to accommodate his stomach.

'How are you Will? Keeping well I trust and your wife, is she in good health?' Nathan asked.

'Yes thank you, Mr Eldine, sir. Mustn't grumble, as they say,' the constable replied. 'in fact it's been pretty easy of late. A few drunk and disorderlies, some minor thievery and a few family disputes but nothing serious. You know what it's like when the sun's shining. Everyone becomes happier and at peace with each other and with the summer we've had, it's been pretty quiet, until now that is.'

The two men chatted on in this light vein, until the barman brought Nathan his drink and departed, when the constable took on a sombre expression and said, 'This is a rum do, Mr Eldine, sir. A stone mason and his son found the body early this morning. They were on the way to a quarr they are working up by Dancing Ledge. He sent the boy straight down to fetch me. There weren't much to see when I got there, no footprints or anything like that, I mean, so I arranged for the body to be taken to the undertakers at Langton and for the man with it to carry on and fetch you.

'It's weird that Parkes should be killed in exactly the same place as Jack Downley was last year. We never found out who done that but many people thought Sam Parkes was involved. Now he turns up butchered in the same spot. I've been asking questions around the village but nobody seems to know anything. There's a lot of talk about it being Downley's ghost what's taking his revenge.

'Not that I believe in ghosts you understand, leastways I've never seen one, although there were that one night when I was walking down Cow Lane and I heard a great whooshing sound behind me but when I looked round there was nothing there. Gave me a turn, I don't mind ...'

'Quite so,' the squire cut in, 'but I think we can rule out ghosts, this was done by human hand and from the look of the wound a pretty adept hand with a sword. One swift and deadly accurate stroke is all it took.'

'You've seen the body then, sir?' Burt asked.

'Yes I called in at Elias Small's place on the way here to take a look at it,' Nathan replied.

'Well sir,' the constable said, 'if it weren't a ghost, it's a strange coincidence that we have a second killing in the same spot. Do you think it could be the work of the same person? A footpad, perhaps, who's chosen that spot to waylay lonely travellers.'

'No you're not thinking clearly, man,' Nathan spoke gruffly. He was disappointed in Burt who, normally a very efficient constable, was clearly addled by the eeriness of this crime and was letting his imagination run away with him.

'For one thing footpads don't usually wait for a year before striking again,' he continued. 'Downley was stripped of all his valuables, whereas, Parkes didn't have much to steal but what he did have was not taken, so we can rule out robbery in this case. I do not usually believe in coincidences and, anyway, there are too many differences between the two killings for them to be connected.'

Having noted the squire's ill disposition the constable chose to keep quiet, although he was thinking that this brought them back to ghosts.

'It's probable that the crime was committed by someone with a grudge against Parkes and maybe they chose this spot to confuse the issue,' Nathan said.

The constable now found his voice, 'Parkes was a bad lot, that's for sure. There would be plenty that had a grudge against him, so that doesn't help much. Mind you, as you said, the culprit knows how to handle a sword and there ain't many as have that knowledge amongst country folk.'

'You forget we've been at war quite a lot recently and there are plenty of fellows who served in the army for a while. They would have been trained how to use a sword,' Nathan said in a more affable manner. It seemed the constable was getting his wits back. 'But your right, it does reduce the possible suspects.'

'So where do we go from here, Mr Eldine, sir? I could start by compiling a list of old soldiers in the area and then ask some questions to see which of them knew Parkes and might have a grudge against him. It would have to be a pretty big grudge to warrant murder. If I find anyone to match this, I could then see what they were up to last night and if they had the opportunity to lay in wait and kill him. It's a lot of work and I can't guarantee I'll find anyone to fit the bill.'

Nathan was pleased, the constable was now reasoning clearly and his remarks had triggered a new thought in the squire's mind. 'Good man, yes by all means start along those lines but when you said they were lying in wait for him, it struck me that this would suppose they knew he would be on that road on that night. How would they know that? And what was he doing on that road? Coming from Langton presumably. Parkes was not a regular visitor to Langton, as far as I know, so it's unlikely that it was a planned ambush. Much more likely, they saw Parkes leaving Langton on his journey home and followed him, waiting for an opportunity to strike.

'They would wait until they were well clear of Langton,' Nathan was picturing the events that had led up to the crime as he tried to work out the dynamics of the attack. 'Then there are a couple of cottages before Downley's Stone.

'Yes that would be it, the stone happens to be about the first place they would risk striking. That would make it simply coincidence after all. Maybe it's the same reason Jack Downley was killed there.' A brief silence followed.

'That's where you should start,' Nathan spoke again. 'Make enquiries at Langton as to what Parkes was up to. Start at the inn, his corpse still smelled of ale, so he had been drinking. Find out who he was with, who he talked with, who else was in the inn and whether there was any trouble that might have led to this.'

'I'll get on to it straight away,' said the constable. He downed his beer, stood up, put his hat on before adding, 'I'll let you know how I get on as soon as I can, Mr Eldine, sir. Good day to you.' Now he had a plan of action and with all thoughts of ghosts out of his head, the constable was a new man and he passed out of the room with a real air of purpose.

Nathan was not so cheered. He remained seated with a sombre expression, not touching his ale, for an unpleasant thought was building in his head. Burt's phrase of an old soldier had caused him to think of Ridley. Parkes was an associate of the White brothers, often serving in their crew. John Ridley knew this, Nathan had told him as much. He might well feel he had reason for killing the man and Ridley was a professional soldier well capable of striking the type of blow that had felled Parkes. Although he barely knew Ridley, Nathan had formed a strong liking for the man and he felt saddened at the thought of this as a possibility.

He did not have long to brood on this, however, as suddenly the door flew open and in rushed constable Burt, looking very flushed. 'They've found two more bodies,' he blurted out as he entered. 'Up at Finley Copse, I'm going up there to take a look, I expect you'll want to as well.' In his excited state, he had lost his normal obsequiousness and had forgotten to add his usual 'Mr Eldine, sir'.

'Two more bodies! Oh Lord, this is turning out to be damnable day,' Nathan said. 'Yes we will go up and inspect the scene but first calm yourself and tell me who found the bodies and do they know who the victims are?'

'Oh right, Mr Eldine, sir,' Burt was getting his composure back, obviously. 'Young Peggy Miles, what does the housekeeping up at Tam's Cottage, found them. It was that Tom Carter and Lemuel Jones, they had spent the night and morning at the cottage and went off to the copse after their mid-day meal to gather wood.

'When they hadn't returned after a couple of hours, she went up there herself thinking they'd just gone off some place. That's when she found them. It seems she was scared silly and ran back to the cottage for help but she remembered there was no one there. Tam had gone off somewhere, so she set off to Corfe to fetch me. She had just reached here and was about to go down the hill when I stepped out. She was well relieved to see me but it took some time before she could get her words together properly.'

Nathan had stopped listening now as his thoughts had returned to the matter of Jack Ridley and the wreckers, for although neither of these men were known to him personally he was aware that they were two more of Josh White's accomplices. 'Get the boy to bring my horse to the front, please Will. We will go and see what we can ascertain from the scene before it gets too dark, but I think I might know what this is all about.

'I cannot tell you anything for the moment. I have my reasons. You will just have to trust me. I need to find someone and speak with him before I can say more. There won't be enough time today so I will seek him out first thing tomorrow.'

The constable looked enquiringly at the squire but decided to say nothing and went out to fetch the horse.

The two men met at the front of the inn and as the constable was on foot, Nathan decided not to ride. Leading his horse by the reins, he set off with William Burt about their grim business.

The scene that greeted them at Finley Copse was gruesome indeed and Nathan was not surprised that it had terrified Peggy Miles when she had stumbled upon it. The first corpse was Lemuel Jones, although it was hard to discern this as his face was virtually all shot away. He had fallen straight back and death must have been instantaneous for he still clutched the axe he had brought for chopping wood. Carter had died a different death. A single sword stroke had accounted for him, similar to the one that had done for Parkes the previous night.

'My God, this was a violent act,' Nathan said. 'Look around carefully, Will, see if there is anything here to help identify the perpetrator of this terrible deed.'

Constable Burt, who was ashen faced, made no reply but simply began to search the area for any clues. Nathan did the same but after a careful and thorough examination of the scene and the corpses, during which neither man spoke, they had found nothing of any significance.

'This tells us no more than that which is clearly evident,' Nathan finally said. 'The attacker picked his moment carefully. He must have got as close to them as he could without being seen. Then he dashed out with pistol and sword, shooting Jones as he came and without hesitation taking the sword to Carter. It must have been all over before they even had a chance to defend themselves.'

'No doubt about that,' said the constable. 'I presume this was done by the same hand as did for Parksie, in which case this is a fearsome man we have to find. I don't relish the thought of arresting him, not on my own, sir.' He hesitated a moment before adding, 'Definitely a skilled swordsman, more proof that he's a trained man, what's clearly used to hand to hand combat, moving from one victim to another like that. What do you think he's up to, Mr Eldine, sir? What connects these killings with that of Parkes?'

'Good questions, Will! Maybe you'll throw some light on them when you find out who Parkes was with the night he died. There is also the question of how our murderer knew where these men were to be found. Just like with Parkes, he could not have been lying in wait. No, once again, he must have followed them until the perfect opportunity arose. And you are right, we need to move carefully against this man, whoever he is,' Nathan continued, not giving away the sick feeling he had that he might know the identity of their killer or what it was that connected the crimes. 'Certainly you must not attempt to tackle him on your own, nor I for that matter. I will send word to the Sherriff at Dorchester to apprise him of the situation and ask him to send some militiamen to help us.'

'You will have to get some volunteers to remove these bodies. You can still make your enquiries at the Ship but if you get any leads do nothing until help arrives. I think you had better stay there tonight. I am going to go back to Kingston to speak to the girl - Peggy you said, wasn't it? I'll see if she has anything more she can tell me. I will send word to the militia from there and get them to report to you when they arrive. I expect it will take a day or two for them to get here.

'Once I've spoken to the girl, I'll go home. I need to get some sleep. I haven't had much lately what with one thing and another. Then first thing tomorrow, I will head down to Corfe. There is someone there I need to speak to.

'I'll get back to you as soon as I can to compare our findings. In the meantime, as I said, make the Ship your base so I know where to find you. If you discover anything significant, you can send a message to me via Dr Palbrey at Corfe. I will check in there from time to time. If you do find something out, don't forget under no circumstances are you to take this man on before help arrives.'

'Right you are Mr Eldine, sir,' Said Burt.

The two men made their way down to the Langton and Kingston road. Here they parted company, going in opposite directions. The constable, on foot, towards Langton while Nathan set out for Kingston on his horse, which he had previously tethered to a tree by the roadside.

Finley Copse was only a short distance beyond Tam's cottage, which was set some two hundred yards back from the road, roughly half way between the villages of Kingston and Langton Matravers. Nathan had considered inspecting the cottage before returning to Kingston but, remembering that the girl had not gone back there because it was empty, he realised that there would be nobody for him to question. So he decided against the idea and he and the constable had walked on past it. He had no idea how much he would come to rue this decision.

When he got to Kingston, Peggy Miles was nowhere to be found. He asked around but no one was able to shed any light on her whereabouts. He wrote a brief letter to the militia and despatched a local man on horseback to deliver it. He also wrote to his fiancée, Madeleine, advising her that recent developments had complicated his enquiries and this would further delay the visit he so looked forward to paying her. He did not detail these developments deciding to spare Madeleine any ugliness but he did say that should she wish to reply she could do so via Dr Palbrey. Then, somewhat disgruntled at not finding the girl, he made his way up the long winding road that led to his house at Holme Matravers.

Without realising it, Nathan passed Peggy Miles on this road. Peggy heard the horse approaching before it came into sight, so she scrambled into some bushes where she remained hidden until the unknown traveller moved on out of view. This was because Peggy was running scared. She did not know everything that had happened since the night the men had returned from the wrecking but she knew enough to believe that she was in terrible danger. The deaths of Carter and Jones had been frightening enough but when an old lady in Kingston had told her of the killing of Parkes, she had guessed that someone was punishing them either for their part in the wrecking or for the murder of Jack Downley. Being a simple-minded girl, she was half convinced that it was for the latter crime and that it was Jack Downley's spirit that was taking this terrible revenge.

Although she had played no part in either of these dreadful crimes, she had been living with Tam for the last year or so and being aware of his evil deeds she realised that, by not disclosing her knowledge, she was as guilty as he and the rest of the White gang. Now it seemed they were reaping the rewards of these crimes and she did not want to be next on the avenger's list. Therefore, she had fled.

At first, she did not know where she was going but as she hid in the bushes, she thought of her aunt who lived in an isolated cottage, outside the village of Corfe. So, after the horseman had passed from sight and hearing, she returned to Kingston and then ran down the hill heading for this refuge.

CHAPTER 12

She knew it was ridiculous, for he hardly noticed her and anyway he was way out of her class, but Molly had fallen hopelessly in love with Major Jack Ridley. She first saw him at the inn when she arrived for work and Sam Butler had told her of his arrival with the doctor the previous night. He then told her to be careful of the stranger.

'Keep away from that one, Moll, he's in the back snug and drunk as a merry monk he is,' Butler said. 'I've got a bad feeling about him. The Doctor said he be a gentleman but I bain't be so sure, he's in a black mood and capable of anything I shouldn't wonder. So I'll look out for his needs, you make yourself scarce as far as he's concerned.'

This was quite the wrong thing to say to an impressionable young girl. Not used to such excitement, Molly was naturally intrigued, and as soon as Sam Butler was off about his business, she hurried into the kitchen. From here, she crept down a corridor until she reached the hatch that served the back snug and, without exposing herself too much, she peered into the room.

What she saw did not impress her at first. The man at the table, who was oblivious to her presence, was in a terrible state - dishevelled bleary eyed and clearly very drunk. He looked a total villain. His clothes were covered in blood and she could make out bandaging on his chest where his shirt was open or torn. His right arm had been in a sling, which he had discarded although it still hung round his neck.

He had clearly been involved in some violent adventure and this set her adolescent imagination running wild. Perhaps he had been set upon by footpads and had fought them off, killing some before the others fled for their lives. Maybe he had received his wounds by rescuing a beautiful maiden from kidnappers who were intent on ravishing her.

As these thoughts raced before her mind, she began to warm to this man, having put him in a heroic role. Why had she done this? The doctor had said he was a gentleman. Sam had not been so sure and Molly had to admit first impressions were that he was a drunken oaf who had been in a scrape but somehow this did not ring true.

As she looked at him more closely, she noticed that, although he was slumped forward in his drunkenness, he had a solid, athletic body and there was a rigid quality to his back, like that of a strong man or a soldier. He was unshaven and his hair was bedraggled yet Molly realised he was very handsome and clearly not as old as she first supposed. Yes, she had begun to warm to this man and, rather than fear him, she felt sorry for him.

This had been four days ago and since then two things had happened. The drunk had transformed and Molly had become besotted with him. The transformation had begun the day Captain Eldine had visited them. The captain had spoken with Ridley before moving him back to his quarters then he had sought out Molly and asked her to take the man some food.

This done, the captain gave her a note to take to the local outfitters who, had set about putting together a complete set of new clothes, including a jacket, two shirts, breeches, stockings and shoes. Molly had then returned to the inn with these riches, which she had delivered to the stranger.

Sam was cross that Eldine had asked Molly to fetch and carry for the man and that she had acquiesced, especially after he had warned her to have nothing to do with him. Molly had no fears on that score. She trusted the captain's judgement and told Sam so.

When she reached Ridley's room, she knocked on the door and, without waiting for an answer, walked straight in. She was carrying the huge bundle of clothes in front of her and could not see much of the room as she entered, nor could she see where the man was. She presumed he would be on the bed unconscious. She made her way to a table set against the wall on which she placed the clothes and then on turning around was shocked and embarrassed to find the man was standing at another small table on which was a basin and water jug. Stripped of all his clothes except for a pair of torn and dirty long johns, the only other covering on his body was the bandaging the doctor had put about his ribs.

For a moment, neither spoke, apart from a short gasp from Molly. They just looked at each other in some confusion. After what seemed like several minutes to Molly, although, in reality, it was only seconds, the man said, 'I'm sorry, I'm not dressed!' and grabbed up his old trousers from the bed holding them in front of him.

Molly had elder brothers and had often observed them washing themselves in the yard behind their cottage, so she was not unfamiliar with the sight of the male torso. Even so, she still felt bashful in front of this stranger and surprised herself by replying, quite cheekily, 'I can see that.' Realising this was not appropriate, she said, 'I mean... I should have waited for you to answer, I should never have barged in so. I thought you'd be out of it... with the drinking that is.' She was gabbling now and what she was saying was making things worse. 'I don't mean you was drunk. I just thought...' she came to a whimpering stop as she saw that he was chuckling at her discomfort.

'That's the first time I've laughed for a long while,' he said. 'Perhaps you could turn your back for a moment.' Molly turned. Moments later, he continued, 'There, you can turn round now and perhaps you will do me the honour of telling me your name after all its customary for people to be introduced before they.., well let us not dwell on that.'

Molly turned and was surprised to see he had put on his trousers but had done nothing to conceal his upper body, which was heavily bruised. And a fine body it is, she thought.

Surprisingly, the only indication of his earlier inebriated condition was that he spoke with a slight burr and perhaps what he said was a little risqué for a man of breeding. Molly was, however, quite certain from his manner, the way he spoke and the language he used that the doctor was right and that he was a gentleman.

'Well, sir,' she replied automatically taking on the role of servant, 'they call me Moll but my name is Mary, and I work here. I just brought you these clothes from Captain Eldine, well not from him, from the outfitters. The captain sent me for them, though how they knew your size or what fashions you wanted I don't know.'

'Thank you, Mary that is most kind of you,' he said. 'My name is John Ridley, although my friends call me Jack,' he added, mischievously copying her offer of a choice of names, 'and I am delighted to make your acquaintance. I seem to remember the captain asked me some questions as regards my measurements before he left, as to the style I am sure they will do admirably. Beggars cannot be choosers, you know. Not that I am a beggar, I simply find myself somewhat discommoded at the present. These clothes are most useful to me, as I shall need to make a good impression on your local banker later today. I need to get to see him as soon as possible but first I must get myself cleaned up, which is proving quite a difficult and painful exercise in my present condition.'

'You must let me help you, sir,' Molly said. 'You just sit in that chair and leave it to me.' Whereupon, Molly set about the delectable task of sponging Jack Ridley down from head to waist and then assisting him in donning one of his fine new shirts. She then left the room in search of a comb. On her return, she again shocked herself to find that, she was disappointed to see that while she had been away he had discarded his old breeches and long johns, donned a new shirt and, presumably, some underwear from the pile before struggling into his new breeches. Berating herself inwardly for being a hussy, she now set about bringing order to his tousled hair. She actually made a good job of this and when she was satisfied, she put the comb down and pulled a cutthroat razor out of the pocket of her apron. Brandishing it in the air, she perkily said, 'I borrowed this from Sam, the landlord, I'll get some fresh hot water, but I'll need to have that shirt off you again if you don't want it to get messy.' With a sparkle in her eye, she then hurried out of the room before Ridley could respond to this latest intimacy.

Having shaved him, she then assisted him in putting his shirt back on as well as pulling on white knee length stockings and finally his shoes, for he found bending very painful. At last, she stood back and assessed her efforts. He looked a new man. He was indeed very handsome and, in his new clothes, he looked every bit the English gentleman. Molly felt a sudden hollowness in her tummy, which she recognised as a sign that this man was having a significant effect on her emotions.

'So, how do I look, respectable enough to pay a visit to a banker?' he asked. 'All this grooming has quite sobered me up.' As he said this he realised that Molly might think he was referring to her earlier remarks. Remembering the discomfort those remarks had caused her,

101

he added, 'You know, I was very drunk, but the food you brought me and your kind efforts have quite restored me. Well almost, that is, for it seems talking of food has made me hungry again. I don't suppose you could rustle up a little something before I go about my business, could you Mary?'

'Of course, sir. I'll see to it straight away. Would you like a pot of ale with it?' There was nothing that Molly wouldn't do for this man, even if she were wasting her time on such an impossible dream.

'Best not,' he answered as she swept out of the room.

Since that day her feelings for him had strengthened, so much so that she felt weak whenever he was around and when she spoke to him she would get all tongue tied. Nothing like this had ever happened to her before. She seemed to spend every minute thinking about him - imagining him holding her in his powerful grasp and her succumbing to his desires. Her thoughts were often lewd and very explicit and she marvelled that she was able to think such lascivious thoughts without a conscience. What would the vicar say if he knew? These thoughts were tearing her apart, making her both deliriously happy and yet full of torment.

It had started slowly at first. When he set out to visit the banker, she had a slight feeling that she did not want him to go. She did not want him to be out of her range so that she could not steal the odd glimpse of him. She told herself not to be silly but when he returned she found herself hurrying up to him, to see if there was anything that he wanted. She realised he was unaware of her feelings as he acted quite normally in her company, perhaps showing a little amusement in her over attentiveness.

He obviously liked her and considered her as a friend for he confided in her regarding the outcome of his meeting with the banker. It seemed that it had been a successful meeting. On Nathan Eldine's recommendation, the banker had agreed to write to Ridley's bankers in Yorkshire to arrange a release of funds to cover his debts and future outlays while he was here in Dorset. In the meantime, the banker had given him a generous advance to meet his immediate requirements.

'It must have been a fair amount he lent you, for you to be able to buy a sword as fine as that. Molly had remarked looking at the blade that now hung by his side. 'Though why you need such a weapon in peaceful old Corfe I don't know.' He did not bother to reply to this but simply smiled at her and the churning feeling in her stomach returned.

He had spent the rest of that day and most of the next sitting in the public bar making light conversation with almost everyone who came in only interrupting this activity to take his meals, which he did in the snug bar, or when he finally retired to bed. He did not drink during this time, at least not excessively, one pot of porter lasted the whole of the first evening and only two the next day.

Whenever she could get away from her chores, Molly found a spot from which to watch him, relishing his every move and gesture. She was at her happiest when he took his meals for here she was able to wait upon him and had an excuse for being near him.

Late in the afternoon, of the fourth day, he started speaking quite agitatedly with a fisherman from Swanwich. Having finished speaking with the man Ridley got up and went off to his room. A few moments later, Molly who was in the passageway saw him come out of his room. He was sporting his new sword and she gasped as she glimpsed, beneath his coat, one of Captain Eldine's pistols tucked into his belt. He was carrying a bundle wrapped in one of the sheets from his bed, though what it contained Molly could not imagine. Without a word to anyone, he hurried straight out of the inn and Molly watched him from the window striding purposefully down the road in the direction of Swanwich.

Molly then went into the bar to find the fisherman and ask what it was that he had said to cause Ridley to leave so suddenly but there was no sign of the man.

That evening Molly fretted for his return but he did not come before she left work and went home.

The next morning, she hurried along to his room on the pretence that she needed to know what he wanted for breakfast but he was not there and his bed had not been used.

By midday, Molly was in a fearful state, bursting into tears when Sam Butler reprimanded her for not paying enough attention to her chores. Sam considered her a strong willed young woman as tough as they come and was surprised at her response to his chastisement. Women! he thought. Must be her time, I suppose.

It was around six o'clock when Jack Ridley finally made his appearance. He crept in to the inn quietly, without anyone seeing him, and hurried along the passageway to his room. Molly, who had been regularly coming out of the bar where she was serving drinks to check for any sign of him, did so again just as he was closing the door. Her heart raced with excitement and she called back over her shoulder, 'I have to take a break Sam, won't be long.' Sam grunted a reply and decided in line with his earlier thoughts that she obviously needed to attend to female needs.

Molly hurried along to Ridley's room, knocked and waited for his reply.

'Who is it?' he called out.

'It's me Jack, I've been so worried about you, where have you been?'

He opened the door. 'Worried about me! There's no need to fret yourself I'm fine,' then looking at her agitated state he added, 'best come in and sit yourself down.'

She entered the room but did not sit. The first thing she saw was a sword on his bed. It was an old sword, not the one he had purchased and lying next to it was a blood stained cloth. 'What have you done, Jack? No don't tell me I don't care as long as you're safe,' She gasped.

Ridley looked at her sharply. What was she saying? Had she feelings for him? If so, it would make it easier to ask the favour he had in mind.

'Do you trust me, Mary? For I have done something that could put me in a lot of trouble. I cannot tell you more but I will say that what I have done is right, it is just that the law may not see it so. I have enemies, they are murderous cutthroats and I'm dealing with them my way but, Mary, you must believe that I am on the side of what is good.'

104

'Oh, I believe you Jack, of course I do,' she said.

'Then, do you think you could do something for me, it could get you into trouble so I will understand if you say no. What I want is, if anyone asks, you don't tell them I was away all night and the best part of today.' Ridley felt awkward saying this and struggled to get the words out. As he did so, he took a sovereign from his pocket saying, 'There's a sovereign in it for you if you can do this.'

Although this was more money than Molly had ever had at any one time in her life, she pushed it back at Ridley saying, 'I don't want your money. I would do anything for you, Jack. If anyone asks I'll say you were here all the time. I'll say I served you your meals in your room and don't worry about Sam he wouldn't say anything to help the law and if you give him that sovereign he'll certainly back up my story.'

Ridley was moved by the compassion and support this young girl was giving him and he lent forward and gently kissed her on the cheek saying, 'You're a lovely girl, Mary, I don't know what I've done to deserve your kindness.'

Her desperate passion for this man caused Molly to misinterpret his intentions completely and, to his absolute amazement, she threw her arms around his neck and kissed him passionately on the lips. As she kissed him, she squirmed against him and the warmth of her, after all the horrors he had been experiencing, totally overwhelmed him as he felt himself responding to her sensuality. Without considering the consequences and forgetful of his true love for Ayala, he put his arms around the girls waist and returned her kisses before lowering her on to his bed.

CHAPTER 13

Ridley woke early the next morning and was surprised to find himself alone. For the first time since the night of the massacre his wakening thoughts were not those of a tormented soul. He felt much more at peace with himself, almost content as he recalled the warmth of the young girl who had shared his bed.

The initial frenetic love making of the night before had not lasted long, driven as it was by all the pent up emotions that her tender kindness had released. It had not been a romantic affair more an uncontrolled melee of passion amidst a flurry of petticoats. She did not seem to mind, however, and when his lust was spent she had placed her hand behind his head and drawn him close to her, holding him tightly to her breasts. Neither spoke - words had no place here. After ten minutes or so she gently rolled him to her side, stood up, tidied her dress and petticoats and still without speaking she left the room.

At first, Ridley did not even think on this, he simply lay there comfortable and satisfied but then he began to wonder why the girl had left so suddenly without so much as a farewell. Now he wanted her back. He wanted to hold on to her, make love to her tenderly, to lose himself and all his mental anguish in her embrace. So strong was this yearning that he began to get angry with her for going.

At last the door opened and she came back into the room, walked over to the bed and sat down beside him. To Ridley, who had been oblivious of anything of beauty these last few days, she looked absolutely radiant, glowing as she was from their earlier deeds so that his anger totally dissipated.

'Sorry Jack,' she said, 'I just had to go and let Sam see me, so he wouldn't be worrying where I'd got to. He hadn't noticed my not being there but he would have eventually. So, I told him I was finished for the night but as it was so late I'd sleep in one of the spare rooms rather than go home. I often do that when I work late, so nobody's going to worry or ask any questions.'

With that Molly stood up and quickly removed all her clothes before pulling back the blankets and jumping into the bed. She pulled the sheets up to her neck then, cheekily she giggled and said, 'Well, Mister Ridley, what are you waiting for, or don't you want second helpings?'

Molly was as happy as she had ever been.

It took Ridley a moment or two to recover from this surprise, the brief view of her naked body and the delights it offered followed by her saucy lewdness had quite thrown him but now he too stripped and joined her under the covers.

This time their lovemaking was gentle and lasting and Ridley was so engulfed by its tenderness that he lost all sense of time. The pleasure seemed to go on and on before he finally gave way to a deep and untroubled sleep.

Now, as he sat up in his bed and thought back on this night of passion, a melancholy began to slowly creep up on him as the reality of what he had done nibbled away at the contentment he was experiencing. All too soon he was engulfed with remorse. What had he done? How could he have taken advantage of an innocent young girl for whom he had no true feelings? Especially with Ayala only lost to him within the last week. The thought of Ayala and her cruel death horrified him when he considered his behaviour and he felt he had totally abused her love. It was as if he had committed adultery. He realised his motivation had simply been lust driven by despondency but clearly this was not so for the girl. He had to force himself to think of her by name, Mary. No, her emotions were those of genuine love even if it were only childish infatuation.

He had to explain to her that what they had done was wrong and could not be repeated and he had to tell her soon before she got too deeply involved. He also knew that this would need careful handling for she might easily turn against him and then who knows what she might do. She might tell young Eldine everything she knows. A terrible thought rushed into his head, he could kill the girl, that would silence her. It was only a flash thought, which he immediately rejected but the fact that he even considered it made him cry out with anguish. 'What am I thinking? What the hell am I turning into?' he roared.

'What's the matter, Jack? What troubles you so?'

It was Molly who spoke. She had entered the room at that very moment. Dressed but without any petticoats under her skirt, she was carrying a tray of breakfast food, which she put down on one of the dressing tables before hurrying across the room to Ridley. She took hold of his hands and lifted them up, pressing them against her cheek. 'What is it my love?' she asked.

'It's nothing,' he said. 'Don't call me that.' He wanted to add, 'I'm not your love' but looking on her young and adoring face he could not bring himself to speak unkindly to her. Instead he said, 'Someone might hear you.'

'No one's going to hear us, it's much too early. Nearly everyone is still sleeping. Anyway, I don't care if they do hear. I got up early so no one would see and got some breakfast. I thought we could have it in bed,' then wickedly she added, 'there will just be time for another serving of seconds afterwards, if you fancy it, that is.'

Forgetting his earlier remorse, Ridley was sorely tempted and as he looked at her pretty and cheeky young face. He realised now was not the time to end their affair but he was resolved not to let it go any further. So he simply said, 'You'll have to excuse me I'm afraid. My wounds are not as well healed as I thought and I'm in too much pain for any more exercise.'

He meant this to be a way to avoid further involvement. Unfortunately, it solicited quite the wrong reaction.

'Oh! My poor darling,' Molly cried, 'how selfish of me I never gave it a thought.' She clambered up the bed, threw her arms around him and nearly hugged the breath out of him. Then without releasing him and with a complete disregard for morals she said, 'Don't worry my love, you won't have to do a thing. You can leave it all to me.'

Despite his determination to end things, Ridley could not help chuckling at this as, breaking free of her grasp, he pushed her off the bed and mockingly said, 'You madam are a terrible hussy, now fetch our breakfast, I need nourishment before any more shenanigans.'

'Shenanigans, is that what it's called?' Molly laughingly mused as she collected the tray and brought it back to the bed. Then having slipped off her shoes and skirt she got in with Ridley. She was dreaming of what was to come, while he was desperately wondering how he could avoid it.

As it happened, he was saved the worry, for while they were eating they heard Sam Butler walking past the door and calling out for Molly. Once he had passed, Molly got up, dressed and made for the door. Before leaving she smiled at Ridley and said, 'Oh well, it's probably for the best, give those ribs of yours time to mend. I love you, Jack. See you later.'

To her slight disappointment, he did not return the feelings. He simply said, distractedly, 'Yes, later,' then he added, 'I don't know when, though. I may have to go out again today.'

He was cross with himself, he knew he should not have let this affair happen and that having done so, he should have ended it this morning. He had been to weak but it would have to wait for now as he had other matters to attend. Maybe it's as well not to offend her before I've finished my business with White and his gang, after that it doesn't matter what happens. I must not get embroiled with this girl or let her distract me from my intended revenge, he thought. I have to plan my next move and maintain my resolve or risk failure. He realised he needed to be stronger minded with this endeavour than he had been with Molly. Stop thinking of her, he said to himself, she'll muddle your brain and cause you to make mistakes.

Slowly he felt his resolve returning and with it his consuming anger. The girl moved to the back of his mind replaced by the cold cruel logic he needed in order to continue with his mission. He sat down on the chair to carefully consider and plan his next move. He stayed deep in thought for sometime before he was interrupted by Sam Butler knocking on his door and announcing that Captain Eldine was here and would like to see him.

Ridley opened the door and ushered Sam inside. He took the sovereign he had offered to Molly from his pocket and held it up for Sam's eyes to linger on it. 'I wonder if you would do me a small service, Sam,' he began.

Chapter 14

For the second time in four days, Nathan Eldine strode into the Bankes' Arms and demanded to see the enigma that was John Ridley. An enigma because Nathan was all but certain that this man was a murderer but the squire could not find it in him to dislike the man, indeed he was aware that under other circumstances they could easily become good friends. Yet here he was with a duty to do and the East India man had best have a good account of himself for the last forty-eight hours or Nathan would have to put him under lock and key.

Sam Butler ushered the squire into the nearest snug and said he would fetch Major Ridley at once. Nathan sat down at the one small round table in the room. It was one of the smaller snuggeries with three more chairs crammed in around the table although in truth only two people could sit comfortably here. As Nathan waited, he mulled over the fact that Sam had been much more diffident when referring to his guest than he had been on Nathan's previous visit. What had happened to bring about this change in respect, he wondered?

His question was answered the moment Ridley walked into the room. No longer the bedraggled drunk, here was a true gentleman, resplendent in his new outfit, upright and clearly sober. Ridley smiled at Nathan as he pulled out a chair from the opposite side of the table but before sitting down, he said, 'Captain Eldine, I am pleased to see you. I have much to thank you for and am also keen to hear how your enquiries are progressing. However, I forget my manners. Can I offer you some refreshment before we go further? I think the morning has progressed enough for some sherry or perhaps you would prefer something more substantial to slake your thirst? Have you travelled far this morning in order to get here?' Without waiting for a reply, he moved to the door and called down the corridor, 'Mr Butler, some service if you please.'

'A dry sherry would be very pleasant, thank you,' Nathan replied.

Ridley turned to face Sam Butler who had appeared at the door. 'A decanter of your finest Fino Sherry and two glasses please Sam,' he said, before returning to the table and sitting down.

Nathan had been studying Ridley during these niceties and despite the remarkable transformation in the man's appearance, he felt there was a falsity in this air of benevolence. His close inspection revealed an intensity behind the man's friendly expression. Ridley looked tired but at the same time resolute. Bodily he seemed as if he had made a complete recovery. Given the extent of his injuries, Nathan knew this could not be the case and realised that he must still be suffering a great deal of pain. The fact that he gave no sign of this was testimony to the man's strength. This strength was emphasised by his new clothes, which, although not made to measure, fitted Ridley well, perfectly highlighting his fine physical stature. Once again Nathan found himself thinking this man would make a powerful enemy for anyone who crossed him.

Aloud he said, 'I accept your gratitude but in truth, I have done no more for you than any humane person would have done, so we need talk no more of that . As for my enquiries, they have progressed little I am afraid. This is because I have been distracted by other events. Events that may, however, be related to your misadventure and it is about these events that I wish to speak with you, Major Ridley.'

'Please, why so formal? As I told you I am no longer commissioned so the Major bit does not apply anymore and, anyway, after what you have done for me, you can at least call me John, although I would prefer it if you called me Jack.'

'Very well, Jack,' Nathan acquiesced, 'the reason I sound so formal is because the events of which I speak are shocking in the extreme. Three men have been brutally killed in a most violent and seemingly professional way. The men all crew for, or are associates of, the White brothers. This fact and the manner of their deaths means that I have to ask you to account for your movements since I last saw you.'

'My movements?' Ridley enquired in a surprised but not reproachful manner. 'Yes of course, I can see why you would think I have a strong motive for killing theses people and if by professional you mean such as a soldier, well I fit that bill all right. However, we only agreed that White's crew were suspects not certainties, also, unless someone has been killing Sam's customers, I cannot be your culprit for I haven't left this establishment. Oh! that's not true, of

111

course, for I did go to see Mr Bonfield, the banker, to sort out my finances.

'After that, I also popped in to see Marsh, your tailor chappie, to thank him for his services. He has been most helpful, had these clothes sent round for me, based on your instructions. Not a perfect fit nor my first choice in fashion but pretty smart don't you think? He has taken some more accurate measurements, shown me some swatches of cloth and is in the process of making me a few bits and pieces, more to my liking. Which reminds me, I have a fitting later today.

'Anyway, you are not interested in all that. The point is, that's the only time I've left here and both those gentlemen can confirm how long I was with them. I expect Sam or the girl, Molly, can vouch for me for the rest of the time. They have been most kind, looking out for my needs, especially as I must have been pretty desperate looking when I first arrived.' Ridley concluded his rather long reply, leaving Nathan taken aback. Ridley's answers had been delivered in such a matter of fact way, with no hint of underlying guilt, that Nathan's original certainty now seemed entirely foolish. If the alibis held up then there was no case against Ridley and Nathan realised he would be starting from scratch. Stymied in this way, Nathan could think of no further questions but something, he knew not what, told him this was wrong.

'So,' he pointlessly tried, 'you have not been to Kingston these last two days?'

'Kingston? Where's that? There is such a place in Yorkshire, near Hull, also southwest of London there's a village by that name, in Surrey I believe but you cannot mean either of these.'

'No, this is a village in the downs above here. You passed through it when Dr Palbrey brought you from Stockwell's farm but I doubt you would have noticed. It's on the road to Langton Matravers. That name doesn't mean anything to you either I suppose? You've not been to the Ship Inn, for instance?'

'No I'm sorry. I cannot say that any of that means anything to me,' Ridley lied.

At that moment Sam Butler returned with the sherry, he placed the tray he was using on the table and without a word made to leave.

112

'Just a minute, Sam,' Nathan said. 'I have been asking Mr Ridley here about his movements over the last few days, since I was last here that is. Can you tell me what you know of this?'

'Well, if you've asked him, I'm sure you know the answer,' came Sam's surly reply. 'I don't know what I can add. As far as I know, he never left his room except to take a drink in the bar.'

'You didn't see him leave to go to the bank then? Nor notice his return?' Nathan asked. 'So you cannot say how long he was away.'

Sam shot a quick glance at Ridley as if to ask what he should say, but Ridley avoided his eye. So Sam looked at Nathan and making it sound as if the matter was irrelevant he said, 'Oh! Yes of course. He went out to see Mr Bonfield, of course he did and he saw old Marsh, the tailor, I remember him saying so when he came in - about midday it would have been.'

'That isn't what you said at first is it?' There was a hint of anger in Nathan's voice. 'Are you sure you haven't forgotten his going out on any other occasion?'

'No he did not!' Sam grunted and again looked to Ridley for approval.

Afraid Eldine would become suspicious of these looks from Sam, Ridley who had sat quietly through the interview now said, 'Perhaps Sam feels uncomfortable speaking about me in my presence. If he has anything he wishes to tell you, it may be easier for him if I am elsewhere. So, if it is all right with you, Nathan, I will go to my room. If you need to speak to me further, that's where you will find me.'

With the wind taken out of his sails by Ridley's consideration and friendly manner, Nathan was further doubting his initial surmise that this ex soldier was his main suspect. 'Thank you Jack, that is most accommodating of you, by all means return to your room,' he said rather lamely.

Before he did so, Ridley poured them both a glass of the sherry, picked his up but without drinking it he said, 'When you are done with Sam, perhaps we can talk some more. As you can imagine, I am most interested to hear more about these events of which you speak.' Carrying his glass, he left the room.

Nathan was silent for a while, still trying to come to terms with this latest turn of events. Why do I feel so uncomfortable? he wondered, I feel like I have been sidelined somehow. Is Jack Ridley a clever manipulator of people or is he truly innocent?

His thoughts were interrupted by Sam, who now said, 'If you've got nothing else to ask me, I've got customers who need my attention.'

'Not so fast!' Nathan said as Sam started for the door. 'Is there anything else you wish to tell me?'

'No there isn't. I don't know what the Major meant by that but I've got nothing more to say. I didn't see him go out again or come back from anywhere for that matter. That's all I know.'

'Well, now we know what you didn't see, perhaps you can tell me what you did see. I mean just how often did you see Major Ridley. Where and when? In detail, please,' Nathan pressed.

Sam sat down on the chair vacated by Ridley and, while Nathan sipped his sherry, he slowly began to recall the various moments during the last two days when he had seen the Major. He added a couple of fictitious encounters to reduce the larger gaps but was clever enough to accompany these with the words 'I think.' If the squire was able to disprove these moments then Sam could fall back on his vagueness and say, 'I might have got the time wrong on that occasion,' or something similar.

It was some time before Sam finished reminiscing, as he had craftily made it seem as if he was struggling to remember exact details, which he felt would give greater authenticity to his narrative. Most of the encounters had occurred when Ridley had visited the bar for a drink but there was still a lot of time unaccounted for. Sensing Nathan's dissatisfaction with this account, Sam added, 'You should talk to Molly, she was with him a lot, serving his meals and fussing over him all the time.'

'Yes I will speak to Molly; perhaps you can send her to me?' Nathan said.

'Is that it then? Can I go now?' Sam was clearly relieved his ordeal was over.

'Yes Sam, that's it, for now anyway!' Nathan chuckled. 'Off you go and send Molly along.'

The interview with Molly was no more productive than that with Sam. She was much warmer in her manner and appeared keen to help Nathan if she could. Her evidence, however, was far from helpful. She was adamant that, apart from the visits to the banker and the tailor, Jack Ridley had not left the Bankes' Arms over the last two days and that there was no way he could have done so without her knowledge. 'He hardly left the room at first, taking his meals in there and brooding over his troubles,' she said. 'He seemed less moody the second day, after he got his clothes and had sorted out his money. It seemed to give him a lift. That's when he started coming into the bar. He just sat there drinking. Not heavily, mind you, not like that first night. Quietly, by himself. Although he occasionally talked to other customers.'

Having achieved nothing, Nathan let Molly go and was surprised to realise it was lunchtime already, so he made his way to the main dining room, where Molly served him a light meal and a pint of ale. As he ate, he reflected on the morning's work. It had not been at all productive. My only suspect appears totally innocent in his demeanour and has two witnesses to provide him with a seemingly watertight alibi, he thought. They cannot account for his every waking hour but they can account for sufficient sightings to make it impossible for him to have gone to Kingston, kill three men and then return to Corfe! Could he have done it in the night, while everyone was asleep? No, that will not work, how would he have found his quarry? Anyway the two men in the copse were alive in the morning when they went off to cut wood!

Nathan's thoughts, which were tumbling around his head, now turned to the two witnesses. What about those alibis? Do they hold up? There were a couple of times that Sam claimed to see Ridley when Molly said he was in his room but either one of them could be mistaken about the time. They were both a little vague on that aspect, but that is only natural, people do not watch the clock all the time. Sam's evidence is probably not that reliable. I would not put it past him to say anything if the price is right and his attitude to Ridley has certainly changed, much more amenable, as would befit a man who has received a nice payment. Of course, it could just be because Jack has money now and is paying his bills.

Molly on the other hand is an honest little thing. There is no way I would   expect her to lie for money. She might do so out of friendship, she is an impressionable young woman and there was something different about her today. She was much friendlier, cheery, not the sullen little girl I met last time I was here and she did refer to Ridley as Jack once. That was odd. A little too personal for a serving maid. Still, I cannot see her lying for someone she hardly knows. Her changes of mood could be down to anything. Who knows what makes young people behave the way they do?

Nathan had finished his meal and was feeling over comfortable. Almost dozing off as he contemplated these issues. Lack of sleep, a good meal, sherry and a pot of ale all combined to slow him down. His reveries were suddenly interrupted by the cheerful voice of Jack Ridley, 'Hello again, do you mind if I join you? I would very much like to know more about these events.'

Ridley was in fact less cheerful than he appeared. Internally he was still suffering terrible bouts of depression interspersed with the fearful rage that accompanied his consuming desire for revenge. However, he knew it was vital he seemed calm and resolved to his loss, for that way the squire was more likely to accept his innocence in these affairs and so talk openly with him about recent developments. Ridley wanted to know how much the squire knew and what he intended as his next line of enquiry. He hoped the answers would give him time and space to complete his avowed mission. He especially wanted to know when the squire was planning to next visit Swanwich, for Ridley knew it was here that he would find his next victims, the White brothers.

Unaware of these motives, Nathan was perfectly happy to discuss the case, there was always a chance it might trigger a memory of something important he had overlooked and he was keen to observe Ridley's reactions to the tale.

He began with the discovery of Parke's corpse by Downley's Stone describing the wounds in detail. He then went on to speak of the murders in the copse and again stressed the brutality of the attack. Throughout this, he watched Ridley closely but observed no sign of emotion. He was completely unaware of the slight concern his listener felt when the copse was mentioned. Ridley had hoped these murders would remain hidden for a while. Nor was Nathan aware of the contrary feeling of relief when it became apparent that the roadside killings remained undiscovered.

Nathan described the wounds to the victims in the copse with the same attention to detail that he had shown when describing Parke's attack. He pointed out the similarity of the sword wound in both cases.

'It was these single blows inflicted with such great accuracy that convinced me they were delivered by a skilled swordsman,' he said. 'When I realised they were all part of the White gang and given the possibility that the gang were responsible for the wrecking, I wondered whether there might be a connection between the two events. Naturally, my thoughts turned to you and although I did not like the direction my thoughts were taking, I felt I had to find out what you had been doing these last two days.'

'Of course you did! I would have done exactly the same thing in your shoes,' Ridley reassured Nathan, 'I hope your enquiries have dispelled any such suspicions, however.'

'Yes, it seems they have,' Nathan said. Deep down he was not fully convinced.

'Tell me who found the bodies in the copse and what were the men doing there?' Ridley now asked.

Nathan described how Peggy had discovered the bodies and, having no one to turn to, the other men having gone to Swanwich, she had run off. Only meeting with constable Burt by chance.

Nathan finished speaking but Ridley remained quiet. The two men just sat for a minute or two considering their thoughts. Ridley was thinking he had been very lucky as both the young squire and the constable had travelled the Langton to Kingston road on the day of the killings. Both would have passed the spot where he had killed Tam Smith and Trevellis. The constable would have done so three times. Twice before the killings, when he took Parkes's corpse to Langton and then when he returned to Kingston. The third occasion would have been when he made his way to the Ship Inn following the grisly discovery in Finlay's Copse. This was after the killings but fortunately it seemed he had not noticed the bodies.

117

The squire must also have passed the spot shortly before the killings and could only have narrowly missed encountering Ridley and his victims as they joined the road from the path that led to Tam's cottage.

'You say these other men that went off, were part of the gang too,' Ridley finally spoke. 'I wonder if that's your explanation! Perhaps they killed the two men in the copse and then ran off themselves. Maybe the gang have fallen out over the spoils. The *Golden Nile* was not carrying a particularly valuable cargo as far as I know. The captain said something about oils, spices and carpets, I seem to recall, but I think ballast filled a lot of the hold. The main commercial venture had apparently been the outward voyage, though what they carried I do not know. That's irrelevant though. My point is, if there was little profit to be shared they might well have set about each other to gain a bigger portion.'

'It's possible!' Nathan responded but with little enthusiasm for this alternative explanation. He was finding it difficult to come to terms with his feelings. He wanted Ridley to be innocent but no amount of evidence or theorising in support of that could persuade him that this man was not behind the killings. He had the motive and he had the skill but how to prove he had the opportunity.

After a short pause, Nathan continued, 'Yes it is possible. Based on what you witnessed, I impounded the wreck. At first I allowed no one to remove any cargo, but then, rather perversely, I delegated White and his crew to the task of removing it. It is now all in store in Stockwell's boathouse under lock and key and guarded night and day. That is upsetting White and his crew, because they have no idea why I've impounded it but it does mean they know the cargo has little value. This could be a cause of their falling out but somehow it does not ring true to me.'

'Maybe you are right,' Ridley came back. 'There is no reason for them to fall out if they haven't even got their hands on the goods but I still think their fighting amongst themselves is the most likely explanation for all these killings. Given the crime they have committed, they are clearly an evil bunch and who knows what they might find to argue about or to kill for.'

'That's true, but I must not forget that we still haven't proved they were involved in the wrecking, although it seems most likely.' Nathan pondered aloud. 'I could still have two different crimes on my hands. With you ruled out, I have no other leads to follow so it looks like my enquiries will have to be around the gang and their movements. I can start with Tam Smith and Simon Trevellis, see if they saw anything or anyone up by the cottage. I'll pay them a call in the morning, I'm going to see Constable Burt at Langton first thing but I can go to the cottage afterwards. If they have returned that is, if not I will have to seek them out in Swanwich. It would give me a chance to have another chat with White if I do.'

The two men chatted on for a while before Nathan pulled out his fob watch. 'My word this day is passing too fast for my liking,' he said. 'I don't suppose I will get much more done today. I best check in with Dr Palbrey to see if there are any messages for me and decide what to do after that.'

'Dr Palbrey!' Ridley chuckled. 'Queer old cove isn't he? A good doctor mind you, for all his oddities. He certainly looked after me well enough. Give him my regards won't you.'

'I certainly will,' said Nathan as he took his leave.

Jack Ridley stayed where he was, going over the conversation in his mind. So, he thought, the young squire will probably be in Swanwich tomorrow, I best delay calling on the Whites until the day after.

On reaching Dr Palbrey's house, Nathan found that the only message was from Madeleine, inviting him to dinner that evening. Madeleine wrote that she was concerned that with all his rushing around he would not be looking after himself nor eating properly. Feeling full from his late lunch, the last thing Nathan wanted was a heavy meal but the chance of seeing Madeleine was too enticing for him to decline the invite. The letter also suggested he stay overnight, as he would no doubt be weary from all the travelling he was doing. He decided to go home, change into some fresh clothes and pack an overnight bag before making his way to the Armitage residence. It might mean he would arrive a little late but once he explained the circumstances he was sure they would forgive him.

119

In fact, he entered the house half way through dinner and was pleased to find that the only other guests, outside of the family, were the local vicar and his wife. They were an unassuming couple with little to say for themselves. The vicar was an amateur lepidopterist, when not concerned with church matters, and the little he did say was all about butterflies. Madeleine's fourteen-year-old sister, Rosemary was the unfortunate recipient of most of his remarks, which she acknowledge with admirable politeness considering how boring she must have found this conversation. On Nathan's arrival, Armitage played the part of the congenial host by insisting that the other diners delay their dessert course while Nathan caught up. Consequently, Nathan declined the first two courses going straight to the main course of game pie.

Conversation throughout this and the remainder of the meal was polite but insubstantial the most animated moment being when Armitage announced that the King and some of his family would be visiting Weymouth in the near future. However, as yet it had not been formally announced, so everyone was sworn to secrecy.

Madeleine, her sister, her mother and even an excited vicar's wife had then spent some time speculating on the likely events that would surround this royal visit and the clothes they would need, assuming they were invited.

Their chatter amused Nathan, especially when they determined that there was bound to be a grand ball, for which they would need completely new outfits. Particularly amusing was the nervous way Armitage received these tidings as he considered the cost.

Eventually the meal ended, whereupon Armitage offered Nathan and the vicar a glass of his fine brandy and suggested they have cigars to accompany it. The vicar declined, saying that he and his wife had to be on their way and their carriage was duly summoned. Mrs Armitage and her daughters then withdrew leaving the men to their deliberations. Nathan normally favoured this custom as he always enjoyed a good conversation. On this occasion, however he was less happy, partly because Armitage would not be his first choice of company, but more pertinently, because he had spoken with Madeleine for such little time. Knowing he would have to leave early the following day, he had hoped Armitage would have had the wit to realise this and dispense with the formalities.

The change in his host's manner, once the ladies had left, depressed him further for it was clear that Armitage had a very definite agenda and that this conversation would eat away much of what little time he and Madeleine did have.

'It's imperative you bring this whole sorry business, to a swift conclusion, Eldine,' Armitage said in his most pompous manner. Nathan wondered what had brought this on. 'Not least because of the royal visit but also because of the effect it could have on trade,' Armitage continued. 'We cannot have the world thinking that Purbeck is a lawless wasteland with murderers roaming freely. I mean, Eldine, three murders in less than a week, doesn't look good, don't you know? Not good at all. How are your enquiries progressing? Have you apprehended any of the killers yet?'

'I'm afraid there is worse news to come out yet,' Nathan replied. 'Besides these murders, there is the matter of the ship that was wrecked the night of the storm.'

'What do you mean? I know about the wreck, that's not news and although it's a tragic business it doesn't reflect badly on Purbeck, surely.'

'I'm afraid it does,' Nathan said. He proceeded to tell Armitage everything that had happened starting with the wrecking.

'The only good thing is that it seems likely that we only have one killer roaming the land as you put it,' Nathan finished his narrative.

Armitage had listened to this account looking more and more aghast as the tale developed. It was not the horror of the crimes that was upsetting him. It was concern for the damage such events could have on the prosperity of the area.

'My God!' he said as Nathan fell silent. 'This could have the most serious repercussions, man. What his Lordship will make of it I don't know. As I said before, you must clear this up as soon as possible, preferably before the story gets out. If the palace hears of this, they could cancel the whole visit.

'Can't you arrest and confine this man Ridley, until your investigations are complete that is. Then you can charge him or not accordingly. If he is the assassin, such action would stop the killings, at least. Equally if there are more murders while he is in your custody that would eliminate him from your enquiries.'

'I had considered doing just that but with the evidence being purely circumstantial it would be hard to justify such action. Ridley is, it seems, a wealthy man who could afford a good lawyer and they would easily get him released. Now that he has an alibi for the time of the killings, such action is even less feasible,' Nathan replied.

'Well you had better do something and be quick about it. I cannot emphasise how important the Royal visit will be to the whole county. Once the King has visited our resort, it will become the rage with fashionable people to do the same and it will give our merchants the ideal opportunity to market their produce. It could do wonders for our trade, times are good at the moment and we must make the most of it.

'The country is entering a new age. Towns and cities are expanding, which means a massive demand for building materials. With all these inventions of milling machines, the woollen industry is growing beyond all recognition and there could be a huge demand for leather to equip the army in boots, belts and pouches.

'Stone, wool and leather, three industries in which Dorset is ideally equipped to compete and now is the time to do it, while the country is prosperous, because that could change if war comes.' Armitage had been walking up and down as he spoke. Now he turned and faced Nathan. 'We certainly cannot allow this problem of yours to frighten prospective customers away.'

Typical of the man, Nathan thought. A carefully worded politician's speech, making sure that the responsibility was passed on so that he could not be blamed if things went badly. I had better be careful lest I become the scapegoat for all of Dorset's problems.

Not wanting Armitage to think this speech had discommoded him, Nathan chose to ignore the thinly disguised threat. Instead, he took up the subject of war. 'You speak of re-equipping the army and of potential war, is that likely do you think?'

'From my experiences in London and the various conversations I had with people in powerful positions, I would think it most likely, if not inevitable,' Armitage pompously replied. 'The Corsican upstart is behaving intolerably he has already broken many of the agreements he signed at Amiens and he treats our protestations with contempt. Not that we have protested much.

'Addington is such an appeaser. He will do almost anything to avoid a confrontation with the Emperor,' Armitage placed a derisive emphasis on Napoleon's title as he spoke. 'If Pitt were still there, we would be at war already. He would never have suffered the little man so. Even the republican, Fox, is losing faith in Bonaparte and the libertines and talking of possible war with France.

'Amazingly, it's Fox whose complaining of the sad state of our army and navy. He hasn't got round to suggesting an expeditionary force but he is strongly calling for our defences to be tightened. He says the navy should be our first priority. Since the declaration of peace most of it has been laid up and, it seems, half the ships are rotting away from lack of attention. Then the other day he spoke in the House, saying we should be building more coastal defences and increasing our army with a recruitment drive. Fox of all people!

'Well, his words have had one good effect, in that they have forced Addington out of his shell and I understand he is meeting with Pitt for advice on the situation. He cannot afford to get this wrong. His party is none too popular as it is, what with all the reforms, and Fox would make much capital out of any dithering. Well as I said, we know what Pitt will say, as to whether Addington will act on his advice is anybody's guess.'

'Do you really think Napoleon would attack us? An invasion would be a highly dangerous move for him surely?' Nathan broke in on Armitage's rant.

'Who knows what the little Corporal would do!' Armitage still refused to pay any respect to Napoleon but he could not deny the man's military capability. 'He could walk through most of Europe at his leisure. There is no one to stop him, no army big enough. His only real opposition is from Russia and ourselves of course. The Russians probably won't bother with him as long as he leaves them alone and if he gets his boot over the rest of Europe there is little we or the Russians could do. Logically, that's what he should do and it would not make sense for him to antagonise either of us in the meantime. However, once he has that much power, he may well look further afield,' Armitage said.

'Our colonies would be a very attractive prize. He's definitely looked at India, before now. His agents were always stirring up the tribes,' Nathan interposed.

'Exactly,' Armitage rejoined. 'So he is more likely to attack us than Russia, I should say. As I said before, it seems to me that one way or another, war with France is inevitable and we should attack them sooner rather than later when they have become too powerful.'

'What of the Prussians or the Dutch, surely they would oppose him?' Nathan asked as he digested this latest information.

'They might try, but I doubt either could resist the French, not on their own that is, but if we were to move against the Emperor they may well join us in an alliance against him. The Dutch would make a good ally. With the help of their navy, we could blockade the French ports. Then we should set about invading France, maybe through Holland.'

Nathan, was not surprised by Armitage's seemingly impressive grasp of international affairs. He knew his future father in law moved in high circles and was adept at picking up the latest news and more importantly the underlying fervour of popular feelings. He was a born politician, only repeating views he had heard aired in London rather than any he had formed for himself.

'This is all conjecture, naturally,' Armitage continued, 'nothing will happen if Pitt cannot persuade Addington to act. We shall just have to wait and see. In the meantime, you need to sort this local trouble out. You will want to retire soon if you're to make an early start, which doesn't leave you much time to appease the ladies for your lack of presence, you'll find them in the withdrawing room. I've some paperwork to attend to, so if you will excuse me...'

'Of course,' Nathan said, happily making his exit to seek out the ladies. He was pleased to find that Lady Armitage, being more tactful than her husband, had already retired for the night, as had Rosemary, so that he had Madeleine all to himself, if only for a short time.

124

CHAPTER 15

It was six o'clock in the morning when Nathan woke to a gentle knocking on his door. He was normally a light sleeper and early riser but he had managed little sleep the last few days and this, combined with all his exertions, had caused him to fall into a deep slumber. The knocking seemed like a distant irritation at first slowly getting nearer until it finally pulled him out of unconsciousness. Still, he did not open his eyes, the bed was warm and comfortable and he did not want to surrender these last moments of luxury. Grudgingly he sat up and called 'Come in.'

He was surprised to see Madeleine enter the room carrying a breakfast tray. 'I hope you are decent,' she said as she entered. 'I had such little time alone with you last night, what with father questioning you so. Now your sergeant is here to whisk you off again. So, I decided to deliver the tray myself and sit and chat with you while you eat. I hope you will not think it too immodest of me.'

As she spoke she made her way to the bed placed the tray in his lap and then discreetly moved to the foot of the bed before sitting on it with her hands in her lap. She was already dressed for the day and Nathan thought she looked beautiful in her white muslin dress, with its high waistline marked by a pretty blue and white striped ribbon that was tied in a bow beneath her bosom. She had on a black Spencer jacket with large blue and white striped collars to match the ribbon. In line with the fashion of the day, the jacket did not meet at the front, leaving a delightful view of her cleavage, exaggerated from the pressure caused by the high waistline of the dress and the fact that she was sitting on the soft bed. Nathan found himself a little discommoded by this, especially as he was naked beneath the sheets, a practice he had adopted while serving with the army in hot climes, and it was all he could do to answer her.

'Not at all,' he blustered. 'I think it most kind of you and I'm delighted we shall have a chance to talk. But first, did you say my Sergeant was here?'

'Yes, I think his name is Sergeant Gaddie, a most peculiar name isn't it?' Madeleine said. 'He's from the militia and says he was told to report to you this morning. No doubt you are going after these villains, do be careful Nathaniel.'

He loved the fact that she was the only person since his mother to call him by his full name and even his mother had only done so when he was little and she was cross with him. As a rule, he much preferred Nathan but when Madeleine used his full name, it sounded different, poetic even.

'Reg Gaddie, eh! Splendid.' Nathan said brightly. 'I hoped they would send him. You need have no fears on my account my dear - Gaddie is the most competent soldier I have ever known. No harm will come to me while I'm in his company. It's not that peculiar you know, his name I mean, in fact it is a very old Scottish name. Not that you would think him Scottish from his accent, that's firmly west country. He told me once one of his distant ancestors settled down here after serving in the King's army during the civil war. So you see there have been Gaddies in these parts a lot longer than there have been Eldines or Armitages for that matter.'

'Quite!' Madeleine interrupted him, 'but I did not bring you breakfast at the risk of my good name to talk of Sergeants and their ancestry.'

'No, of course not,' he said and they fell into talking the most delightful nonsense, while Nathan tucked into his breakfast. When he had finished and they had chatted some more, he sadly ended this happy interlude.

'Now my dear, as wonderful as this has been, I'm afraid I can keep the Sergeant waiting no longer I must be off about my business and if you are to save what's left of your modesty you must leave me for I need to get dressed.'

Madeleine blushed, she did not want this moment to end so soon and secretly would not mind watching her beloved getting dressed. However, being a woman of excellent breeding she gave no hint of her emotions as she said, 'Yes, duty calls and the sooner you rid us of these terrible people the sooner you and I can meet again to talk some more.' At that, she rose, picked up the tray and left.

126

Once she had gone from the room, Nathan jumped out of bed and set about washing himself at the jug and basin provided for this purpose. As he did so, he thought of Madeleine and was amazed to find he could not recall any of their conversation. All he could see in his imagination was her beautiful face outlined by her long brown hair, her lips were moving as she chatted away but what she said he knew not. Then to his shame, her face moved out of view as first her lovely long neck and then her smooth inviting bosom came into focus. Quickly he poured cold water over his face and forced himself to concentrate on the present and to plan the day's events as he finished washing and got dressed.

Sergeant Gaddie, who was waiting for Nathan in Armitage's library, came smartly to attention as he entered. A strongly built man, about five feet ten inches tall, Gaddie had a lived-in face although he was only in his late twenties. He had long jet-black hair, worn in a ponytail, heavy dark eyelashes and a long straight nose. There were laughter creases at his eyes, which together with deep smile lines suggested a contented man who enjoyed life yet there was a quality to him that said he was not a man to be taken lightly.

'Sergeant Gaddie reporting for duty,' the soldier barked out.

'Alright Reg,' Nathan countered. 'No need for formality between us, we'll work more efficiently if you act naturally and don't wait for orders from me.'

'As you say, sir, it is good to be working with you again I must say.'

Nathan and Gaddie had worked on a number of cases in the past, mostly smuggling related, and had developed a strong bond, with each man coming to respect the other and their abilities. They were in fact friends. Both men inwardly acknowledged this, but their difference in class would never allow either of them to say so and Gaddie would never dream of calling Nathan by his Christian name.

'How did you know to come here and what of the other men from the militia, have they gone to Langton?' Nathan asked.

'That's right sir, just as you asked', Gaddie said. 'We set out as soon as we got your letter. I could tell from your words that this was a serious business so I didn't hang around. We got to Corfe last night and Dr Palbrey told me you were here. I hired a horse first light so as not to miss you. The rest of the squad I sent on to report to the constable. There's twelve men under the command of Corporal Wallace, he was with you the other night.'

Gaddie noticed a slight frown on Nathan's brow and, quickly reading his thoughts, added, 'He's a bit surly, sir, but he does what he's told and he's a good man to have at your side if it comes to a fight. In fact, they are all good men. I picked them myself.'

'That's good enough for me, Reg,' Nathan said.

'Wallace is to report to Constable Burt and to take orders from him. Provided Burt's up to it they will do a good job,' Gaddie added further assurance.

'If you say so, then I'm sure they will.' Nathan hesitated then went on, 'Now you will want to know what this is all about and what has happened to date. It's a nasty business, Reg, probably the nastiest we have ever faced. There are too many dead people already and we need to act before it gets worse. You'd better sit down for I've got a lot to tell you.'

Nathan related the whole story to the Sergeant, from Stockwell's gathering of information, through his own fool's errand, to the wrecking and the subsequent murders. He left nothing out, not even the fact that Ridley had survived or the discrediting of his suspicions as to the identity of the killer, for he trusted Gaddie implicitly.

Gaddie listened intently never interrupting or asking questions and when Nathan had finished he remained silent for a while as he pondered over the facts. When he did finally speak, his grasp of the details was impressive. 'It does not hold water,' he said. 'It certainly seems as if they spread the story of the smuggling to get you out of the way but it couldn't have been because they were planning a wrecking. They could not have known there was going to be a storm that night or that there would be a ship to wreck. It is a busy sea-road but there would be no certainty to it. No! Wrecking is a haphazard activity. You prepare for it but you have to wait for the right circumstances and there's no knowing when that will be.

'As for the killings, your man certainly seems to be a prime suspect, although it could simply be a falling out of thieves. How reliable is the girl? Could she be lying? I would not put it past Sam

Butler to provide a false alibi for a price but not knowing the girl I cannot comment on her.'

'Your first point is a good one,' Nathan replied. 'I had the same thoughts myself but I put them to one side, now I see you are right and it means that they must have had another reason for deceiving me but it stumps me for the moment. As to the girl, she is young and impressionable and I sensed that she was quite taken with Jack Ridley, maybe more than I imagined. Maybe enough to lie for him. As it stands, we must assume he is innocent but we should keep an open mind. Perhaps we should have another talk with her. It should not be hard to break her if she is lying.'

The two men sat in quiet deliberation for a few moments then Nathan stood up. 'These questions will have to wait for the moment,' he said. 'Let's get ourselves to Langton to see what Constable Burt has unearthed, if anything, then we can plan our next moves. I'll speak to Armitage to see if he will lend you a fresh horse from his stable, one of his lads can return yours to the ostler at Corfe.'

Armitage was most obliging and in no time at all a stable lad appeared at the front of the house leading Ridley's mare and another for the Sergeant both saddled and ready. Then, after polite farewells to Armitage and his daughter, they set off for Langton Matravers.

Nathan and Sergeant Gaddie did not get to Langton for they met William Burt on the road. He was with the men of the militia who had discovered the bodies of Tam Smith and Matthew Trevellis on their way to report to the constable.

'It was just luck that we found them, sir,' Corporal Wallace told Nathan who had dismounted in order to inspect the bodies. 'We stopped for a break a little way back, some of the lads lit up their pipes but some of the others started messing about and threw Perkins's hat over the wall. He climbed over to fetch it and on his way back he noticed something odd by the wall in the far corner of the field. He didn't say anything cause he couldn't make out what is was but when we started up again and we reached this point, his curiosity made him stop and take a look. Well you can imagine his reaction, he went all pale and called for me to look and a right gory mess it is. I guessed it might be something to do with why we were here and sent for the constable. I decided we shouldn't touch anything till he arrived.'

'I got here only ten minutes or so before you, Captain Eldine, sir,' Burt took up the story. 'I haven't disturbed them, they are just as we found them. I have had a good look at them though, it's Tam Smith and Si Trevellis, two more of White's gang, and it is the same story as before, one man shot and the other killed with a sword.'

'Except this time the man who was shot was also put to the sword,' Gaddie said. He too had dismounted and was inspecting the bodies.

'That's Smith, Sergeant,' Burt said.

'Right, then this is Trevellis and it looks like he took a wound before he was run through. I would say that our killer wasn't quite so efficient this time and found he had a fight on his hands though he still seems to have made short work of it,' Gaddie said. Suddenly he pulled out a broken sword blade from under the bodies. 'Hold on, what have we here, seems our man broke his sword on one of them, that might be the clue we need. It looks like a fairly new blade. I can't see the hilt anywhere though, which would be more useful for identifying the owner, but it's something to go on.'

They looked about some more until Nathan was satisfied that they had seen all there was to see. 'There is no more for us to learn here, Corporal,' he said to Wallace. 'We need to get these bodies to the undertaker. Can you arrange that? You best start by sending a couple of your men to fetch a cart from Langton.'

'Yes sir,' the Corporal replied. Carrying out his orders, the Corporal detailed two men to fetch the cart and four others to lift the bodies over the wall where they carefully and reverently laid them on the ground.

While this was happening, Nathan took Gaddie and Burt to one side then he asked Burt what, if anything, his enquiries had revealed.

'Not a lot I'm afraid, sir,' Burt reported. 'You were right, Parkes was in the Ship the night he died. He was there with Carter and they got quite drunk but it seems they kept to themselves and didn't have any arguments or upset anyone. They stayed late and left together. I asked the landlord about any strangers and he said there were a couple of people he had not seen before but he wasn't much help in describing them. One was dressed like a tradesman and the landlord seemed to think he was involved in the stone business. He was fairly stout it seems wore a blue coat and had a white wig. He only had one drink and left long before Parkes. The other was scruffily dressed and didn't say much. He was a bit of a hard case apparently, who didn't talk much and the landlord didn't see him leave.

'I did find out the names of some of the others that were there that night and I sought them out but I had no luck questioning them. One said that the scruffy stranger was slumped at a table near Parkes. He also said the man had a beard but when I checked this with the landlord, he disagreed. However, they did agree that the man had brown hair, quite long and tied at the back. Neither felt they would recognise him again, though, as they hadn't paid him much attention. Not much to go on I'm afraid, Mr Eldine, sir,' the constable finished up.

'Never mind Will, I didn't expect too much from that line of enquiry anyway but it does fit in with our picture of events,' Nathan said. He was thinking that the description could fit Ridley, apart from the beard, but it was not conclusive.

'It gives further reason for our man to have waited until he was well clear of Langton before he struck,' Gaddie said. 'Carter was staying at Tam's cottage, that much we know. Presumably he and Parkes went that far together. Our killer waited until they parted company because he did not want to tackle them both.'

Gaddie thought for a moment. 'That would also mean that Carter led him straight to the cottage and the rest of the gang,' he said. 'After disposing of Parkes he must have come back to the cottage and waited for his chance. It seems certain now that it is White's gang the killer is after.'

'And it appears they played right into his hands,' Nathan carried on from where Gaddie had left off. 'Two came out to gather wood and he takes care of them in the copse. Then the other two leave together, no doubt oblivious of the fate of their mates, and he follows them before surprising them here on the road. Strange he held off from taking on two men first time but he hasn't hesitated on the other two occasions. Perhaps he didn't have the opportunity to use the pistol sword combination.'

131

'Or he's getting bolder and more confident,' Gaddie rejoined.

'What about you, sir, did your enquiries fair better? What did Peggy have to say? Was she any help?' Burt now asked.

'Unfortunately not, she disappeared, there was no sign of her at Kingston when I arrived and nobody had any idea where she might have gone. She didn't go back to the cottage or I would have met her on the road,' Nathan said. He sounded frustrated at all these dead ends. 'It's a damned nuisance as I have a feeling that she could answer a lot of our questions.'

'How about your lead at Corfe? Any joy there?' Again, it was Burt asking the questions.

'No, I did have one suspect, at least he is a man who would have a motive for attacking White's gang, but it turned out that he hadn't left the place and had two witnesses to vouch for him,' Nathan replied. He decided not to mention his doubts as to the veracity of this statement but Burt noticed a lack of confidence in Nathan's voice.

'You don't sound too convinced, sir,' he said.

'To tell the truth, I'm not but without any proof there is little I can do against such a strong alibi.' Nathan was clearly dispirited, two more killings and he was no nearer to solving these crimes and he seemed to be running out of leads.

He was fairly sure he had a good grasp of all the salient facts since the wrecking. He was convinced that was the work of White and his crew. He was equally convinced that it was Jack Ridley, taking his revenge, who was guilty of the murders since then. There were a few areas that did not fit well together but he was sure these could be accounted for once he had made his arrests and could question the guilty parties more vigorously. The trouble was he had insufficient proof to make those arrests and if he tried to question White or Ridley too deeply, without arresting them, he would give his hand away and they would no doubt flee the scene.

While Nathan was mulling over these thoughts, the constable, who had noted his dejection, had also been thinking and now he said encouragingly, 'That Peggy, she's got an aunt, I seem to recall, lives in a cottage beyond Corfe. I think it's down a lane off the Wareham Road. I don't know, of course but I reckon that's where she will have gone if she's running scared. I can't think of anywhere else she would go. It's worth a try anyway, sir. Dr Palbrey will know where it is exactly, he had to attend her aunt for some ailment about a year ago.'

'Splendid!' Nathan was clearly relieved to have something to grasp at. 'Well done Will. I was going to go to Swanwich to talk some more with the White brothers. Not that I had much hope of discovering anything new. Now I think it best if Reg and I go and seek out this girl and see what she can tell us. Yes, we will get down there straight away. In the meantime, you and these men can start asking questions at every house and farm hereabouts. See if you can find anyone who saw anything at all on this road the night Parkes died or since. Any strangers on foot or horse, you know the sort of thing and don't forget to ask if anyone has picked up a broken sword hilt.'

Once again, Nathan and Gaddie rode off together leaving the constable busy organising the men, while a little way off the two militiamen could be seen returning on the farm wagon to be used to carry off the gruesome consignment.

CHAPTER 16

Nathan and Gaddie found Palbrey at home and in an unusually affable mood. He had just finished his elevenses, having had a large breakfast earlier and was about to partake in a glass of sherry when they arrived. He was not the least put out when they declined to join him in refreshment and quickly gave them precise directions to the cottage before coming to the door to see them off.

The directions had proved to be very accurate and necessarily so, for the cottage was tucked away behind bushes and trees some distance from a second lane leading off the first, which itself was not obvious from the main road.

Peggy's aunt was a frail woman, clearly not capable of making much of a living from the small amount of land that went with the cottage. As a result the cottage was in poor condition, desperately in need of thatching repairs and the paint on the doors and windows was cracked and peeling off. She was fortunate, however, for it was a tithe cottage and while her landlord clearly paid little heed to his responsibilities he must have a kind heart for he had not evicted her, despite the fact that she must be well in arrears with her rent.

Having tied their horses to the rickety fence, Nathan and Gaddie were now sitting at an old table in a barren kitchen. Peggy sat opposite them. Her aunt was standing at a large ceramic sink, washing some mugs.

'I have a little tea, if you gentlemen would care for some,' the old woman said.

'That is most gracious of you I am sure,' Nathan replied, 'but we will decline this time thank you, our business is most pressing and the sooner we hear Peggy's story the sooner we can leave you both in peace.'

Nathan was careful in the choice of his words. By including Peggy in this statement, he meant to put her at ease and make her understand that she was not in any kind of trouble with the law.

'Now Peggy, what you saw at Finlay's Copse was terrible indeed but I must tell you that even worse events have occurred,' Nathan began. 'I think you may know something that will help me to understand what is going on,' he continued. 'Besides Carter and Jones, Sam Parkes was murdered the night before.'

'I know!' Peggy interrupted him. 'I heard about it when I was waiting for you at Kingston. That's what scared me, so I ran.'

'I understand, Peggy, and I don't blame you for being scared because it gets worse. We have now found the bodies of Tam Smith and Simon Trevellis, butchered in much the same way.'

'Oh God!' Peggy cried out. 'I knew it - they are punishing us because of the woman.'

'Steady girl, get a hold of yourself!' Gaddie said sharply. 'What are you talking about? What woman?'

Peggy didn't answer him, she was crying now and just looked from one to the other of her inquisitors in obvious dread.

'Peggy,' Nathan now spoke gently. 'I have no idea what you are referring to but I am equally sure you have nothing to fear.' As he said this, he took a handkerchief from his pocket and held it out for the girl. 'I believe these killings are to do with the wrecking of a ship the other night and as you surely had nothing to do with that, then you need have no worries. However, four of these men were staying at the cottage with you and I need to know how long they had been there and if they said anything about the wrecking.'

Peggy took the handkerchief and then, after wiping her face and with a loud blowing of her nose, she began to speak and the words tumbled out incoherently at first but getting more lucid as she cleared her conscience.

'Oh, they spoke of it alright, talked of little else, how clever they'd been, how they were going to be rich, what they would like to do to her. They brought her back with them, the night of the wrecking. They was full of it. Said she would fetch them a pretty penny.'

'I had to look after her, feed her and wash her, you know, tied up as she was. I didn't like it. I said I didn't want anything to do with it but Tam said they would cut me if I didn't do as they asked.'

Nathan was beginning to make sense of what the girl was saying and he was horrified. 'Do you mean they brought the woman from the ship back to the cottage? They hadn't killed her?" he asked roughly.

'That's right, it seems she was amongst the survivors and none of them could bring themselves to kill a woman as hard as they are, so they brought her back that night and they were waiting to see what Josh White wanted done with her,' Peggy answered him.

'You mean she's still at the cottage, tied up and unable to move? My God, she's been there two days since you left her, we must go to her at once,' Nathan said getting up from the table as he did so.

'I didn't know Tam was dead,' Peggy whispered. 'I thought he would be coming back to her after he'd seen Josh. I'm sorry.' Her voice petered away and she started crying again.

'Reg, you stay here get the full story from this creature. I'm going to fetch the woman. I'll take her straight to Palbrey. If she's still alive she will need his services. When you've finished here make your way to the doctor's house.' Nathan was very angry and agitated but his mind was working well.

Gaddie stood up, moved towards Nathan and bent to his ear asking quietly, 'What about the girl? She's guilty of abetting these crimes, shouldn't we arrest her?'

'Question her here and then use your own judgement,' Nathan whispered back. 'If you think she was unable or too scared to get away then let her stay. We can always pick her up later if we change our minds. On the other hand, if you think she helped them willingly then bring her back to Corfe with you and put her in the lock-up.'

'Now, I must be going,' he said aloud. 'I do not want that poor woman left a moment longer than necessary. Good Lord, Ridley will be so relieved when he finds his wife is still alive, that's if she is! If only I had checked the cottage, I must have passed it three or four times these last few days,' Nathan said this last over his shoulder as he was leaving.

'Now then, you,' Gaddie turned on the girl. 'I want the full account from the start. Stop your snivelling and start talking and if you leave anything out or try to lie to me, you'll be very sorry indeed. Unlike your chums, I have no qualms when it comes to hitting a woman, least ways not a miserable creature such as you.'

He was pretending, of course, as he did not believe in violence unless it was necessary but his threats clearly impressed the girl for she pulled herself together and began her tale.

'It all started last Sunday, a whole gang of landers, led by Josh White came to the cottage and had a few drinks.'

Gaddie interrupted her, 'Names, I said a full account, give me their names.'

'I don't know all of them, there was Josh and Tam, of course and Josh's brother Frank. Then there was Parkes, Carter, Trevellis and Jones, you know about them and Si's brother Matt, he crews for Josh on the *Mary Jane*. The other two I don't know. Though, I think, one of them works the *Mary Jane* as well. The other was a big man, no one said his name, not so as I could hear anyway. That's all of them,' she stopped.

Gaddie had taken a pencil and some paper from a pouch that hung on his belt and was writing down the names as she spoke. 'Alright, carry on with your story,' he said licking the end of the pencil.

'Well as I said, they waited there drinking until it got dark, then they all went off together, they hadn't told me what they were up to but it was clearly no good. I guessed they would be bringing back some smuggled goods but I didn't know for sure. During the afternoon the weather had started to get bad and by night time it was blowing a real gale so I was expecting them back at anytime. I was surprised when they didn't return, least ways not until the early hours of the morning. I don't know what time it was as I had been sleeping but they made such a racket that they woke me. It would have been an hour or so before sun up, is all I can tell you.

'Anyway, that's when I found out they had wrecked a ship and had brought this woman with them. She was a proper fireball I can tell you. Several of them had scratches and Tam had a black eye. She was struggling so, it took two of them to hold her and even then, they were finding it difficult. Eventually they got her into the small room at the back and tied her hands behind her back and they tied her feet together. Not before she kicked Lem Jones in the face. They put a rope around her neck and tied that to a hook on the wall. She was screaming and shouting so they gagged her as well.

'That's when Tam told me I had to look after her until they found out what Josh wanted to do with her. Josh hadn't returned with them nor his brother or the two lads from the *Mary Jane*.

Gaddie had been making notes as she spoke. Now he asked, 'The *Mary Jane*, that's White's fishing boat, is that what you said?'

'That's right, he sails it out of Swanwich,' she replied. 'I said I wouldn't do their dirty work and that I wanted no part of it. I said as soon as it was light I was leaving. That's when the big man hit me. He hit me several times, he said I was to do as I was told and that I was going nowhere and if I gave them any trouble or if I tried to leave, it would be really bad for me. Tam told the big man I would be no trouble and that he would take his knife to me if I were. I was very frightened so I decided to do as they said.

'There was a bit of a do the following day, they saw a man approaching the house on a horse. Got all alarmed, worrying that this man might see or hear the woman, though how he would do so I don't know, so they went out to meet him. It turned out to be one of Stockwell's farm lads, drumming up help. The wreck had been discovered and they wanted volunteers to go down and help with the bodies and stuff. Tam and his men were not very happy about this. They hadn't expected the wreck to be discovered so soon and couldn't work out why. They were afraid that Josh might have been beaten to claiming salvage. The big fellow told them they should offer their help, said it would look suspicious if they didn't and that way they could find out what was going on.

'So that's what they did. They all went down except him. I remember I thought it a mockery that they should go all innocent like to help clear up their own crime.

'They had a long meeting when they returned but I don't know what was said, they made me wait in the other room with the woman. I guessed it must have been all right though, for they did not seem to be upset in anyway,' Peggy said.

'Well, three days passed and we had heard nothing from Josh,' the girl continued. 'The big man had left after the first day, where he went I don't know. Tam was getting agitated, not just about the woman but he also wanted to know when he would get his share of the spoils. So, he sent Parkes and Carter to The Ship at Langton. Josh White usually goes there of an evening and they were to seek him out and find out what was happening.

'Carter didn't return until late. He was drunk. Apparently, they had waited all night but Josh didn't show. Carter said Parkes had gone back to his cottage to change his shirt amongst other things. He's fussy like that, not like most of them.

'Parkes had told Carter that he would go to Swanwich, first thing the next day and would be back at the cottage about lunchtime. He never showed.

'In the afternoon, Jones and Carter went to cut some wood. While they were away, Tam got fed up with waiting for Parkes and he and Simon decided to go to Swanwich themselves.

'After they'd gone, it felt eerie in the cottage on my own, with that woman in the other room. She'd given up struggling by now, we removed the gag but she kept quiet just sat there looking scared. Never spoke, not even when I was trying to feed her, not that she took much, even though I spoke kindly to her. I tried to ease her bindings once but Tam saw and tightened them again, then he gave me a whack. I felt sorry for the woman, she had such a look of fright in her eyes, I did not want her to be harmed but there was nothing I could do.

'Waiting there, in that silence, well it began to get on top of me and the fire was going out so I decided to see where those two had got to with the wood. I went up to Finlay's Copse and .....' she hesitated now as she recalled the terrible scene.

Gaddie looked up from his writing. 'That's fine, Peggy,' he said. 'I think we know what happened after that. That's all I need to know for the time being. You know you have been party to a terrible crime don't you? And you could be in serious trouble for it. No doubt, you were coerced by fear and, in your shoes, many would have done the same, so I'm not going to arrest you and I'm pretty sure Captain Eldine will feel the same. However, you should not leave Corfe until this is all over, we may have further questions for you.

'I hope you have spoken truthfully and I can trust you to stay here with your aunt. If I find you've lied, in any way, I will not be so tolerant again. You do understand, don't you?'

'Yes, sir,' she said fearfully. 'I haven't lied and I won't run away again.'

'Best not, besides anything else, you are relatively safe here. Don't forget there are still members of this gang at large and if they think you are a witness against them they will be looking for you. So keep your head down,' Gaddie finished speaking. He packed up his writing materials and, without further comment, he left.

The girl was, it seemed, an unwilling accomplice and he felt little good would be served in punishing her, especially as the punishment would certainly be death if she were found to be guilty of any part of this heinous crime.

While Gaddie interviewed the girl, Nathan rode as fast as he could back towards Langton and Tam's cottage. He could not press his horse too hard as most of the journey was up the steep hill that rose from Corfe to the village of Kingston. When he finally arrived at the cottage, he leapt from the horse and, without stopping to tether the reins, rushed straight inside.

He entered into the main living area that Ridley had spied on through the window, and only hesitating long enough to confirm the room was devoid of any people, he made straight for the first of the two doors in the dividing wall.

This opened into a small scullery and a cursory glance told him this too was empty. As he reached the second door, he became aware of a fetid smell which hit him with a full blast as he opened the door. It was the smell of human detritus and he gagged as he entered.

She was sitting on the floor in a corner of the room, still bound hand and foot with her hands behind her back. There was a further cord around her neck and this was attached to a large hook, fixed to the wall, above her head. Hunchcd up, her knees were close to her chest and her head was resting on them. There was an old blanket around her shoulders and under this Nathan could see her badly tattered and torn clothes, covered with her own excrement.

At first she showed no signs of life, not even looking up when the door opened, but as Nathan approached her, he detected a slight rise and fall of her body. She was alive and breathing!

He did not know what to do and her terrible condition repulsed him. Where to start? How to handle her? Was she in a feint or just too exhausted to move?

140

'Can you hear me?' he asked. 'I'm a friend. I have come to release you. Don't be alarmed,' he tried to reassure her but she showed no sign of recognition or understanding.

'I'll start by cutting these ropes,' he said. 'I need to get a knife from the kitchen, I won't be long, your terrible ordeal will soon be over.'

On returning with a knife, he knelt down beside her and started cutting her bonds. 'Your husband, Jack, survived the wreck, he's made a fine recovery but he thinks you are dead. He is going to be so happy when he sees you.'

Nathan was not sure if she could hear him and was only talking to allay any fears she might have if she were conscious. However, his words did register with her, for, very quietly and shakily, she said 'Jack?' Then after a short pause, 'He's alive?'

'Yes, yes,' Nathan said soothingly. 'All is going to be well, just see if you can lift your head. I've cut your bonds, now we must try and get you up and out of here.'

He was very relieved that she had spoken but her condition concerned him greatly. She had not reacted in any way to his cutting of the ropes retaining her position as if she were still bound. He gently coaxed her arms round to the front, then putting one arm around her, under her shoulders, he slowly began to lift her to a standing position. It was unpleasant work, given the state of her clothes, and he had to force himself not to show too much disgust.

When she was upright, he had to retain his hold for fear her knees would buckle under her. He was wishing he had brought Reg with him for this was an awkward task for one person. How am I going to get her to Corfe?, he wondered. At that moment, she finally lifted her head and looked at him. There was no expression in her eyes - neither fear nor happiness for her release. Despite this it struck Nathan that they were beautiful eyes that would be even more radiant when and if joy should return to them. Then she lowered her eyes and looked down at her condition and began to cry. There was no sound to her crying, just tears that poured profusely from her eyes dripping onto her dress.

141

'Come, let's get out of this room.' he spoke gently. 'Can you walk with my support? We will get you into the other room at least, when we will see what we can do to clean you up.'

She put her left foot forward in compliance but as she did so, her right leg buckled and she would have fallen had Nathan not been holding her tightly. He pulled her up until her legs were straight and she tried again with the same result.

'It's alright,' Nathan said. 'It's only natural that your legs will be weak after being bound for so long. You'll soon get your control back, you'll be walking normally in no time.' He tried to sound reassuring but inwardly he was concerned that she seemed to have no strength at all throughout her body, not just her legs.

Slowly they progressed until he got her out of the room that had been her cell and they moved into the main room. Leaving the cell seemed to give her confidence a boost. She now started to manage two or three hesitant steps before needing his support. Nathan saw the old armchair and guided her to this and she gratefully collapsed into it.

'Good!' he said. 'Now let us see if we can clean you up somehow, you just rest there while I see what I can find in the way of soap and water.'

He disappeared into the scullery and then returned brandishing a bar of soap and a water jug. He pulled a small three-legged stool up to the side of the chair, put the soap on this then went outside to fill the jug from the pump in the yard.

When he came back, he put the jug down with the soap and looked about for a suitable cloth to use. There was nothing obvious but he did see a small chest in the corner. Suspecting this might be a linen chest he went over and opened it.

'Well, what have we here?' he exclaimed and turning round he held up a black dress. Nathan laid this over his arm before returning to the chest from which he now extracted some petticoats. He inspected these before saying, 'Not your finest I'm afraid but respectable and certainly a great improvement on what you are currently wearing.' In fact, it was Peggy's Sunday dress and her spare petticoats that he had discovered.

Feeling pleased with himself he walked over to Ayala all ready to administer to her when the thought struck him that she was in no condition to tend herself. She needed to get out of her soiled clothing and to wash all over, before donning these heaven sent robes. The pleasure he was feeling seconds ago had turned into angst as he was struck by the terrible realisation that he would have to assist her in all of this, indeed the bulk of the work would fall on him. Even in his full and varied life, he had never encountered such a daunting prospect. He was embarrassed and did not know where or how to start.

He tried to tell himself that he was being foolish to be so discomfited. Here was a human being in need of his aid and there was nothing of which to be ashamed. He must forget she was a woman, imagine her to be a wounded soldier and get on with the task.

In this, he was only partially successful, for as he gently started to disrobe her he could not help but notice her smooth tan coloured skin or her finely proportioned body. He was surprised to find that she did not react to his administrations not even when she was totally naked. It was as if she knew he meant no harm to her and he was only doing that which was necessary.

Wishing to avoid further embarrassment, he gave her one of the petticoats to hold against her body. Even in this, he had to put the cloth in place and to guide her hands to hold it there. He then set about washing her and made a good job of it, using a strip torn from another of the petticoats as a flannel and the remainder as a towel. He could not bring himself to wash her most personal areas, despite the obvious need. Having satisfied himself that he had done all that he could he was about to tackle the task of getting her into the dress, when she suddenly reached out for the flannel. Taking it under the petticoat in her lap, she began washing herself. It appeared as if it took all her strength and will power to do this but she managed it and then dropped the flannel to the floor.

Getting her into the clothes was easier than he expected, although he had to lift her to slide a petticoat up to her waist and again for the dress. It was a high necked, long sleeved dress, with a tight waist and buttons at the front. Only after he had pulled it up her back and placed her arms in the sleeves, did he remove the petticoat she had been using to protect her modesty and then, as delicately as he could, he buttoned the dress.

With a sense of great relief, he stepped back and looked at her. 'It's not the height of fashion, but it fits you quite well and I believe you would make even the drabbest of dresses look good.' His chivalrous remarks were intended to cheer her spirits but were wasted, as again she showed no reaction.

'My horse is outside. We need to get you mounted on it so that I can take you to our doctor's house where you will get more suitable treatment. The question is are you up to it?' Nathan was speaking more to himself than to Ayala, so he was quite startled when she replied in a faltering whisper, 'I think I can, with your help, ...and thank you for your kindness.'

It was the first time she had spoken since those first three words when she had discovered her husband lived. Nathan was greatly encouraged by this and without a word, he bent down put his arms under her knees and shoulders and lifted her from the chair. Carrying her in his arms, he took her out of that fateful cottage and placed her on his horse. He would have walked the horse with her on it except that, in her weak state, he was afraid she might fall off so he climbed up behind. Then putting his arms around her he picked up the reins.

CHAPTER 17

The ride was difficult, not least because it was all downhill from Kingston to Corfe, and the hill was extremely steep but also because Nathan had to keep a very tight grip on Ayala as she was in a state of near collapse. Eventually, however they arrived at Dr Palbrey's rather grand three storied house, which stood alone in a lane running off the main square. Palbrey did not have a houseful of servants, he kept just a husband and wife, Mr and Mrs Gamble, who acted as manservant and housekeeper respectively. Both, like the doctor, were well advanced in years so they were little help to Nathan in getting Ayala into the house but they were efficient in marshalling the operation. Mrs Gamble made up a bed in a spare room and once Nathan had got his charge into the room, the housekeeper ushered all the men out so that she could prepare Ayala for the bed.

Until now, Dr Palbrey had shown professional concern but had been only discreetly attentive. Now, with the domestic arrangements taken care of, he took over. Nathan waited in the study while the doctor gave his patient a thorough examination.

Nathan was sipping a glass of sherry provided by Mr Gamble, when Palbrey finally joined him.

'The lady has suffered a very debilitating experience,' he reported 'Were she not so young and in good health she may not have survived such an ordeal and would certainly have taken many weeks to recover. As it is she shows amazing resilience and I am confident that with some good nursing and plenty of Mrs Gamble's fine cooking she will make a full and speedy recovery.

'How it will affect her mentally, I cannot say, much will depend on her moral fibre and not knowing the woman I cannot make a judgement on that. The nursing will, however, be something of a problem. While Mrs Gamble will easily cope with another mouth to feed, she is not a young woman and cannot be expected to undertake the onerous business of attending to the lady's toilet for example. We have a young girl that comes in on a daily basis to do parlour maid duties but she is a scatty little thing who I would not trust with such responsibilities.

'As I say I expect the patient to make a relatively speedy recovery but she will need close attention and nursing for at least two weeks. I dislike being mercenary about this but there is also the matter of the costs of keeping her to say nothing of any fees.'

'I will speak to my fiancée as regards the nursing, she knows most of the young girls in the area and will no doubt know who best to recommend,' Nathan answered the first of the doctor's concerns. 'As for her mental recovery,' he continued, 'I think that will be greatly helped when she fully realises that her husband, whom she thought dead has also survived their ordeal. With him by her side she will be much fortified. You realise that he is the man you treated at the Stockwell farm of course. It seems he is a man of property and will have no problem reimbursing you for your professional services, Doctor.'

'That is good news, Mr Eldine,' the doctor said, quickly adding 'that he survives that is. I had not realised the connection. So this is the wife he thought lost. It is indeed wonderful that they will be reunited. I would have attended the lady in any case - out of Christian charity of course. You understand.'

Tactfully, Nathan let this subject drop without further comment. 'Yes as you say he will be delighted to hear that his wife has been found,' he said. 'With that in mind I will waste no time in telling him. So if you will excuse me, I will take myself to the Bankes' Arms without delay.'

'Yes, yes of course, by all means,' Palbrey said. Nathan emptied his glass, placed it on a side table and left.

The evening was drawing in as Nathan reached the inn. He went straight to Ridley's room but received no response to his knock. He went to the main bar and looked around but there was no sign of the man. Nathan spotted Molly collecting some dirty glasses from the tables. He walked over to her. 'Molly, do you know where Major Ridley is?' he asked. 'I've tried his room but I got no response. I need to find him, I've got some good news for him.'

'He's not here, I don't know where he's gone,' Molly said abruptly. She turned and made to leave but Nathan placed a hand on her arm encouraging her to turn back and face him.

'What do you mean, he's gone out? Last time I was here you said he was sulking and seldom left his room, what's brought this change in him, do you suppose?'

'I don't know! How should I, he's nothing to me,' Molly spoke quickly with an edginess to her voice. This was because Molly was feeling both confused and aggrieved. She was dispirited because Ridley had paid her little attention since their night of love making. In fact he had been quite boorish with her whenever she approached him and now he had gone off without even telling her where he was bound. She knew where he had gone because Sam had told her and she was annoyed that Jack had confided in Sam but not her. The different emotions she was experiencing had put her off guard and she realised she had spoken rashly and could see from the squire's face that he had picked up on it.

Why did she say that? Nathan wondered, somewhat taken aback by her vehemence. "He's nothing to me!" She did not need to say that, unless, of course, he does mean something to her.

Nathan spoke gruffly now. 'I think you are lying, Molly,' he said. 'Though I do not know why. I think you know where he has gone and I think he has gone out before, although you said he hadn't.' Getting no response, Nathan pressed her. 'He did go out before, didn't he?'

'No, I told you, he never left his room. Ask Sam, he will tell you,' Molly said.

'I did ask Sam, and he lied too, just like you. That he lied does not surprise me. It comes naturally to him especially if he can make a penny or two from it. But you Molly, I thought you had more sense, it's a serious business to help a wanted criminal, you could go to jail or even be transported to the colonies, if I prove you are lying.'

'I'm not lying, I'm not,' she spoke like a child, protesting its innocence, when obviously caught in the middle of some naughty deed. There was no conviction in her words, just panic. Trying to change the subject she said, 'What do you want him for anyway? What's he supposed to have done?'

147

'I believe he is responsible for the deaths of five men, that's how serious it is Molly. I think he killed these men as an act of revenge and I don't think he's finished yet. He won't stop until he has slain everyone that he believes was involved in the murder of his wife. The irony is his wife was not murdered. She survived her ordeal and is over at Dr Palbrey's now. That is what I came here to tell him.'

Molly had turned pale. She clutched at the table and tears formed in her eyes. 'His wife! He's married! She's alive, no she can't be! She can't be!' she wailed.

Nathan was shocked at the intensity of her emotions. A moment ago, he had begun to suspect that she had feelings for Ridley but her reaction now suggested that those feelings were much greater than he had supposed.

'Oh, she is alive alright,' he said. 'Although she has suffered terribly at the hands of her captors. However, Dr Palbrey assures me that she will make a full recovery. What I want to know is why that discommodes you so, have you got some fanciful idea that Jack Ridley might be interested in you?'

Molly did not reply, she simply lowered herself into a chair by the table and began sobbing with her head in her hands.

Nathan was exasperated by her. 'Come on Molly, you're not stupid,' he shouted. 'You know there is no future for you down that road.' Then more calmly he added, 'He wouldn't look twice at you and you know it.'

'Well that's where you are wrong,' Molly shouted defiantly. 'He did more than look the other night, he was lovely and he likes me I know he does.' Then realising she had said too much the girl jumped up from the chair and flounced out of the room.

Having got nowhere with these enquiries, Nathan pondered his next move and realised he had no idea as to what to do next. He needed to speak to Ridley, so he decided to settle down with a glass of ale and await the man's return.

Jack Ridley did not return that night, however, so eventually Nathan sought out Sam and booked himself a bed for the night.

Nathan slept well and deep so that it was relatively late in the morning when he emerged from his room. He took breakfast before seeking out the serving maid once again.

He found Molly in the corridor and, grasping her by her upper arm, he dragged her into an empty snug. The girl struggled and demanded to know what he thought he was doing but he forced her to sit at the solitary table. Then, not letting go of her arm, he pulled a second chair up close and sat down next to her. Nathan had been intentionally rough with her, hoping such treatment might shock her into realising the seriousness of her position. He was equally rough with her when he spoke, angrily demanding to know what she knew of Jack Ridley's whereabouts.

For Molly, this rough treatment was the last straw. Unlike Nathan she had not slept well, indeed she had hardly slept at all having sat up all night waiting for Ridley to return, occasionally nodding off, only to awake with a start as her head dropped. Her emotions were all over the place. She was tired, angry, sad and scared all at once. Angry at Ridley for his neglect of her but at the same time she longed to see him and have him hold her in his arms once more. This was what made her sad. For she knew it would never happen no matter how much she loved him.

On top of this she was afraid, worrying what his non-appearance might forebode. She did not know the truth of everything that had happened but she did know that Ridley was engaged in a dangerous mission against violent men. She fretted that maybe it was his turn to be left lying in a pool blood.

These were the mix of thoughts that had been troubling her all night and through the morning. Now the squire's rough questioning made her snap and she burst into tears, wailing, 'I don't know! I don't! I don't know where he's gone or what he's doing.'

Nathan let go of her arm and the girl sat there sobbing with her head down and her hands in her lap. He felt sorry for her, she seemed little more than a child now, but he knew he had to press her. As he was about to ask again what she did know, she surprised him by saying, 'What you said last night, about finding his wife, was that true?'

'Yes it was true and she was...' Nathan did not finish his answer for Molly again started crying profusely and was clearly not listening. Once she had calmed slightly and the sobs were not so fierce, Nathan continued, 'Mrs Ridley has been very badly treated and is lucky to have survived,' he said, 'That is why I have to find Jack so that they can be reunited as quickly as possible. You would not want the poor woman to suffer further, would you? You must tell me what you know.'

'I don't mean her any harm, honest I don't but I can't tell on Jack, please don't make me do that,' Molly said between sobs before breaking into another burst of full on crying.

Feeling he was getting somewhere Nathan pondered on his next words, he handed Molly a handkerchief but before he could speak, a commotion started up outside.

A carriage had arrived and, looking out of the window, Nathan saw that it was Madeleine who had alighted from it and, accompanied by a footman, she entered the inn. Nathan left the room and made his way to the hallway to meet her.

'Madeleine, my dear, what brings you here?' he said, as he held out his hands to greet her.

Taking his hands into hers, she kissed him on the cheek before replying, 'You do Nathaniel, you do. I could not sit at home like the dutiful woman fretting about you out hunting this awful killer. I simply had to come to town to find out the latest news and to assure myself that you are safe. Not that I expected to see you, I just thought this the most likely place to pick up any news. I have moved into my aunt's house until this is over, that way I won't be so cut off.' Madeleine's aunt was the wife of the local vicar and they lived in the vicarage, a fine house not far from the centre of town. 'I know it's not seemly, but I decided to come here anyway to see if Sam Butler had heard anything. He's usually the first to know what's happening.'

'Well, I should chastise you for coming to a place like this of all things!' Nathan said in a disapproving manner. 'Although, despite your foolishness, I'm delighted to see you as always,' he said more warmly. 'Much has happened since I last saw you that's for sure, come into the snug and I'll tell you all about it. Actually, I think your

150

arrival may be most fortuitous, for I have a delicate situation on my hands, which may best be unravelled by a woman's touch.'

They entered the room and sat at a small round table set in a bay window. The footman did his best to be invisible by huddling in a corner. He was under express orders from Madeleine's aunt not to let the young lady out of his sight and knew better than to disobey that formidable lady. Nathan quickly outlined the events that had occurred, starting with the discovery of Ayala and the terrible condition she was in, although he refrained from telling of his role in cleaning and dressing her. Then he explained his suspicions regarding Molly and her reaction to the news that Ridley's wife was alive.

'I need to make her talk, I know she is lying for Ridley and I'm sure she knows where he is,' Nathan said. 'I must get to him before he commits any more crimes. The trouble is she is being stubborn and all she does is weep. When I saw you arrive, it made me think that if she had another woman to confide in, someone who was sympathetic to her feelings, then maybe she would tell what she knows,' he concluded.

'That's very perceptive of you Nathaniel Eldine,' Madeleine said. 'Most men would not be so aware of the bond that can exist between women, I can see I shall have to be very subtle when I want to use my female charms on you. I won't be able to twist you round my little finger as I do my father,' Madeleine chuckled. She became serious again, 'It may well be that you are right and I will see what I can do. However, my first priority must be to arrange the nursing of Mrs Ridley, from what you tell me I imagine she too will need the female touch. Palbrey may be a good doctor but he is no nurse.' She paused for a moment considering the situation. 'I shall call on her straight away and I think I shall take Molly with me. The catalyst to start Molly talking might well be the sight of another woman in distress, even her rival. I shall see how she reacts and if I deem it appropriate, I shall put her to the nursing duties. Where is she now? I will speak to her briefly before we go.'

'She's in another snug bar opposite this room.' Nathan told her. 'There is no one else with her, so I suppose it's alright for you to go in there. Take your man with you though. I'll go and speak to Sam to see if he knows where Ridley is. I also need to find Reg Gaddie. I wonder if he learned any more from questioning Peggy Miles.' Nathan left the room.

Madeleine sat pondering the situation before she too got up and left followed dutifully by the footman. On entering the room where Molly was waiting, Madeleine found the girl sitting on a chair weeping quietly into the handkerchief that Nathan had given her. Realising that kindness was the key to dealing with this situation, she gently touched the girl on the shoulder, before saying, 'Now, now Molly, calm yourself. I do not know what Captain Eldine has been saying to you but I'm sure it cannot be so bad. He can be very heavy handed at times, like most men, but he has a kind heart and would not want to cause you unnecessary distress.'

'It's not the captain, ma'am,' Molly answered between sniffs. 'He's not being unfair, it's just that he said, well I can't say what he said but something he said, well it can't be true. It just can't. I don't know what's going to happen if it is true!' She fell silent for a moment or two then she wailed, 'It can't be true, can it, ma'am?'

'What cannot be true? What are you referring to?' Madeleine was mystified.

'He said that they had found her, Mrs Ridley that is, Jack's wife. I didn't know of her, honest I didn't.' Molly was gasping now as she spoke between sobs.

'I see,' Madeleine said. 'I think I'm beginning to understand. They have found Mrs Ridley, it's true, and the poor lady has had a very terrifying experience, which has left her very weak and in need of careful nursing. That's what I came to see you about, I cannot think of a better person to give her the kindness and attention she needs! I will speak to Sam and I'm sure, when he hears the reason, he will be amenable to the idea and allow you any time you need. It will be a chance for you to redeem yourself with Captain Eldine for the way you have deceived him.'

Molly looked horrified. 'Me!' she said. 'You want me to nurse her? Oh no, I can't do it. You don't understand it can't be me.' She was very agitated now, jumping up off the chair.

'Calm yourself, Molly, I believe I do understand. How far things have gone I do not know and it's best that it stays that way but you must realise, for your own sake that this turn of events makes any thoughts you may have regarding the Major totally fanciful. In truth they always have been, whether or not Mrs Ridley returned. You must forget all about him - in that way anyway. You do understand this don't you? And you must help this lady. I think you owe it to her.

'I will leave you now. I need to speak to Sam to arrange things. You must pull yourself together. When I return, we will go to Dr Palbrey's house to put things right,' Madeleine said firmly. 'Do you understand?' she added.

Molly did not speak she simply nodded then buried her face in the handkerchief.

Madeleine found Sam talking to Nathan. Getting him to agree to let Molly tend the patient, without stopping her pay, presented no problem. Initially Sam began to object but Nathan made it clear that his lies had been seen through and that, if he did not behave like the good Samaritan, the full force of the law would be brought down on him. Not just for wasting official time but for being an accomplice to murder. Sam was then all 'yes ma'am, no ma'am anything you say ma'am' Nathan and Madeleine left him looking very crestfallen.

Molly was a simple girl but she was not stupid. She had been overcome by her emotions but by the time Madeleine returned she had pulled herself together and taken stock of her situation. She knew Madeleine had spoken truly and she realised she must put all hopes of a future with Jack out of her mind. She realised now that she had always known it was a hopeless dream and that their affair had simply been an indulgence of passion. Wonderful as it was, it never really had a chance as an ongoing relationship. She also realised that she would nurse his wife back to health. She would do this for anyone in distress but she had the added incentive of knowing that she had done wrong by this woman and needed to make amends.

She also thought that it would be what Jack wanted, so she would do it for him. Molly still loved him and resolved that, despite everything, she would not tell the squire where Jack had gone. She would not give him away no matter what the consequences might be.

Molly need not have worried on this score for Sam had no such loyalty and rather than risk his neck he had quickly told Nathan that

Ridley had set out the previous evening, bound for Swanwich. Sam did not know what business Ridley had there but he had hired a horse and Sam had heard him tell the ostler where that horse was bound. Sam also added that Ridley had said he might not return for a day or two.

Hearing this, Nathan quickly sought out Reg who was enjoying himself talking with a couple of farm maids outside the Inn. As the two men hurried off to the stables behind the coaching inn, Reg told Nathan of his questioning of Peggy Miles, although there was little to add to what they now already knew.

Some minutes later they emerged from the stables on horseback and set off down Corfe High Street in the wake of Jack Ridley. At the same time, Madeleine and Molly made their way on foot to Dr Palbrey's house, closely attended by the footman.

CHAPTER 18

Dr Palbrey was veritably gushing as Madeleine, Molly and the footman entered his house. 'My dear Miss Armitage, I am so pleased to see you,' he said. 'I have done all I can as regards treating Mrs Ridley's physical hurts. It is her mental state that concerns me now. She will need attentive nursing and gentle companionship if her spirits are to be revived. Not my forte, I'm afraid.' Remembering his manners he added, 'Oh, I'm sorry I forget myself in the relief of your arrival. Good day to you Miss Armitage, do come in, perhaps we should go to my consulting room, so that I can brief you before you meet the lady.'

Mr Gamble had opened the front door to the ladies but had been brushed aside by the doctor in his eagerness, now the old retainer stepped forward and took Madeleine's hat and shawl. Molly also wore a shawl but of far poorer quality than Madeleine's, and she now held this out but Gamble ignored her. So she wrapped it over her left arm and stood there holding it. Madeleine had hardly time to reply, 'Good day to you, Dr Palbrey,' before he turned, crossed the hallway, opened the door to his consulting room and ushered her in. 'This way, Miss Armitage, this way,' he said.

Madeleine entered the room, followed by Molly seemingly unnoticed by the doctor as he closed the door behind them, leaving the footman in the hall with Mr Gamble. Molly was not offended by the doctor's lack of acknowledgment, as it was standard practice for the gentry to totally ignore those waiting on them and Molly was clearly of that rank in the doctor's eyes.

It was a typical consulting room. The walls were lined with glass fronted cabinets sitting on top of an assortment of chests of drawers. The cabinets which reached to the ceiling were home to a plethora of leather bound books mostly covering the sciences, particularly those medical. One cabinet was given over to the storage of medicines in different forms. The chest of drawers beneath this cabinet consisted of numerous small drawers each labelled as to its contents. Another cabinet contained shelves crammed with jars and phials of various

155

coloured liquids, powders and pills as well as a whole range of boxes, no doubt containing more pills.

A single shelf held two mortar and pestles and a microscope, while on another, the doctor's bag, stethoscope and sundry surgical instruments could be seen.

The books appeared never to have been taken out for reading but appearances can be deceptive. Palbrey was in fact extremely well read, having in his time consumed the knowledge of all of these texts as well as most of the great works of literature. He was extremely fond of the classics especially the Greeks.

There was a solitary but large leather covered desk with two wooden fiddle back arm chairs either side of it and a matching fiddle back dining chair against a wall. Apart from these, the only other furniture was a couch behind a Chinese screen for the more intimate examinations.

Being at the front of the house, the room would have been well lit as it had a large bay window. However, drapes were drawn across to protect the doctor's patients from the prying eyes of passers-by. Even though the house was not on the main street, it had no front garden and the lane outside led to some further dwellings. As a result people often walked close to the window as they passed. To overcome the gloom the doctor had a fine candelabra on his desk. This served its purpose well as it could accommodate four candles. They were not lit at the moment, so Dr Palbrey hurried across the room and quickly pulled the drapes aside. The room was immediately plunged into dazzling sunlight to which its three occupants took a few moments to adjust.

'That's better,' Palbrey said. 'Now we can see what we are doing. Please take a seat, dear lady, although what I have to say will not take long.'

Madeleine sat herself in the chair opposite the doctor who had taken up his usual consulting posture, sitting at the desk with his elbows on it and his chin resting on his clenched fists. Molly, uncertain of her place remained standing.

Madeleine was having none of that. 'Come Molly,' she said, 'pull that chair up and sit next to me.' Addressing the doctor she said, 'Molly will be doing the main nursing duties, so it is important she hears what you have to say. Also I would be grateful if you would advise Mr and Mrs Gamble to treat her with the respect appropriate to that role and that they should afford her every assistance she may require.'

'Oh yes, yes, of course,' Palbrey answered. As if seeing Molly for the first time he added, 'Molly, isn't it? Yes of course. Make yourself at ease and rest assured every convenience of the house will be at your disposal while you are nursing Mrs Ridley. She is a fine lady you know, even if she is foreign!'

'Foreign?' Molly said rather abruptly. She looked as if she was about to burst into tears as she reacted to the mention of her lover's wife.

'Oh yes, she's definitely foreign. Indian, I think but you must have no qualms on that account.' The doctor was surprised at Molly's strong reaction and, having no idea as to the cause, had misinterpreted it entirely. 'As I say she is a perfectly respectable lady and speaks English fluently, so there is no cause for concern,' he concluded.

'Quite so!' Madeleine now interjected, ignoring the confusion. 'You wish to tell us something of her condition and the treatment she will require, isn't that so, Doctor?'

'Yes indeed, Miss Armitage,' the doctor continued, having remembered his thread. 'Well its quite simple really. The lady has been very badly maltreated by her captors. She has a number of cuts and lesions, particularly where she was bound. Her wrists, ankles and throat, that is. These will need dressing each day for about a week or until they are healed. There are two salves that you will need to use - one for the cuts the other for the bruises. They are by her bedside and I have clearly marked which is which. Can you read and write, my dear?' the doctor asked turning his head towards Molly.

'Yes I can,' Molly answered bluntly, as if such a question were an impertinence, although , in truth, she was a poor reader and struggled with her letters.

'Good, good, yes indeed,' Palbrey patronised, not noticing Molly's irritation.

'She is also somewhat undernourished,' he continued. 'I do not think she ate whilst in captivity although her condition would suggest

157

it was longer than that since she last ate. Perhaps she had mal de mare on the voyage. This may have exaggerated the situation. Like the abrasions, this is hardly life threatening. Gentle coaxing to eat and a steady build up of her food intake will soon have her back to normal. I have instructed Mrs Gamble as to an appropriate diet.

'But it is not her physical condition that concerns me. More worrying is the fact that she is very disturbed mentally, she hardly recognises my presence and says very little when she does. Such appalling behaviour and disregard for humanity is it seems quite, um..,' the doctor was going to say "foreign to her" but decided this was not appropriate and struggled for an alternative, finally settling for, 'abhorrent to her. Being exposed to such violence has quite unhinged her. She witnessed the murders of the crew you know or so it seems, according to young Eldine. Then to be subjected to such ghastly treatment whilst in captivity. Well, it seems to have seriously undermined her will,' he said.

'Her spirits were revived when she learned of her husband's survival but that was short lived I'm afraid,' he continued. 'She soon regressed back into her state of despondency. Perhaps we shall see a better and longer lasting recovery once he starts visiting. Do you know when that might be? Captain Eldine said he was going to see Ridley last night and I had expected a visit by now.'

'No, I don't know when Mr Ridley will be visiting,' Madeleine answered. 'My fiancée was unable to locate him, so as yet he still knows nothing of his wife's rescue,'

'The poor, poor man, he must be feeling so hapless. Let us hope the captain finds him soon so his misery can be lifted and as I say he can visit his wife and maybe help to lift her misery too,' Palbrey said. He was almost talking to himself as he said this, then, more coherently, he said, 'Time, kindness and good company are the only cures we have at our disposal and I fear there is no certainty that they will work. Mental illness is such an unfathomed science.

'Be that as it may, besides the nursing there is a more mundane task for which I would be grateful of your assistance. When the lady arrived she was most immodestly clad. She was wearing a very threadbare dress and nothing else. The dress was clearly not hers, leastways in did not fit her properly and was of quite inferior quality.

What this means she suffered at the hands of her captors I dread to think,' the doctor said. He remained quiet for a moment as if he were trying to imagine the horrors.

'The point is her luggage was, I presume, lost with the wreck so she has nothing suitable to wear,' he began again. 'Mrs gamble has lent her a nightdress, not her size of course nor of a quality fit for a lady. It will suffice for now but as she recovers and wishes to ....'

'Do not fret yourself, Doctor,' Madeleine interrupted. 'I will handle that. It will be my pleasure. I always enjoy a visit to the haberdashers and this will give me a good excuse.'

Secretly she was thinking that Nathaniel had neglected to mention anything about Mrs Ridley's state of undress. Madeleine was not concerned or jealous in any way but she was happily tucking this piece of information away, to await an opportune moment when she might have some fun confronting him with it and amusing herself at his discomfort.

Molly was also deep in thought. Her deliberations, however, were of a quite different humour. She was a good person with a very generous nature and a warm disposition. As she listened to the doctor describing Ayala's condition and the ordeal she had endured, Molly could not help but feel for the woman. This woman who not so long ago was her rival and who Molly would have cheerfully strangled was now a hapless victim of a heinous crime and Molly's heart went out to her. She recognised that she would do everything she could for Ayala, without a moment's hesitation and the emotional torment Molly had been undergoing lifted slightly at each mention of mistreatment. Molly still loved Jack. She had no regrets for what they had done but the jealousy she had initially felt had begun to dissipate slightly. Their affair had been a wonderful moment of passion but it was over, a thing of the past and she knew she had to accept this.

It was when the doctor mentioned that Ridley would be visiting his wife that her despair took hold again. How can I give his wife the strength of mind she will need when I have no hope myself, she thought. What will I do when he visits her and takes her in his arms? No I could not bear to watch them embracing each other like that.

'I can't do this!' she suddenly blurted out.

Dr Palbrey was again startled by the girl's outburst as he wondered about her sanity and whether she was a good choice for the job. 'What is she going on about?' he asked Madeleine.

'Don't be silly, Molly,' Madeleine quickly reacted. 'Of course you can.' She then turned to the doctor and calmly said, 'There are a few things Molly and I need to discuss, Dr Palbrey, women's things you understand and I'm sure a busy man like you will have urgent matters to attend to, so if you wish to excuse yourself perhaps you could tell us where we can find the patient before you go. We will make our own way there when we have finished talking.'

'What? Oh yes, of course,' the doctor said. He did not understand at all but was happy to be excused of any further involvement. 'You'll find her on the first floor, the door opposite you at the top of the stairs. I'll leave you to it then,' he said and left the room.

'Now Molly!' Madeleine said firmly. 'I realise that this is hard for you but you must not let Mrs Ridley suspect that anything may have happened between you and the Major. I know you, Molly and I know you are a very generous and well intentioned young girl. That is why I selected you for this task. For your part, what you have done was wrong and the only way you can put it right is to give Mrs Ridley your total care. Time will heal your grief but only if you do the right thing now. Consider how painful it is for you to give him up. Would you inflict such pain on his wife by coming between them. Would you add that pain to her already terrible condition?'

'It's not that I don't want to help her, ma'am, I do and I'm resolved to the fact that I can't have Jack. But how can I see him again? How can I watch him embracing her and loving her?' Molly said. She wanted to add, 'especially knowing he can't have her either, after what he's done,' but she held her tongue. Instead she began crying openly now and Madeleine took Molly in her arms and comforted her.

'You poor thing, you have been badly used in all of this, I don't know what the future holds for the Major and his wife but I do know it is not right that you should suffer such ill out of it, Madeleine said.

'I am sure that if you do right by this lady, you will be the better for it,' she said. 'When this is all over I will look after you, that I promise. You're a smart girl, Molly, too good to be wasted working at that inn. Perhaps, if you are up to it, you may become my lady's maid. I shall need one when I marry and I would be there to help you recover your heart. It's a big world you know and you are very young. I'm certain in time you will meet someone else, who you will love just as much as Jack Ridley if not more and they will love you. I know you cannot imagine that could happen but it will I'm sure. Maybe not tomorrow but maybe not so far in the future as you might suppose.' Madeleine's kindness helped and Molly stopped crying, although she still looked extremely unhappy.

'Come we must go and see our patient now but first you must wipe your eyes and change that expression. She must not be aware of your pain or realise that you have been crying. No that would never do. Come along now, deep breaths.' Madeleine was quite the strict matriarch when she wanted to be.

Molly did as she was told. 'I'm ready,' she said.

CHAPTER 19

Once again things seemed to fall into place for Ridley when he reached Swanwich. He was here to seek out the White brothers but, having no idea as to what they looked like or where to find them, he was uncertain as to where to begin. To get here he had hired a horse from the stable at the Greyhound Inn and now he sort out the local hostelry to have his mount looked after, before making his way down to the harbour area. The Whites were fishermen after all and this seemed the most likely place for his enquiries.

As he approached the jetty, Ridley noticed a well dressed gentleman sitting on a bench and staring out to sea across a large pool of water. This was in fact a reservoir of fresh water collected from the flow of the numerous springs located in the southern hills above the village. The reservoir was manmade and served two purposes. It was initially built as a sluice to protect the lower part of the village from flooding when tides were high. Without it the streams from the springs would be forced back and so overflow their banks.

Later generations had stocked it with fish to supplement the village's food supply but it was now used more for sport than a larder as evidenced by two young lads Ridley observed fishing off one of its stone built retaining walls.

Sauntering over, Ridley studied the man on the bench. He was middle aged wearing a black suit with grey stockings and a pair of handsomely buckled black leather shoes. His right arm was held out in front of him supported by an ebony cane topped with a fine silver lion's head. He had a black tricorn hat resting in his lap so that his very white, freshly powdered wig was strikingly evident.

He was clearly a professional man and local at that for him to be so at ease in displaying his evident wealth. A stranger would take care to be less conspicuous in an unfamiliar environment. Through his profession, this man, Ridley surmised, was almost certainly well acquainted with and no doubt respected by the residents of

Swanwich. The ideal candidate to guide me to the White brothers, Ridley thought.

'Good day to you, sir,' Ridley said as he approached the bench. 'Do you mind if I join you for a moment? You look like a man of some importance who may well know many of the inhabitants of this town and therefore possibly able to point me in the right direction.'

'Please, please, seat yourself by all means my friend,' the man replied. He then added, 'Ahem.' This was a sort of guttural clearing of the throat the man made a habit of. 'It's most agreeable here in the sun I must say, so unusual for this time of year. I am Dr Small, and indeed you are right in your assertion. I do not mean that I claim to be important but that I do know most of the people of this village, if not all of them, for I have been helping them into this world and looking after their ailments for nigh on fifty years now. As to whether I can help you, sir, that depends on whom you may be seeking?'

'You stagger me sir, I would not have thought you anywhere near old enough to have practised for so long,' Ridley flattered him, 'and I would say that makes you a very important person.'

Dr Small? Ridley wondered if he were related to the undertaker at Langton who's doorway had been so foully used by Parkes and Carter. Pushing these thoughts aside he said, 'I seek a man called White. I have some business to carry out with him but have no address. I believe he is something of a character, so perhaps you can indeed help me.'

'Yes, yes, ahem! I'm sure I can but I need to know which White you refer to, there are a number of them in Swanwich, you know.'

Before Ridley could respond the doctor continued, 'There's old Jeb White. His real name is Jeremiah but everyone calls him Jeb. He's the patriarch of the family, if you know what I mean. Although his wife is the real boss. Anyway he is the eldest, must be well into his eighties by now and no I did not deliver him, before you ask,' the doctor chuckled. 'Ahem! Then there are his brothers James and Joshua.

'Old Jeb married Sally Black. Quite a joke at the time people saying that black was white after all, ahem, kept the village amused for weeks before and after the wedding. Well they had eight children, everyone a girl except the last one and that poor mite only lived three years. Died of consumption, I'm afraid. Ahem!

'James never married but Joshua did. He married the Knightly girl, Agnes. Lovely girl she was. I could never understand what she saw in Joshua, ahem, you'd find it hard to meet a more surly character. Still they must have had something going for she bore him six sons, nary a daughter don't you know! Strange how things work out. Poor Sally would have given anything for a healthy son and Agnes desperately wanted a daughter. She died giving birth to her sixth boy, Francis she named him just before she left us. A sickly child he turned out to be and never really got over it, ahem, always hiding behind his older brothers' coat tails.

'Three of the boys are dead now, two died at sea, fighting the French. The other one, Jack, fell ill one day and nothing I could do would save him. I bled him several times but to no avail, ahem!' The doctor fell silent for a moment or two and Ridley was about to interrupt his thoughts when the old man suddenly continued his account, 'the eldest son is still going strong. That's Jeremiah, named after his uncle, but he will have nothing to do with his last two brothers, Joshua and Frank. You see, Joshua didn't just take his father's name, he inherited much of the old man's demeanour as well. Ahem! He's a nasty piece of work, always getting into trouble both as a child and now as a grown man and Francis, Frank that is, just follows suit, worse in fact. He drinks too much and gets into scrapes, then Joshua steps in to protect him.

'They work a fishing boat out of here but if you ask me that's just a cover for the more nefarious practices they indulge in. Ahem! Mind you I have to admit I've taken a bottle or two off their hands from time to time. Brandy that is and good stuff too.'

'They would be the gentlemen I'm looking for,' Ridley said. Taking advantage of this latest break in the doctor's rhetoric. 'Do you know where I can find them?'

'Gentlemen, ahem!' the doctor rejoined. 'I don't know about that but as to where you can find them that's easy. They are out there, on their boat. They've just got back from salvaging the cargo from that unfortunate ship that was wrecked.' As he spoke the doctor pointed to a small fishing smack that was anchored up a short way out to sea.

Ridley looked out to where the doctor indicated and could clearly see the vessel and three men on it who were busy tidying up its rigging and various ropes. They were obviously going to be out of his reach for sometime so he studied them carefully. He wanted to be sure he would recognise them once they came ashore.

'Which are the brothers and who is the other man?' he asked.

'Joshua's the big fellow in the bows, the fatter one bending next to him with the red bandana is his brother Frank and the fellow in the stern is Roger Bowles, he crews for them from time to time. But I thought you said you had business with them, ahem, how is it then that you don't know what they look like?' The doctor stumbled over these last few words, afraid he may have spoken out of turn. He was aware he had a bad habit of being over garrulous and wondered if, once again, he had said too much.

Ridley, on the other hand, realised he needed to be careful and not make the doctor suspicious, after all, the news of the murders must be spreading by now and the doctor was no fool he might well put two and two together. Knowing most of the local people, he might easily see the connection between the victims and the White brothers and a stranger asking questions about members of the gang might well set him thinking.

'No I don't know them,' Ridley said trying to sound casual. 'I've got some goods that need transporting along the coast and someone suggested White as someone likely to turn his hand to other things, that's all.'

Dr Small was indeed suspicious on hearing this but he was not thinking of the murders. Rather he presumed Ridley had some contraband to move. He was too wise to say anything that may give a hint of these suspicions, however, for he did not know this man nor what he might be capable of. 'Of course, of course, ahem,' he said amicably. 'I understand that they had to stow their claim on the cargo for a few days, so no doubt Joshua will be glad of the work.'

A nervous silence ensued as both men fretted over the turn their conversation had taken. Ridley worried that his interest in the Whites had made him too conspicuous and the doctor was afraid he had spoken too openly to a stranger who was probably a complete villain if he was doing business with the Whites.

After an uncomfortable delay, Ridley finally spoke, 'Well thank you for your time doctor, it looks like they will be out there for some time, so I best get on with other matters and leave you in peace. Good day to you.'

'Yes, yes, ahem!' said Dr Small rising from the bench. 'I too must be about my business.'

In truth neither man had anything to do or anywhere to go and both would have preferred to stay sitting in the sun but the discomfort they felt over their conversation forced them both to leave. Ridley started walking further along the seafront towards 'The Bankers' while the doctor set off up the hill towards his house in Langton.

Before coming to Swanwich, Ridley had visited the tailor in Corfe to pick up the new clothes he had ordered. Although they had served him well the night he had visited the Ship Inn, what remained of his original clothes were too torn or shabby for everyday use and would draw attention to him as much as the flamboyant new clothes the tailor had sent him. To the disappointment of Marsh, the tailor, Ridley had deliberately ordered more sombre fabrics for the bespoke garments as he did not want to be too memorable. Even so, when he went back to his room to change he had decided that the black frock coat looked too new and he had discarded this for the old brown coat the Stockwells had given him. Finally, satisfied with his appearance he had set off confident that he would not draw too much attention. Now he cursed himself for having undone these precautions by his foolish behaviour with Dr Small.

Ridley need not have worried, for the doctor's only concern was that he might have caused an unpleasantness by talking too freely with this stranger. He had been reassured, however, when the man had simply sauntered off, clearly having taken no offence. In no time the doctor had put the encounter out of his mind and was soon enjoying his walk home through this beautiful valley on a pleasant autumn afternoon.

He was particularly anticipating a stop for refreshment in the gardens of the Ship Inn, a peaceful retreat that contrasted so strongly from the interior of this notorious establishment.

Dr Small was not the only one enjoying this lingering vestige of summer. Having left the bench well behind him, Ridley had looked around for somewhere discreet to sit and wait for the White brothers to come ashore. He had finally settled on a low brick wall, which seemed to serve no purpose other than to divide the road in two.

On one side of the wall it was quite busy with carts carrying stone and other goods passing regularly. There were several people on foot who all seemed to be involved in trades associated with the harbour. The road was much more poorly maintained on the other side of the wall and was clearly far less used. It appeared to only serve traffic that was headed out of Swanwich to a solitary cottage on Peveril Point or to a destination beyond that and out of site.

There was no traffic on it now as Ridley basked in the afternoon sun, looking far out to sea, beyond the vessels in the bay, to the white cliffs of what appeared to be two islands. His geography of the south coast was not great but even his limited knowledge told him that this was a false impression. He knew there was only one island out there - the Isle of Whyte and these two crops of land must be joined by a lower strip of land, invisible on this day. The Isle had been something of a mystery to the early residents of Swanwich, as it was capable of taking on many different forms depending on the prevailing light.

Some days it could be seen in its full pomp with the whole stretch of the Island from North to South and its magnificent white cliffs appearing quite clearly. At other times it would disappear altogether so that, in less enlightened times, it had been known as the vanishing Island and people had even claimed it was inhabited by Giants who occasionally sailed it out to sea.

Ridley knew nothing of these stories but was transfixed by the sheer beauty of the scene. Eventually he pulled his attention away from the distant island returning his gaze to the boats in the bay and in particular the White's fishing smack. To his consternation the boat was clearly deserted and he quickly scanned the harbour for any sign of the men. There was none.

Alarmed, he jumped up only to sit down again almost immediately as he saw the White brothers with arms over each other's shoulders, walking down the road straight towards him. There

167

was no sign of the third man, Bowles. As they walked they laughed and boisterously chatted with each other and the people they passed, including a pair of comely lasses to whom the brothers made lewd suggestions.

Ridley felt his anger rising as he watched these two loud and offensive braggarts approaching, his demand for revenge surged and the blood lust took hold.

Until now, Ridley had killed his victims with a cold, calculated and savage efficiency. The sight of Josh White sauntering along with his brother, laughing and joking as if he were a complete innocent was an affront and changed everything. The nightmare of his wife being assaulted and abused by her attackers had escalated in Ridley's mind to such an extent that a demented rage overtook him and without considering a plan of attack, he simply rushed forward drawing his sword as he went and lashed out at Frank White before throwing himself on the skipper of the *Mary Jane*.

The sword stroke slashed across the younger brother's chest, opening a long cut which immediately flowed with blood but it was not a fatal blow.

The surprise of the attack and the horror of his blood-drenched shirt was enough to send Frank White sprawling to the ground clutching at his chest and screaming with fear. The time it took for him to realise he was not dying and that the wound, whilst bloody, was not life threatening was the difference between him saving his brother's life and the actual grisly outcome.

It was probably the fact that the sword Ridley was using was the one he had taken from Trevellis on the road to Langton that spared Frank White. It had not been sharpened for some time and the blunt blade had not cut as deeply as it might. This sword had a metal hand protector on its hilt and it was this that Ridley used to attack Josh White, smashing it into his face as he leapt upon him. The two men tumbled against the wall of a whitewashed warehouse. White with his back to it, his nose broken and bleeding.

Before his victim could react, Ridley struck a second blow with the hilt of the sword, this time against the man's temple paralysing him in momentary unconsciousness. Time enough for Ridley to grab White by the shoulder and spin him around so that his face was pressed against the wall and, moving the sword to his left hand, Ridley began punching the man in his kidney. Although White was a strong well built man, the ferocity of the surprise attack and the succession of blows rendered him helpless to defend himself and his knees sagged as each blow sent violent pain through his body.

Ridley was holding the man up now and pummelling him with blow after blow. He could have let the man slip to the ground and then finish him off with the sword but in his madness for revenge Ridley did not want White to die so easily. He wanted the man to suffer as he imagined Ayala had and so continued the frenzied attack. At last, exhausted from his efforts, Ridley paused, then he spun White around again and kneed him in the groin. All but unconscious, White screamed in agony before falling to his knees, his right hand against his kidney while his left hand clutched his groin. All the fight had gone from him - he was totally unaware as to what his assailant might do next and incapable of defending himself against further onslaught.

Panting from his efforts, Ridley watched the man sprawling before him, then, almost reluctantly, he took the sword in both hands held it over his victim for a moment before plunging it down in what was meant to be the coup de grâce. As he did so, he felt a sharp pain in his side. Spinning around to identify its source, his thrust was averted, and instead of delivering a deathblow, his sword drove in to the side of White's body passing right through him.

The source of the pain was a fisherman's knife, which Frank White, gathering himself together, had thrust into Ridley's back as he rushed to his brother's aid. It was not a big knife, so that the wound was not overly serious but a lucky strike or a succession of strikes with this blade could kill and Frank White was preparing to strike again.

Ridley kicked out at the man, which caused the younger brother to step back and gave Ridley time to pull the sword free. The two wounded men now squared up to each other and stood like a pair of rutting stags, their shoulders sagging with weakness from their wounds and their efforts.

It was not an even contest. Frank was the more seriously injured and his blade was no match for Ridley's sword. Realising this, like the defeated stag, White turned and sought an escape from this encounter. All thought of saving his brother had gone and on seeing a break in the buildings, where an alleyway led off the main road, he fled. Oblivious of a few stunned observers that had gathered, Ridley gave chase and caught up with Frank in the alleyway. This time Ridley struck with more control. White tried to defend himself with his knife but the outcome was inevitable. After a couple of lunges, which White managed to avoid, Ridley's sword finally passed over Whites despairing parry and struck his neck, slicing the jugular vein. Blood gushed out. Frank dropped his blade, clasped at his neck in a futile effort to staunch the flow and with a petrified look stared at Ridley. Then, faintly, he asked, 'Who are you?' before sagging to his knees and falling forward unto his face. He was dead. Ridley stepped forward and with the blood now pumping proudly through his veins he cried, 'I am Jack Ridley and I will have my revenge.'

Drawing breath Ridley stood shaking having surprised even himself with this theatrical outburst. 'Pull yourself together man,' he muttered. He turned and hurried back down the alley. He intended to return to Josh White and make certain that the man was dead but when he reached the road he found that a crowd of people had formed and that a constable was with them. On seeing Ridley, a cry went up, and several of the men, including the constable started towards him. Not knowing where it led, Ridley rushed back up the alley, almost falling over Frank White's body as he made his escape.

The posse followed Ridley up the alley but came to a halt over the body. It was probably the great pool of blood that caused them to stall their pursuit as they realised how dangerous their prey was. Constable Burt forced his way to the front and he too was appalled by the sight.

He thought of Captain Eldine's words and said, 'This man is very dangerous, it's not for ordinary folk to tackle him.'

Spotting a young boy in the melee, he went on, 'Tom, go get the militia, there's a group of them waiting on me outside the Methodist Hall.'

The boy ran off as Burt called out, 'The rest of you go back about your business, clear this alley, go on, move along.'

Remembering Josh White, he selected a couple of men from the crowd. 'Except you, Adam Carberry, and you Pete, you can go back and get Josh White, take him to the inn. Get Missy to do what she can for him while you go and get Dr Small from Langton.'

Dr Erasmus Small, who Ridley had conversed with earlier, was indeed the undertaker's brother. His favoured treatment for any complaint was to let blood via the application of leeches. This was thought by many to be the cause of work for his brother rather than the avoider of it. He was, however, perfectly competent when it came to serious wounds having removed many a limb in his time.

The remaining crowd slowly dispersed leaving the constable standing guard over the corpse. After a while he heard the sounds of boots and, on looking up, was delighted to see Nathan Eldine leading the approaching militia men.

'Captain Eldine, sir, I'm glad to see you sir. Our man's struck again and made his escape down this alley, I would have followed him but ..,' Burt stopped speaking, as he could not think of a reason.

'Quite right, Will,' Nathan salved Burt's conscience for him. 'This is not a man for any of us to be tackling alone. Where does this alley lead to?'

'It arcs round and back to the river, sir, it comes out by the jetty where they unload the stone,' Burt answered.

'Alright, let's get after him but steadily we don't want to do anything rash, the boy tells me he's wounded, that could make him desperate and as such even more dangerous.'

'Right, you two take the point, one on either side of the alley,' Reg Gaddie said taking control. 'Wallace you stay here and sort out the clearing up of this mess. Pick a man to help you.' He selected two of the men to lead. 'The rest of you fall in behind the point men. We will move forward slowly and check any doors or gateways before moving on.'

They made slow progress down the alley as there were numerous breaks in the walls for doorways, gates or in some cases just due to disrepair. All of which needed to be checked cautiously. When, at last, they arrived at the river's edge there was no sign of their quarry.

A group of workers were standing by the jetty and on seeing the militia one cried out. 'Over here, he took a boat, he's about half way across, if it's him you're after, that is?'

They hurried to the jetty. There was a pile of cut stone here that the men had unloaded from a barge using an A frame winch. This was not the jetty for sea going barges but one used for unloading stone ferried from Herston, the next village up the valley. Making his way to the front of the group, Nathan studied the small rowing boat that was now almost across the river. He recognised the man as Jack Ridley even though he was slumped in the boat due to his wound. Despite this handicap, he was rowing strongly and would soon be on the other side.

'It's our man alright,' he said. He was about to gives instructions to his men when one of the militia men fired his rifle. The bullet slammed into the rowing boat throwing shards of wood into the air.

'Belay that,' Gaddie shouted at the man. 'Hold your fire,' he ordered the rest of the men. 'Nobody fires without orders, is that clear?'

There was a general muttering of agreement, although nobody answered him directly.

Nathan turned to the mason who had called them over, 'We need to get across, can we take this barge?' he asked.

'I don't know about that,' the man replied. 'It needs sailors to handle it and the crew is away for some victuals. We're stone cutters not sailors, I'm afraid.'

Nathan looked back to the river and saw that Ridley was jumping from the boat although he was not right across. Lifting his knees high he strode through the water up onto the bank and started hurrying away across an open field. Judging by his stride and the fact that he was still creating splashes, Nathan discerned that this must be a saltwater marsh, which stretched away for some hundred yards before the ground turned into grassland rising slowly at first and then quite sharply up and over Ballard down.

'We could head back up to Herston and take Mill's ferry across,' Burt ventured. 'It will give him a bit more of a start on us but once across we will be on the Studland road so we will make much quicker time than he can across country. There's only the sea ahead of him, to escape he would have to turn inland and, unless he does that soon, we will be able to cut him off. Then it would just be a case of closing in on him.'

'By God, you're right,' Nathan said. 'Come on all of you.' Whereupon he and the rest of the posse set off along the riverbank towards Herston, which lay back down the valley about a mile from Swanwich.

The village of Herston comprised little more than a few thatched cottages for farm workers and took its name from the nearby manor house, Herston Lodge, which was one of the residences used by Lord Aldwin during his rare visits to Purbeck.

It was also the point where the river became no longer navigable for deep-hulled sailing boats or for the broad sail barges used for transporting stone to Swanwich quay.

Up-stream from here, the river broke up into small rivulets fed by the numerous springs emanating from Nine Barrow Down. These streams, although easily crossed by travellers on foot or horseback, created a barrier to wheeled transport. They also meant this area was regularly shrouded in low lying mist.

The river was not very wide at Herston and the construction of a bridge was forever being discussed but it had never passed the point of proposals. Consequently, a tow-rope ferry operated at this point to provide the link for a well used roadway connecting the villages on the southern side with those of Ulwell and Studland across the water as well as the lodge itself, which nestled in the foothills of the downs.

It was just on mid-day when Nathan and his men arrived at Herston. Here there was a jetty with an A-frame hoist similar to those at Swanwich. There were some large stone blocks awaiting the next barge but there was no sign of any of the masons who had cut these stones or the labourers who had moved them here.

In fact, on first sight, the village seemed to be devoid of any human life but this was not the case. The workers were simply taking a break while they waited for a wagon loaded with more stones. This was about a mile off, coming slowly down the valley road, but was hidden in the mist. There was a distinct chill in the air and this had caused the workers to take refuge behind a small building on the end of the Jetty, where the road ran up to the river. They were huddled together out of the wind and out of view.

The building was Ferryman's House. Although grandly named, it was in fact the smallest cottage in the village. In front of it, on either side of the road, were two large capstans round which were wound the ropes to guide the ferry.

A simple device, operated the ferry. One rope attached to the portside end of the ferry was wound round the capstan. The rope then went back across the river where it was wrapped around another capstan. It then travelled back again until fastened to the other end of the ferry. Both capstans were well greased. This rope did nothing more than to ensure there was no drift downstream with the current.

A similar rope on the starboard side was not tied to the ferry. Instead, it passed through holes in stanchions set on both ends of the ferry, like eyes in a needle and, with its two ends woven together, this rope formed a continuous loop.

The ferryman would simply stand in the middle of the vessel, facing the direction he wished to go. By hauling on this rope with his feet firmly placed against raised struts in the deck, the ferry was propelled forward. It was hard labour and the ferryman had to have powerful arms and legs to carry out the operation.

Jack Mills was such a man, only just five feet tall he had an enormous barrel chest with arms and legs to match. He seemed to have been the ferryman here as long as people remembered and many wondered if another like him would be found when the job became too much for him. Perhaps, then the long discussed bridge would finally be built, as although there was a good road from Corfe to Herston Lodge along the north side of the valley, it was known that Lord Aldwin would like easier access to that part of his estate on the south side.

Mills, had been sat dosing on a wooden kitchen chair at the front of the house but now jumped up and welcomed his customers cheerfully. 'You'll be wanting use of the ferry I can see and in something of a hurry too, by the look of you,' he said.

It was the constable who answered him. 'That's right Jack, a big hurry,' Burt said. 'We're after a dangerous murderer and need to catch him before he harms any more people, I'll get my men to pull on the rope with you if it speeds things up. We'll settle the toll later on.'

While he was talking, Nathan and the others had been hurrying on to the ferry, which being large enough to accommodate two carts and four horses had plenty of room for them all. Burt and Mills brought up the rear and jumped aboard where upon Mills prepared to untie the mooring ropes. Behind them the stone workers had come out onto the road to see what all the excitement was about and Nathan saw an opportunity to swell his ranks. 'You men get on board the ferry,' he called. 'I'm going to need more men than I've got or he might slip through our fingers.'

The men did not move at first but simply looked around at each other some muttering in discontent but most seeking a leader to take up the responsibility of decision-making.

Reg Gaddie relieved them of their indecision by running back amongst them. 'You heard the Squire,' he shouted forcefully. 'Get moving now, lively with you! We'll square it away with your employers, don't worry about that, but this is King's business and takes priority.' Well used to handling and marshalling raw recruits, Reg gave off such an air of authority that the men stopped their grumbling and positively hurried onto the ferry.

Mills now unloosed the mooring cables. 'Pull away lads,' he shouted, 'As for the toll Mr Burt, that'll be no problem, settling later that is, I see Mr Eldine is with you and I know I can trust him.' This last was said with a cheery laugh to show that he was only teasing Burt. Then he moved to his mark on the deck and laid his hands to the task.

Although two men had been pulling on the rope, the ferryman's expertise was clear as they noticeably picked up speed and were jumping off on the other side in no time at all.

Reg Gaddie again took charge and he quickly began ordering the men to form a line and set off up the hill and over the ridge. Every fifty paces or so he would detail a man to drop off the group. Nathan took up his position on top of the ridge so that he was in touch with both sides of the line. Once all the men were in position, the chain they formed stretched for well over half a mile and, because this was barren windswept terrain with little shelter, their view covered the

175

whole panorama from the southerly riverbank to the coastline of Poole harbour.

There were few places that a fugitive could hide in this land. The ground undulated but any protection it gave would be removed as the line of searchers moved forward. Nathan signalled and the line began to move.

As they did so, Nathan began to worry about the likely success of this manhunt. He was afraid that he did not have enough men and that those he did have were too far apart. They might easily miss sighting their quarry. He worried too that it had taken a long time to travel here from Swanwich and then to set up the line, although, in fairness, it could not have been done quicker. Could Ridley have turned west and already broken through the line?

Then there was the possibility that Ridley had seen them move off upstream and had decided to retrace his steps, get back in the boat and return to the other bank where he could find plenty of hiding places. Nathan dismissed both these possibilities as unlikely.

He was banking on the fact that Ridley was a stranger to these parts and would not be aware that the land would be so inhospitable beyond the ridge or that he was heading to a promontory with no escape except by sea. It was important that they should catch up with their prey as soon as possible because if Ridley could get down to the area around Studland then he would be able to find plenty of cover among any of several copses that grew there or down in the bays where there were rocks and caves to give cover. On top of this, the weather was deteriorating and the beginnings of a mist was forming in the lower hollows.

Nathan was also concerned as to what might happen if they did unearth Ridley. He knew the man had two muskets, he had given them to Ridley himself, and with the men so far apart, Ridley could easily kill two of them and reload before the others could close in on him.

All these worries were misplaced, however, as what Nathan did not know was that Ridley's wound was debilitating him to the point where he could hardly keep moving.

Ahead of the hunt, Ridley had reached the brow of a hill where he collapsed to his knees. Lifting his head, he saw the land ahead of him fell away down to the sea about a mile off. Between him and the sea was bracken-infested heath land. This was Godlington Heath and, in the middle of this panorama, he saw the Aggle Stone.

This impressive rock formation had long been a source of awe. Standing alone on a small hill and shaped like an anvil balanced on another smaller rock, it stood some thirty feet high and weighed several hundred tons. Local legend claimed that the devil or a giant had thrown it from the nearby Isle of Whyte. When the Celts invaded these parts, they thought it was a menhir raised by early Britons and considered it to be a holy and dangerous place and they looked with fear upon the works of their predecessors. Later the Anglo Saxons arrived and they too saw it as a spiritual place, calling it the Helig, or holy stone, from which it derived its present name.

The origins of the Aggle Stone remain a mystery and it retains a feeling of unease for some as they look upon it but it was not fear that Ridley felt on seeing the rock. It was a haven where he could rest up out of sight. So with one last effort he pulled himself up and stumbled on down towards his goal.

The search line reached the edges of Godlington Heath late in the afternoon and the light was fading fast. The weather was deteriorating with a dank thin rain swirling around as the mist thickened, and Nathan's doubts increased. It was imperative that they reached their quarry soon.

The last part of the hunt had become more complicated as the down along which they had been advancing now encompassed a number of hollows before reforming as Ballard Down. The high headland that divided and overlooked both the bays of Swanwich and Studland. Keeping everything in sight had required careful control of the search line.

To maintain his place in the centre Nathan had to drop down into one of these hollows as the line swung round towards Studland before climbing out again. Coincidently, he crested the hill overlooking the heath in much the same place that Ridley had fallen to his knees earlier. As he did so, a cry went up from the man to his left, who now raised his rifle with both hands above his head. This was the prearranged sign to say the fugitive had been sighted and that the line should close up.

Nathan called down to the next man in the line and gave the same signal. Then he hurried to the man who had made the sighting and was the first to reach him. Reg Gaddie quickly followed him.

'Where is he then lad?' Reg asked.

'There, Sarge, under the rock, he's just sitting there. Not trying to hide or nothing but I'm sure it's our man,' the soldier replied.

'I see him,' Nathan said. 'It's odd that he's not bothering to conceal himself. Maybe he's tired of running. Still, we will take no chances. We'll wait for the others to get here before we approach him.'

Steadily, the rest of the party arrived and gathered around Nathan. 'Right men,' he said. 'You masons can go home now. We've found our quarry. Arresting him could be dangerous and that's down to me, the constable and the militia. So, off you go with my thanks. You can use my name if you have to explain yourselves or let me know if you need me to speak to anyone about this.' He turned back to the soldiers. 'We will spread out in a single line then move in, slowly encircling him,' he told them. 'Have your weapons ready but no one's to fire unless I command it or he starts shooting at us. Do you understand? I want to give him the chance to surrender.'

Under the directions of Sergeant Gaddie the men formed a wide circle around the stone before, keeping as low as possible, they closed in on the fugitive who remained unmoved - seemingly totally unaware of their presence.

In fact, Ridley had been watching the men approaching him for some time, ever since they had first crested the brow of the hill. At first, he had considered how best to defend himself against this challenge, checking his muskets to ensure they were both primed and ready to fire. Then he had tried to draw his sword from its scabbard but this movement invoked a searing pain in his wounded side. It was this that brought him to his senses as he realised he was in no condition to take on this fight. Anyway, he thought, I have no grudge with these men or any desire to harm them, especially not young Eldine, who has been so good to me.

Ridley had developed a strong liking for the genial young squire and felt sure this friendship was reciprocated. He did not want his last meaningful action in this life to be the murder of a friend or other innocent men for that matter, so he leaned back against the Aggle Stone and settled to await his fate.

At first he watched the men as they crept forward, smiling to himself at their unnecessary caution but slowly his mind wandered and he found himself thinking of Yorkshire and the peaceful farm in the dales where he had spent his boyhood.

His memory of the area was surprisingly vivid considering how many years he had been away from it. He realised that in some ways it was very similar to parts of Purbeck with its remote stone built farmhouses and a profusion of dry stone walls making a patchwork of the hills. The Yorkshire houses tended to be two storied, as many of the original crofts had been rebuilt, something that had not happened so much in Dorset where the traditional long farmhouses prevailed. This was probably due to the harsher climate of the North and the greater wear and tear on properties. Yorkshire stone was different too, being much greyer in appearance as it was granite rather than chalk based. Combined with the wetter clime it meant that Yorkshire could be a more foreboding place.

Mind you, Ridley thought, Purbeck can be a pretty dour place especially when the sea mist rolls in over the hills. It gives the place a very bleak veneer. That's when it is most like Yorkshire. Not that Yorkshire is always wet and grey. He argued with himself as he now recalled memories of summer months with village fetes and dances on the village green and evening walks up onto the hills overlooking the beautiful dales resplendent in sunshine. He recalled the joy of watching the shadow of a solitary cloud as it scampered across the scene below and the flashes of silver sun reflected from the winding river in the valley's belly. He used to fish in that river and had hoped to do so again.

How Ayala will love it, he thought, she'll find it cold at first, of course, but she will soon adjust to that and she'll be captivated by the strong minded but good natured Yorkshire folk. Then he gave out a loud anguished cry of despair as his mind returned to reality and he realised that Ayala was not going to be there and that he would probably never see Yorkshire again.

He was getting feverish from his wound and could not retain his thoughts, which were beginning to make no sense at all as his mind skipped about.

Now he was back in a Yorkshire market town although he could not distinguish which one. There were a number of stalls selling the usual commodities one finds at a country fare but, incongruously, there was Ayala standing at one. It was a stall selling Indian silks and Ayala was calling out to him from behind it. He was about to run to her when, from out of nowhere, a band of horsemen burst in on the scene.

They were Maharani Cavalry and they came charging down the street, calling out to Ayala that she did not belong here. 'Give yourself up,' they called. 'You have nowhere to go and to resist is useless.'

Ridley shook his head to rid himself of these thoughts. As he did so the call was repeated, only this time it was real and it was to him here at the Aggle Stone that the summons was made.

It took him a moment or two to realise that it was Eldine calling. Then he pulled himself back hard against the rock and, drawing his chest up he summoned the strength and clarity of mind to reply. Before he could answer, however, Nathan called again. 'Do you hear me, Jack? This is no way to end things, give yourself up. That way you will see your wife again and maybe we can sort something out of this mess.'

Ridley's heart was pounding. 'What do you mean?' he gasped. 'How can I see Ayala again?'

'As I said,' came the reply. 'We found her. She is alive and though she's been through a terrible ordeal, she is recovering well, except she's worried about you.'

There was a brief hiatus when all that could be heard was the sound of a slight breeze rustling the heather, swirling the low-lying mist that was creeping in. Eldine called out again. 'Come on Jack, there's a good fellow, tell me you will not harm anyone and we can all get back to Corfe, and your wife, tonight.'

Ridley was bewildered. He did not know what to think. Ayala was alive! Could it be true? Surely Eldine would not lie to him about such an important thing but how could she be? He began to feel terribly weak and empty.

He should be feeling elated at this news but all he could think was, what have I done? Was it all for nothing? Then pulling himself out of this latest trough of despair he at last answered Eldine. 'Come on in Captain, I'll harm no one, I have no strength or will to do so,' he called.

CHAPTER 20

They would not make Corfe that night for it was late evening by the time they returned to Swanwich. Despite the last throes of this Indian summer, the shortening of the days meant it had been dark for some time before their return, which had caused serious problems for the latter stages of their journey. Fortunately, two members of the militia carried simple portable oil burning lanterns for such emergencies enabling the party to make its way back without mishap, if somewhat slowly. Nor had Ridley's wound helped, as he had needed much assistance to complete the trek.

On arrival, they found Joshua White ensconced in the town's primitive lock-up. A small building tucked away in a courtyard behind the big house that acted as the Village Hall. The lock-up was little more than a stone shed with a heavy metal studded wooden door. The door housed the cell's only window, a barred hole, about eight inches square, cut at head height. Josh White was plaintively looking through this and on seeing Nathan, he started shouting for an explanation of his incarceration and claiming his innocence. Nathan ignored him and walked over to constable Burt, who had sat himself on a wooden bench to the side of the square, and was happily puffing on a clay pipe. A street light in the form of a burning torch attached to the wall behind him illuminated the scene.

Another man, who had been sitting there, was now standing, leaning over the constable, with his foot resting on the bench. This was Adam Carberry, the man the constable had left in charge of White. Carberry had not been guarding the prisoner so much as taking his ease after a long day. On seeing Nathan, Carberry removed his foot from the bench and stood upright like an old soldier making a report.

He told Nathan and the constable that Dr Small had tended White's wounds and given him laudanum for the pain but in truth there was little the doctor could do for White, whose condition was serious. So Carberry had locked the prisoner up to await the constable's return.

It was clearly not appropriate to put Ridley in the same cell so they took him to the small Methodist chapel where he was to be kept overnight, under suitable guard, although neither his condition nor his resolve was such as to encourage him to attempt an escape.

Once again the doctor had been sent for and Nathan and Gaddie, satisfied that there was nothing more they could do here for the moment, returned to the lock-up to question White.

There was just enough room in the cell for Nathan and Reg to stand over the captive who was now seated on a stone shelf running the length of the lock up. This was for prisoners to sleep on overnight. There was a bucket in the corner which gave off a strong smell of urine. It was not much of a prison but in truth it was mainly used to house the town's drunks, who would be released in the morning, usually thinking they would not want to spend another night there. A salutary lesson until the next time their thirst for alcohol overwhelmed their good sense.

More serious offenders might also spend a night there before they were marched off by the constable as soon as possible. They were usually taken to Wareham, a dominant Saxon walled town just outside of the region of Purbeck, which offered superior facilities for dealing with offenders.

Joshua White was weak and frightened. He was wearing the same clothes as when Nathan had interviewed him and his brother on the beach, only now his white jumper was heavily stained with blood. He made no more denials when accused of his crimes, especially as Nathan informed him that they had proof in the form of information and witnesses. In fact, this revelation caused him to breakdown completely and he was soon talking freely even though his every word condemned him to the gallows.

'It wasn't our plan to wreck the *Golden Nile*,' White began. 'We didn't even know it would be there. No! We are just landers really, we were expecting a lugger from France with brandy and stuff. That's why we got you out of the way. The beacon was to guide the skipper to Chapman's Cove, he would lie up outside the cove and the ship's boat was to be used to beach the cargo.

'I planned it with Cordone, that's the skipper, a week or so before. The beacon would not have misled him because he knew it was inland. The trouble was the weather broke and that awful storm blew up. We thought it unlikely that he would show. We didn't even know if he had left France but we thought we should light the beacon just in case he was out there somewhere. It took some lighting in that weather, but we got it going eventually.

'We'd just about given up when someone spotted a sail, naturally we thought it was our boat but as it got nearer we saw it was too big and that it had three masts. We watched it struggling out there for a time before I realised it was heading for our beacon. I told the lads what was happening and that they should hurry to put the fire out.' White looked up as if expecting to be disbelieved but Nathan said nothing.

'That's when Avery took over,' White said. 'He's a nasty piece of work, I should never have taken up with him. There's piracy in his blood. He's not from around here, he's from Cornwall, out of Falmouth, I think. Claims he's some sort of descendant of Henry Avery, the old pirate, even has a four striped chevron tattooed on his arm. That was Avery's flag, you know.'

'Keep to the point, man,' Gaddie grumbled.

'All right, you said you wanted to know everything, well I'm telling you everything. "Hold it," he says, Avery that is, "we can make some profit from tonight's work after all." Then he laid out his plan, how we should let the ship come on to the rocks then kill the crew and claim the salvage. I said I didn't like it. Smuggling was one thing but what he wanted to do was not my style. We argued for a bit but he won most of them over, then he said I didn't have to be part of the wrecking if I was too squeamish, I could go along with my brother and two others who were not keen on the idea. Our job would be to claim the salvage.'

'Who were these other two?' Gaddie interrupted.

'Roger Bowles and Matthew Trevellis. Trevellis was one of Avery's men and I think he was picked to keep an eye on us and make sure we did our bit,' White answered. 'We were to go to Swanwich and get our boat ready for sailing as soon as the weather broke,' he continued his tale. 'Avery said if we failed them, it would be the last thing we ever did and I knew he meant it. He's not one to cross I can tell you. I was glad to be out of there but I knew we were not free of the business.

'So that's what we did, for what it was worth. All those murders - and the cargo were not much to sing about. I reckon that's why he's killing us off. There was too little to share and he wants a bigger part of it. Either that or he's afraid someone will talk. Well I've done that now haven't I?'

Nathan and Gaddie had listened intently, without further interruption, but Gaddie, who had been writing notes as he listened, now spoke, 'You think it was Avery who killed your crew. That's possible, but it wasn't Avery who attacked you was it?'

'No I've never seen him before, he's probably some mate of Avery's from Cornwall, there are a few of them hereabouts,' White replied, hesitantly. He was obviously not convinced of the veracity of this.

Nathan, who had been meditating over every word, spoke, 'That certainly explains some of my questions about this case,' he said, 'but it doesn't get you off the hook, Josh White. You may not have been party to the killings but you are still in it up to your neck. Oh, you've got off lightly in the past but that was for smuggling. With the killing of the captain and his crew, there isn't a jury in the land that won't see you hanged. You're lucky that the woman you kidnapped didn't die as well, the way you left her in that cottage without treating her wounds or giving her food and water for two days. No, you'll get no sympathy from anyone this time.'

'I didn't know about the woman,' White claimed. 'Not till Tam told me the day after I'd spoken to you, I was horrified to hear they had her prisoner but Tam said it was all in hand and I shouldn't worry. He was supposed to look after her - and Peggy was there - I thought she'd be alright.'

'And what were you going to do with her even if she was alright, as you put it?' Gaddie roared at the prisoner. The anger in his voice even shocked Nathan. 'You couldn't set her free could you?' he said. 'No you would have to kill her eventually.'

'I didn't know what to do at first but then Avery suggested we give her to Cordone the next time he was here and he could do whatever he liked with her,' White whimpered. 'Avery reckoned he would use her for a bit and then sell her to some Arab slaver. That was the plan ..,' White lowered his voice as he spoke before trailing away altogether.

Speechless for a moment, Nathan finally shouted, 'My God, is there no end to this infamy!' then, controlling himself, he asked, 'So, where is this Avery to be found?'

White did not reply, instead he turned his head nervously from side to side as if he were expecting Avery to step out of the shadows at any moment.

'Come on man, tell us,' Gaddie said loudly and menacingly. 'You are finished anyway and you will suffer far worse at my hands than at Avery's if you don't.'

Then, to demonstrate that this was no idle threat, Gaddie grabbed White by the scruff of his collar pulled him up and punched him hard. Unwittingly, Gaddie landed the blow exactly where Ridley's sword had pierced.

White screamed. Gaddie released his grip and the prisoner sank back onto the stone. All colour had drained from his face. He wore a terrified expression as he gasped to catch his breath and moaned with the pain that was searing through his body.

Gaddie again took hold the prisoner's collar but before he could pull him up a second time White blurted out, 'Stop, don't hit me again, I'll tell, he's held up in the old stone workers caves near Tilley Whim. The ones they aren't working anymore. He's got one of his Cornish mates with him.' White was babbling now, as Gaddie had not relaxed his grip. 'The Cornish stick together,' he said. 'They are armed and they won't come easy, it'll take more than you two that's for sure.' Finally, Reg let go and White slumped back. Blood began to trickle from his mouth.

'That'll do Reg,' Nathan said. He was concerned that the prisoner's wound was bleeding again, not that he cared particularly and he had no qualms as to how Gaddie had extracted this last information. 'We will need to get the doctor to look at him again,' he said. 'We wouldn't to cheat the hangman.' These words were more prophetic than he realised, for Josh White was in a bad way. Bleeding internally, he would be dead before the night was out.

Nathan and Gaddie left the cell, locked the door and went out of the building into the fresh air. It was a cold and misty night by the sea's edge and they could taste the salt in the air. Even so, it was pleasant to be out of the gloomy cell and both men relaxed slightly as they felt the refreshing atmosphere.

They stood there in the small square behind the courthouse neither speaking but both deep in thought as to their next actions. Nathan was impressed as always by Sergeant Gaddie, he was a capable and efficient soldier, quick to pick up relevant points and instinctively knowing when to speak and when to keep quiet. He was sure the man had plenty to say but had the sense not to interrupt upon Nathan's own contemplations.

Eventually, Nathan spoke. 'If they are holed up in those tunnels, it will be hard work shifting them,' he said. 'We will have to move very carefully against them.'

'We could always wait them out,' Gaddie responded. 'They cannot stay down there without food.'

'No I need to get this over and done with.' Nathan was remembering his conversation with Armitage and the pressure he was under. 'You're right they cannot stay down there forever but they will have water, those workings are very damp. They could last for days without food and we don't know that they haven't got some food. We have surprise on our side. They don't know we are on to them yet and they are unlikely to go anywhere for now but once they realise we are, they might try and make a break for it at night. If they get past us without our seeing them we could be sitting there for days not knowing our quarry had fled.'

'True enough,' Gaddie concurred.

'We are going to have to flush them out,' Nathan continued. 'We will start at daybreak tomorrow.' He fell silent as he considered their options.

After a little while, he spoke again. 'First, we will go and arrest Bowles for his part in this affair, he doesn't know we are on to him so he should not be hard to find. Then we will gather your men and billet them down somewhere, we all need to get some rest for we are going to have an early start and a tough day tomorrow.

'You will need to get your men in place on the headland above the caves before the sun comes up. Tell them to move cautiously and not make any sounds that might alert Avery. I'll come to you in the morning with someone to guide us. Those tunnels are extensive and very disorientating when you are down there in the dark.'

In years to come, Nathan would often reflect on this decision and whether Armitage's words had caused him to act rashly, for casualties were to be suffered in the taking of Avery and his men.

Bowles was indeed easy to find he was in the Anchor Inn supping a pint of porter before retiring for the night and was completely taken by surprise when Nathan and Reg approached him.

'What can I do for you, Captain?' he said affably.

'I'm here to arrest you for your part in the wrecking of the *Golden Nile* and the murder of her crew,' Nathan said.

Bowles looked shocked at this. He fretfully looked around but realising he was cornered and that there was no escape, he clutched the table with both hands as if he were about to overturn it.

Then having had time to gather his wits he relaxed his grip and spoke confidently. 'You've got the wrong man, Captain,' he said. I was here in Swanwich, the night of the shipwreck, I was in this pub most of the night, ask anyone, they'll tell you. I know nothing of any wrecking or murders it was just a terrible disaster, one of life's tragedies as far as I know.'

'You are wasting your time and ours with your lies,' Reg said. 'We've got Josh White and he's told us everything, not that we didn't know already. Why do you think the captain impounded the cargo.'

Now Nathan leaned forward over Bowles and spoke quietly. 'I know you weren't there at the time, your role was to sail with White, discover the wreck and claim the salvage. But that doesn't make you any less guilty of this heinous crime and you will certainly hang for it.' He let this sink in before adding, 'You might have got away with it you know, if it hadn't been for the fact that your mates did not kill all the survivors.'

'You mean the woman, has she been found then?' Bowles was totally crestfallen now he knew the game was up. He didn't even stop to think that what he said was further evidence of his culpability.

'No I didn't mean the woman, although she has been found and will live,' Nathan told him. 'No, I was talking of her husband who also survived and told us of the wrecking. Unfortunately, he took the law into his own hands and its him that has been killing your gang. Still you won't have to worry about him now, the hangman will deal with you.'

To Nathan's surprise, Bowles actually looked happy to hear this. 'You mean it weren't Downley's ghost!, he said. 'I can rest easy then, he isn't out haunting us.'

The man was genuinely relieved that he was not going to be haunted to his grave and maybe beyond and seemed not to care that he was going to be hanged. Nathan could hardly credit such foolish but strong superstition. 'What do you mean?' he asked. 'Why would Downley be haunting you all?'

'I suppose it don't matter if you know - not now that is. We had a bit of a falling out last year over the value of some contraband we'd landed. Jack Downley reckoned White was getting more for it than he said and that we was all due a bit more. Tam Smith and Parksie took Whitey's side and an argument broke out and before the rest of us could intervene they was fighting. Downley got Tam on the ground but Parkes drew a blade and stabbed Downley.

'Well we had this large haul to move and we couldn't have you coming round asking questions so we had to get rid of the corpse. Trouble was we were afraid his missus might raise a hue and cry if he just went missing so Tam says we should put him on the highway rip his pockets and take his money and stuff. That way people would think he'd fallen foul of footpads and no questions would be asked.

'We left him on the Kingston road up by the old Saxon cross. I suppose you already know that. Then Parkes was killed in the very same spot we'd left Jack - well you can see why we was scared and then others started dying. But it weren't Jack after all so I won't be haunted in my grave.' Bowles fell silent without finishing his sentence.

'After the terrible crimes you've been party too I doubt you'll rest easy in your grave,' Reg said crossly.

'I can confess my sins to the priest and be forgiven, it says so in the bible but it would take an exorcism, or something like, to stop a ghost coming after my soul,' Bowles retorted almost happily.

'I'll never understand how people can believe such nonsense,' Nathan said quietly. Although he was not a religious man, he knew that, even in this enlightened age, it was not wise to openly question the existence of an afterlife for that could be construed as an attack on the church and its preaching.

'Take him to the lock-up Reg,' Nathan said. 'He can keep Josh White company. They can reflect on the stupidity of their actions together.'

Chapter 21

A clear sky heralded dawn the following day, with a blazing sun rising over the Solent to the east of Purbeck. Nathan wished it were otherwise. Taking these caves was going to be a difficult job and he had hoped there might be some sea mist or at least poor light to give cover to their approach. He need not have worried for, on his arrival, he found ten men under the command of Reg Gaddie, all ready in place at the designated meeting point - the headland that housed the Tilley Whim caves. They had arrived there before sunrise and, as far as Reg could tell, they had not been spotted.

The men were lying down behind what natural cover they could find in an arc formation, half encircling the path that led up from the caves below. Nathan too decided It was unlikely that the fugitives would be aware of their presence. The caves were half way down a three hundred foot cliff face where the land gave way to the sea and from which the soldiers were well out of view.

Even so, Reg had decided not to risk being observed should one of the fugitives decide to ascend the steep path, so he had told the men to lie down well back from the cliff edge. The men happily obeyed this order, welcoming the chance to rest. They had little sleep in order to get here before dawn and it had not been an easy journey from Swanwich across country in the dark. The bumpy undulating terrain was littered with animal burrows as well as manmade quarrs. The larger quarrs were not so bad being more easily recognised but some of the smaller ones, many only half started with discarded stone lying around were quite treacherous. Most of the men had taken a tumble at some point or another and there had been two cases of twisted ankles with the soldiers unable to carry on. Gaddie had told them to hunker down for what remained of the night and that he would get help to them later that day, once the arrests were made.

Everyone was impatient to get on with this business and they were all pleased to see Nathan arrive together with John Tilley a leading stonemason of the area. Nobody knew the exact connection this man had with the caves but it was presumed that they were named after a former relative of his.

It was known, however, that few people knew the caves better, for he had worked here for many years, some said both legitimately as a mason and illegally as a smuggler. For these were not natural caves but huge caverns created by centuries of men extracting stone which in recent years, at least, had been lowered down in large blocks to barges in the sea below for transporting to 'The Bankers' at Swanwich. There was a wide ledge half way up the cliff, which accommodated derricks, for lowering the stone. These were known locally as whims, which accounted for the other part of the name. At the back of the ledge were two rectangular portals, some ten feet high and six feet wide, marking the entrances to the vast caverns beyond.

No one was working The Whim at this time, as there had been a slight collapse in one of the caves. The owners were waiting for a shipment of timber, due any day now, in order to make the area safe so that excavating the stone could continue. John Tilley would be in charge of the shoring up party.

After the initial nods and introductions, it was Tilley who, in a broad Dorset drawl, spoke first. 'Thar be just two ways out of them caves,' he said. 'Up the path thar or through a tunnel that comes out on the coast path back at Durlston Head. If you gain me a couple of men, we can go back thar and flush 'em out. I know them tunnels and I can keep us behind cover so thar should be no chance of them harming us. You wait here with the rest of your men and arrest them as'n they come up. With us behind them they will surely realise the game is up.'

'Sounds like a good plan to me, Nathan answered. 'Only, these are seriously dangerous men, who may well put up a fight even though the odds are all against them. I'm assuming there are just the two of them as White said but for all we know this Avery character may have more men. So, I would be happier if you took more men with you, let's say four. Reg, you will lead the party. Mr Tilley will be your guide but from behind. He is a civilian after all and your first priority is to protect him. I don't want you taking any chances. If it proves too dangerous or there are more of them than we reckoned on, then you're to make a safe retreat, report back to me and we will reconsider our actions. Is that clear?'

Gaddie nodded his reply.

'Good, then pick three men but leave me Corporal Wallace,' Nathan continued. 'I will need a reliable man in charge of the arresting party.'

His ego boosted by this remark, Wallace had the confidence to add his thoughts.

'Excuse me Captain,' he said. 'I've heard that there are other ways out of Tilley Whim. People say it's a veritable maze and there are smugglers' paths that go well in land.'

'Thar be a number of tunnels leading off the main caverns, that's true,' John Tilley answered him. 'Few of 'em go very far, though. They've all been shored up so the miners don't get lost down thar. If any of 'em were ever used for smuggling, they bain't be now.'

'All right!' Nathan said. 'That settles the issue, we will go ahead as planned.'

So Reg, the three soldiers he had selected and John Tilley set off back the way Nathan had recently come, while he and the remaining members of the militia settled down to await their prey. Nathan hoped it would not be a long wait as he was worried that the men were already getting restless and he fretted in case the fugitives might be alerted before the trap could be sprung.

It was just before noon when voices were heard from below the cliff face and, in unison, the militiamen brought their rifles to their shoulders and pointed them at the pathway. The voices grew louder. The sound of boots scuffling on rock could also be heard. Then clearly Nathan heard Reg's voice. 'Hold your fire Captain, it's me, Reg,' he called. We've gone right through the caves and there's no one there I'm afraid.'

Nathan ordered his men to put up their rifles and there followed a comical moment as they all got up on to their feet. Several of the men had maintained the same position for some time. As a consequence some legs had gone to sleep and these men struggled to maintain their dignity as first they rose, causing them to give vent to shouts of surprise and drawing laughter from the other men. Nathan recognised that the men's humour was exaggerated by the release of

193

tension now that a fight was no longer imminent, so he allowed them time to settle down.

The merriment finally died down just as Reg Gaddie and John Tilley appeared over the crest quickly followed by the three soldiers.

'I'm sorry Cap'n, but the Sergeant spoke truly,' Tilley said as the two groups came together. 'We searched every passage way as we made our way through. Thar bain't be anyone down thar now but someone was thar - two of 'em, I'd say. Thar be clear signs that they was holed up for a couple of days, bits of discarded food and the like but I'd say they made their escape a couple of days ago, yesterday morn at the latest.'

Nathan looked at Reg Gaddie who simply nodded to confirm the mason's words. 'Well,' Nathan said, 'it seems there is nothing for us to do then. I don't suppose there is any chance we could track them, is there Reg?'

'No Captain, I had a look around at the base of this path but it's too well trodden to make out any fresh tracks. Anyway, we cannot be certain they left by this exit. It's a dead end I'm afraid, sir.' Reg was clearly deflated to be the bearer of such tidings especially so after the difficult night march.

Nathan too was deflated and he was reminded of his earlier night vigil and how that had been a fool's errand as well.

'Hum! What to do?' Nathan did not realise he spoke aloud as he considered his next move but nothing obvious came to mind. Reg recognised the signs and, knowing this question required no answer, said nothing.

After a while, Nathan spoke again, but this time in a commanding way, he had made a decision. 'Spread your men out, Reg, we will trawl the ground either side of the coastal path until we reach Winspit. Then if there is no sign of our quarry we will call it a day. It's a long shot I know but they have no reason to suspect that we are after them so they may have been careless and left some evidence of their route. Tell your men to keep a sharp eye out for any sign that they passed this way, even the smallest hint.'

'Very well, Captain,' Reg said, 'but if it's alright with you, I'll send Wallace and another man back to pick up our injured men and get them back to Langton. I doubt the men we are after will have strayed far from the coast path if they went in this direction so we will have plenty of men to check the ground.'

Reg's spirits had risen now that action was called for, even though like Nathan he held little hope of success.

'Yes of course Reg.' Turning to Tilley, Nathan said, 'Perhaps you would like to go with the Corporal, John, I'm afraid this has been a waste of your time but thank you all the same. We had to check the caves and, with your help, we have done that in half the time it would have taken us on our own. So your efforts have not been in vain.'

'Right you are, I'll do that. Good luck with your search,' Tilley said.

He, Wallace and one of the militiamen set off back towards Langton while the remaining party spread out and began walking west towards the headland known as Winspit.

Any other time Nathan would have loved this walk, especially on a day like this. The view was magnificent both ahead and behind. Miles of rolling countryside culminating in white cliff faces which gave way to the sea on their left. Today the sea was calm, a vivid blue close to the shoreline turning grey green as it got deeper with only the occasional white horse to be seen.

Being autumn the sun was not too high in the clear blue sky. So, while it gave a pleasant heat, it was not overpowering and with the sea breeze it was as well to keep a coat on. Trudging along with his head down looking for any clues, Nathan was deep in thought, and was slightly startled when Reg suddenly spoke loudly and with obvious pleasure.

'Now there's a sight to gladden the heart and make you proud to be English,' Reg said. He was pointing out to sea and following his guide Nathan saw four fully rigged ships of the line beating their way up the channel. They were indeed a magnificent sight, one not often seen since the peace and Nathan, recalling Armitage's words, wondered whether this was a sign of England's readying for war.

With his spirits lifted by this superb sight, Nathan returned to the business of searching for signs of their quarry but with less and less hope of success as they drew ever nearer to Winspit, where they would terminate their quest.

Before they reached this point they came across, Hugh Twomey, a local eccentric of unfathomable age. He seemed to everyone that knew him to be as old, or as young, as he always had been. All that was known for sure was that his working career was long behind him.

How he existed was also a mystery, there were always plenty of people happy to invite him in for a meal, which he would graciously accept. The odd thing was no one could ever seem to recall feeding him twice in any one year, so he was never considered a scrounger. He also had a knack of acquiring items of other people's discarded clothing just before his current raiment finally gave out.

Today, he was sporting several layers including a dark brown roll neck sweater, over which he wore a yellow corduroy waistcoat held together by the top button, the only one remaining. This was covered by a food stained royal blue tail coat that had clearly seen better days. His jodhpurs were cream coloured, originally, but now appeared as a very pale brown and had leather patches at the knees. Incongruously, these were tucked into an immaculate pair of riding boots, no doubt recently acquired from one of his wealthier benefactors, and the whole ensemble was topped off by a battered black stovepipe hat.

Hugh was a common sight up here with the cows. Being coastal there was always a high salt content to the rain that fell here and that, combined with the fact that the ground was rock based with little top soil, meant it was unsuitable for crops. As a result, most of the land, when not being quarried, was given over to grazing and, although unpaid for his efforts, Hugh loved to lend a hand at marshalling the cattle and bringing them in for milking. He always carried a stout cane for coaxing the cows along and he cheerily waved this at the party of soldiers and shouted at them.

This was no stranger to Nathan who, since childhood, had been aware of Hugh Twomey and the many stories he engendered. Nathan had met the old man on several occasions but had never mastered his broad accent. Once again Nathan could make no sense of what was said.

Not wishing to appear rude he called back, 'Hello there, Hugh. How does the world treat you, my friend?'

To his astonishment, the old man started agitatedly hopping about pointing his stick westwards along the coast path, accompanying these actions with the longest speech Nathan had ever heard him utter.

Whatever old Hugh was saying was a complete riddle to everyone except one soldier. Fortunately this young lad, who could be no more than seventeen, had no problem understanding the old man. The lad stepped forward. 'S'cuse me Cap'n,' he said. 'He says there are men in the priory, villains he reckons, and no doubt that's what brings us here. Sorry to speak out sir but Old Hugh's from Portland originally and he's a little hard to fathom when excited, unless you know their tongue, that is.'

'No, no need to apologise, it's Guillam isn't it?' Nathan said. 'You were with me the other night at the bay in Studland? This is news I need to hear and without you I wouldn't understand a word the old man says.'

With that the old man started up again and before he finished talking the lad began his translation 'He says there are three of them and they are heavily armed. One of them has been there several days, he got there soon after the shipwreck.' The boy broke off speaking.

He listened for a short time and then continued, 'Alice, I don't know who she is Captain, but she saw him there and went to help, thinking he must be a survivor but he shouted at her and drove her off.' Another pause, while the old man rattled on. 'The other two arrived yesterday, at least that's when Hugh saw them, they was on the path between Seacombe and Winspit and he watched them go on to the priory.'

'By the priory I presume they mean the old ruined chapel on St Aldhelm's Head,' Nathan said. 'Ask him what the men looked like?'

Again the old man spoke quickly in his unintelligible dialect.

Guillam listened intently then he translated, 'One of them was a big man dressed like an old pirate with a red tail coat and frilly shirt. He wore a pair of them leather roll top boots. He was armed - no sword as far as Hugh could see but he carried a musket and powder horn. Hugh can't really describe the other one except to say he was

197

smaller and had long hair, it seems the big man was so striking that Hugh hardly looked at his companion.'

Although he seemed to speak a foreign language to most of them, Hugh clearly understood what they said and was nodding his head in agreement as Guillam spoke. Now he interrupted and muttered a few words directly to Guillam. 'He does remember the smaller one had a very pock marked face,' Guillam said. 'One you don't like to look at straight that is and he thinks he had a musket too, though he's not sure on that.'

'Simon Trevellis had a pock face, do you remember Captain,' Reg Gaddie said. 'He was one of the dead men on the Langton road. Perhaps this is his brother Matthew, the man White spoke of.'

'Yes you could be right,' Nathan said. He turned back to Guillam. 'What about the man who was already in the Chapel? Does Hugh know what he was like and whether he was armed,' he asked.

Hugh understood this question and did not wait for Guillam before answering, 'Nay! I'm nare seen im.'

'I got that thanks Guillam,' Nathan said. 'Looks like we have found our quarry after all, Reg. Fall the men in and lets go and see the lie of the land.'

They had come across old Hugh in a small depression. Part of a fissure in the cliff face of Winspit. It was here that the path split in two. One route turning inland towards Worth and beyond to the village where Nathan's house was located, and the other continuing on as the coastal path.

They had expected to give up the search at this point. Intending to take the inland path but now it was the coastal route they took.

They quickly rose up out of the gulley so that they could see the coast line stretching out before them. It consisted of a series of headlands, their white cliffs towering over the ocean below but it was the broad headland they were on that was called St Aldhelm's Head. The ancient chapel standing solitary on the sea most point was clear to see. They set off purposefully. Marching at a quick pace now that the end of their pursuit was close.

As they drew nearer, Nathan realised that this was not going to be an easy proposition. If their prey had stayed in the caves at Tilley Whim it would have been relatively easy to take them. There, he had sent Reg and his party to ensure there was no retreat through the tunnels and to drive the fugitives out by the caves' main exits which he surrounded with the rest of his men, well protected behind the rocky outcrops. This meant that Avery and his men would have to give themselves up. Their only alternatives were to be shot down on the exposed ascent or to dive into the sea, where they would almost certainly have been dashed to death on the rocks.

St Aldhelm's Chapel presented much greater problems. For a start it stood alone on a headland, only reachable by crossing a large expanse of open land with no protection. A veritable killing ground.

The chapel, although in a state of collapse, boasted four crumbling, thick stone walls about six feet high at the highest points. The only entrance being a narrow doorway on the far side. The wooden door had long since disappeared. While the doorway had offered its monastic residents a fine view of the cliffs and the sea beyond, ideal for the contemplation of God's great works, it was hopeless for Nathan's needs. He needed to be able to fire into that doorway if he were to launch an attack but there was no safe route to any place from which to do so.

To call it a chapel was to flatter it, as it was only big enough to accommodate a few monks at prayer. It had no windows, as far as Nathan could see, but the roof had fallen in so that the occupants could stand on the collapsed stones and fire over the top of the walls at anyone attempting an approach. During the recent war Nathan had seen men attacking a small breech in a castle wall. The forlorn hope they were called and not without reason. The death toll of such an adventure was enormous even when there were only a few defenders.

With a forlorn hope the attackers literally sacrificed a large number of men by throwing them at the breech in the hope that a few lucky ones would get through. Sufficient to hold the gap long enough for the main army to advance through it. Nathan had been amazed that anyone would be prepared to do it but such was the glory and renown that awaited the survivors of a successful breech that men happily volunteered for the honour.

There would be no great glory or honours for storming this little refuge nor did Nathan want to sacrifice his men's lives on such folly. He did not know how well armed or prepared these fugitives were but he did know that he did not have enough men to risk storming the ruin even if he were willing to endanger his men so.

Reg, who had also been considering the problem, now stepped up and spoke quietly to Nathan.

'I know you said you wanted this over quickly but the sensible thing would be to lay siege. They can't stay in there forever. There is a problem with that of course, in that we don't have enough men to surround it from this distance nor can we move in much closer without getting shot, there being so little cover. When night comes, if there's no moonlight they could easily slip through our lines and be off without us knowing about it. Lots of ifs and maybes I'm afraid.'

'Yes you are right,' Nathan answered him. 'Too many ifs and maybes. I too was thinking about the night and wandering if we couldn't use the dark to move in closer. The trouble with that is it only needs one person to trip up or make a noise to start them shooting and before you know what's happening you're shooting at your own men in the confusion.

'I've seen it happen,' Nathan said. He was remembering a disastrous night action in the malaria infested swamps of Zealand. 'Men badly led by a foolish young officer looking for glory. No I'll not risk my men's lives if I can avoid it.'

'There is one thing we could try,' Reg said. 'Walter Coppock, is a crack shot. A poacher he was, and a good one before he went into the militia. These Dorset militia boys are all riflemen you know, they don't use muskets, they say their rifles are much more accurate and he's the best shot amongst them.'

'Yes, yes I know all about their rifles but what's on your mind.' It was unusual for Nathan to be so tetchy towards Gaddie, but he was both tired and on edge with the situation.

Reg ignored his captain's irascibility and calmly outlined the plan. 'If we distract them by appearing to advance down that slight trough there, Walter, Coppock that is, could creep round the other side and hopefully get in range. Then we could draw their fire by appearing to rush them. When they put their heads up to shoot at us, Walter can pick them off.'

Nathan studied the land. There was indeed a trough that ran down the hill towards the sea. It headed neither towards nor away from the ruin, simply skirting it, maintaining its distance. Initially, it was little more than a depression but it got deeper as it approached the cliffs until it was a deep gulley. It was never deep enough to hide them from sight of the old chapel but that did not matter as it was always out of musket range. They could safely march along this, distracting Avery and his men who were bound to wonder where they were going. Then, without dropping out of sight, they could turn scramble out of the gulley and make their pretend assault, hopefully, tempting the men inside to start shooting, so exposing their position to the marksman.

'It could work,' Nathan said as he considered the plan. 'The distraction part is easy enough and should work but what about Coppock? Can he find cover near enough and will he hit his target?'

'What about that pile of rocks, there?' Reg said pointing. 'That would do.'

Nathan looked in the direction Reg indicated and saw a stony outcrop. It looked unnatural, probably man made. It was covered with vegetation and must have been created a long time ago, maybe it was from a time when men had quarried the stone to build the chapel. Nathan gave no thought to this now, however. He was more concerned as to whether it would serve its purpose.

'It's in range and it would give Coppock enough cover,' he said. 'Whether it's near enough for him to get an accurate shot and whether he can get there without being seen is another matter.'

'As I said, he was a poacher so he knows all about moving stealthily,' Reg said. 'If anyone can do it, I reckon Walter can. Let's ask him.' Without waiting for a reply, he called the man over.

The plan explained, Walter studied the lie of the land, then he nodded saying, 'That won't be a problem, Sarge. They won't see me, especially if you're distracting them, and if they put their heads up I'll knock 'em off. You can be sure of that.' Then he sat down with his rifle in his lap carefully checking its every part.

'If this works,' Reg said, 'I won't have need of my rifle, so why don't you take it Walter. That way you will be able to get two shots off quickly without having to reload.'

'Right you are, Sarge,' Coppock said. He took Reg's rifle and gave it an equally thorough examination. While all this was happening,

Nathan had been studying the land and going over the plan in his head.

Now he was ready with the final touches. 'I want you to stay here, Reg,' he said. 'Where you can see what's happening. Once we get into that gulley, we won't be able to see Coppock, so you will have to signal to us when he's ready. We don't want to show our hand by going too early.' Then he turned to the old poacher. 'Walter, we are here to arrest these men and bring them to trial, which means you are only to shoot if they start shooting. It's a risk I know but it's one we will have to take.'

Reg would have preferred their roles to be reversed, thinking it wrong for the young squire too be exposing himself to enemy fire, but he knew the man too well to suggest it. There was no way Nathan would not be at the front of his men when they were facing danger. So Reg simply turned away and asked Coppock if he was ready.

Nathan called the men over, there were only seven of them now that Wallace and the other man had gone to attend the injured.

The young squire fell them in, had them shoulder arms and with as much pomp and ceremony as possible he marched them down the gulley, leaving just Reg and Walter lying on their stomachs. Once the detachment was under way, Walter began crawling forward, very surreptitiously.

The rocky outcrop now seemed a long way off to Reg who hoped the captain would not enter the gulley too quickly. If Avery and his men lost interest in the soldiers they might look back this way and see Walter who seemed very exposed to Reg's mind.

He need not have worried for Nathan too was keeping an eye on Walter's progress and realised he would have to allow him more time. About half way along the gulley, he called his unit to a halt and then he strode forward towards the Chapel. He stopped at a point he felt was still just out of range and stood legs apart with his hands on his hips studying the building, as if contemplating how to attack. When he felt he had used up sufficient time he returned to his men, called them to attention and then marched them off down the gulley. Just before they moved out of sight altogether, he again called them to a halt and ordered them to fix bayonets.

Reg chuckled at this fine flurry of activity and Nathan's ingenuity. He stopped chuckling when he looked for Walter. He was shocked to find there was no sign of the man. Reg studied the rocks again more intently and this time he caught sight of the old poacher who was well hidden amongst the stones but now with one hand raised to indicate he was ready. Reg acknowledged the sign and passed it on by waving his arm above his head. Then he sat back and watched as Nathan, followed by his men, clambered out of the gulley and began running towards the chapel.

At first all was quiet as the rushing soldiers narrowed the gap between them and their target. Reg swore, realising that Avery was no fool, and was holding his fire until the soldiers were well within range. Then just as it seemed nothing was going to happen, shots rang out from the stone walls and one of the militiamen fell to the ground, clutching at a wound in his leg. In the excitement a few of the militia fired their rifles but their shots bounced ineffectually off the stone walls.

Reg realised that Walter had not fired. What had gone wrong? Could he not see his target?

Worryingly, Nathan and the militia were still attacking and had a long way to go before they would reach the chapel. A second volley rang out from behind the walls and, almost simultaneously, Walter fired. This time two militia men fell, one lay there moaning from his wound the other lay still and lifeless. Before Reg could take this all in, Walter fired again.

Nathan and his remaining men were now only some twenty yards from the building when to everyone's surprise, a huge man, Avery, came rushing out at them. He had a musket in his hands which he was holding by the barrel and was waving above his head as if it were a club.

As the opponents came together he swung the club ferociously striking young Guillam a violent blow to the shoulder and sending him crashing to the ground. Then a shot rang out as one of the men, who had had the presence of mind not to fire before, now discharged his weapon.

The bullet hit Avery in the stomach sending him staggering backwards. The big man did not fall, however, but gathered himself up and started swinging his cudgel above his head once more. Before he could use it a second time, Nathan roared forward, throwing himself, shoulder first, into the man's chest. Nathan just bounced off, while Avery again staggered backwards. This time he did fall, going down on one knee, but once again he recovered his balance and readied himself for another attack. He was outnumbered, however, and before he could leap up to do any more damage a soldier hit him hard on the head with the butt of his rifle and as Avery slumped from this blow another soldier drove his bayonet into the big man's side.

'Belay that!' Nathan shouted. 'He's down and he's ours. I don't want him killed. I want this man to hang for everyone to see! Bind him up before he starts fighting again.'

There were now only three militiamen still standing and it took all of them to hold and bind the man as he did indeed try to resist.

Meanwhile, Nathan cautiously entered the chapel expecting to be fired upon at any moment. Instead he found the corpses of Avery's two companions. Both had the top of their heads shot away.

'Christ in Heaven!' Despite his experience of warfare, Nathan moaned with nausea at the sight. For several minutes he simply stood there trying to regain his composure. Feeling a presence behind him, he turned to see Reg Gaddie standing at the door.

'I've made a mess of this I'm afraid Reg,' Nathan said. 'Men wounded and the prisoners dead, I'd hoped not to have any casualties but I suppose that was wishful thinking. Your man, Coppock, certainly did his part. Took two of them out, blew their heads right off. They couldn't have known anything about it.

'I didn't mean us to rush them, we should have gone to ground after the first volley but the excitement of the moment just swept us on. It was incredibly exhilarating when they fired and you realised you hadn't been hit.'

Nathan fell silent. Reg had let him speak without interruption, recognising the young man's need to talk the exhilaration and horror out of his system.

Finally, Nathan spoke more rationally, 'I had best go and speak to the men, congratulate them on a good job, well done. I need to check the wounded too, I hope they are not badly hurt.'

'It's worse than that I'm afraid,' Reg finally spoke. 'Sterne's dead. Two others got flesh wounds, nothing serious, they'll soon be up and about, no doubt bragging of their feats of derring-do this day. Oh, and young Guillam has got a bit of a sore shoulder.'

'Oh Lord! Sterne dead!' Nathan anguished as he pictured the face of the soldier and remembered him as one of the men who had been there that night at the cove. It seemed a long time ago now. 'I thought it a good plan, the best we could have come up with anyway. I had hoped that Coppock would hit one of them before they fired and the other two would be so shocked they'd give up without a fight but Coppock didn't shoot, leastways not straight away. Why didn't he shoot?'

'He couldn't. You know what it's like in battle,' Reg sympathised. 'Nothing ever goes to plan. Coppock was in place alright but it seems he couldn't distinguish their exact positions, couldn't tell the difference between their heads and the stones. He had to wait till he saw the smoke from their volley to work out his targets. Before he could fire they dropped down, presumably to reload, but he'd seen enough. Soon as they came up again he fired killing the first one but the other two got their shots off. By then you were so close they could hardly miss.

'Walter had my rifle, as well as his own, so he was able to take a second shot almost immediately.' Reg said. 'It seems Avery ducked back down but the other fellow kept his head up, probably looking to see who'd shot his mate. A big mistake that was. Walter took him out easy like. I guess Avery knew he couldn't put his head up again, not after what happened to these two. So rather than be cornered in here he came out to face you.'

Nathan was only half listening to Gaddie's explanation as he was still anguishing over his decision and the price his men had paid. 'I should have thought this through more carefully. It was madness to take such a risk.' As he spoke, he wondered whether his foolish desire to placate Armitage had caused him to act so rashly.

'I disagree, sir,' Reg said firmly. 'If you don't mind me saying so. These were dangerous men and we've taken them with minimal casualties. It could have been a lot worse.'

'I lost a man, Reg. I'm not sure it was worth that.'

205

'You'll think better of it Captain when you remember how many people these men have killed,' Reg said. They did so without thinking. If we hadn't taken them who's to say what they might do next and how many more people they might have killed. They needed stopping. Sterne's life is a heavy cost I agree, but he was a soldier and a soldier's life is always precarious. We've done good work this day and we should be proud of it, not least because that makes Sterne's sacrifice an honourable one.'

'Maybe you are right at that, Reg,' Nathan concurred but with little enthusiasm. It would be some time before he could see today's events in that light. 'For now we had better see about tidying up here and getting Avery behind bars. All I seem to do these days is organise wagons for removing the dead. Do we know who these two are by the way?'

'One of them will be Matthew Trevellis, the brother of Simon that was killed at Finlay Copse. I don't know which it is though.' As he said this, Reg bent over the corpses, studying them. 'Even if he looked like his brother you couldn't recognise him in this light and with half his head blown off. I've no idea who the other is, I'm afraid. I do remember White said something about a Cornish friend of Avery's though.'

They walked out of the chapel. With the autumn sun low in the sky, it had been quite dark in there and Nathan blinked at the strong afternoon light. The two injured soldiers were sitting on the ground with Coppock, who was tying a bandage around the thigh of one of them. The prisoner was also seated, a little removed from this group, his arms and legs bound. The other militiamen were standing in a circle around Avery, leaning on their rifles joking about the day's events, with a couple puffing merrily on their clay pipes. Nathan was surprised, even shocked, to see that they had done nothing about Sterne, leaving him where he had fallen. 'I take it someone has at least made sure Sterne is dead,' he said crossly.

'Yes, I checked him,' Walter Coppock said getting up as he did so' 'He's dead alright and I'm very sorry Captain, that I did not shoot the bastards before they shot our Walter. I'm afraid I let you down, sir.'

'No, no you did not let anyone down. As a matter of fact I have never seen such fine shooting. No you did your job well. You all did.' Nathan raised his voice to include all the militiamen into his speech. He had been a little confused at first by Coppock's words but then he remembered the men talking earlier and that Sterne like Coppock was also christened Walter.

'Yes you all played your parts well and bravely,' he added. 'If anyone got things wrong it was me, my plan may have been a little hasty.' Remembering Reg's comments he added, 'Sterne's death, while tragic was not in vain. Because of it we have apprehended or killed three very serious villains and Purbeck is a better place for it. Well done men, well done, especially you Walter.' He was looking at Coppock as he said this and the man smiled gratefully at the intimacy of the squire's use of his given name.

'Right pleased with yourself aren't you!' Avery spoke loudly. He had a harsh grating voice. 'A good day's work killing two young men one barely eighteen and an innocent at that!'

'Oh and who might that be and what do you mean innocent?' Reg asked angrily. He kicked the prisoner for good measure. Then he said, 'We know one of them is Matthew Trevellis and that he was a party to the wrecking so he is as guilty as hell. Who the other one is and why he was here with you, shooting at us if he's so innocent, I don't know.'

'He was young Billy Wells and he only got here three days ago,' Avery snarled. 'So he had nothing to do with any crimes Josh White and his gang got up to. He only came to tell me my father had passed away. I know nothing about a wrecking and I don't believe you've got any proof that I do. We didn't know who you were, we was defending ourselves from attack, as is our right. There have been no end of killings around here lately. You should know all about that Squire. Isn't it your job to protect people from such? That's why we were hiding up here. Scared for our lives we was and waiting for things to calm down.'

'I'm sorry if young Wells was an innocent, though I very much doubt it. That's what happens when people get mixed up with trash like you,' Nathan rejoined. 'As to your cock and bull story and protestations of innocence, I've got all the proof I need to hang you. Including confessions from Josh White, Roger Bowles and Peggy Miles, the girl from Tam Smith's cottage. As well as that we have an eye witness to the events on the beach. You didn't kill all the survivors, you see and we have recovered the lady you kidnapped who will also testify against you. Do you still want to claim you are innocent?'

Now Avery looked shocked. He had been hiding out in the caves when all the killings had taken place and although he had heard news of them he had heard nothing of the arrests, so he was amazed at Nathan's knowledge and the case that had been put together.

At first he said nothing, then he sneered and spat at Nathan 'You bastard,' he shouted, 'you think you're clever but I'll get you, you bastard, you see I'll get you.'

It was an impressive outburst, made more threatening by the hideous condition of the man who seemed impervious to the wounds that had left his clothes blood soaked.

Triumphant and elated that this whole hideous affair was finally over, Nathan ignored these idiotic threats and turning away he started giving orders to clear the area.

'You leave that to me sir,' Reg said. 'Why don't you get off back to your home you've been on the go for days now. Time for a rest.'

'Yes, yes, perhaps you're right, Reg,' Nathan acquiesced. 'Get him stowed away in the lock up at Corfe, then get yourself a good night's rest. You can call on me tomorrow when we will get all the paper work tidied up.'

Nathan was only too happy to get away from this scene but he would not be going home just yet. There was plenty of time for him to go to Corfe and see Madeleine with whom he could express his feelings more freely and indulge in her gentle comforting. Besides, he needed to check that the constable had arrived with his prisoners.

CHAPTER 22

That evening, when Nathan reached the Court House at Corfe, he was surprised to find there was no sign of the constable or his prisoners. On leaving Swanwich, following the arrests, he had given orders for the constable to remove the three prisoners to the cells at Corfe. Burt was to await Nathan's return before taking White and Bowles on to Wareham. Ridley was to be allowed to remain in Corfe, for a few days at least, allowing him to visit his wife. Nathan had accepted the man's promise not to make any attempt to escape in recognition of this privilege.

The fact that Burt had not arrived was a little worrying. Although Nathan was not overly concerned, reasoning that any number of things may have caused the delay, he did resolve that he would send one of the militia to Swanwich later that evening to investigate the delay and to give the constable written orders. These were virtually the same as his earlier verbal instructions with a few minor additions, as well as advising the constable of the arrest of Avery. Reg and the militia would be arriving soon and, with all the arrests made, Nathan had intended to let them return to their barracks the following day. They could go via Wareham as support for the constable with his charges.

Now, he assumed that Burt would not be arriving until tomorrow afternoon at the earliest. He could not justify delaying the militia's return so he would need to find some other assistance for the constable. Burt would have four men in tow - White, Bowles, Avery and a wife beater who had been arrested by a court official two days ago. Having completed his orders for constable Burt, Nathan wrote a note for Roland Travis, the constable at Wareham. He then went to the livery stables, which also operated a post service, and sought out a rider whom he immediately despatched with the note.

He got back to the court house just as Reg and the militia arrived with their prisoner.

'Hello again, Captain!' Reg hailed him warmly, with a hint of surprise. 'I thought you were off home last time we spoke.'

'Yes I was but I remembered a few things I had to do,' Nathan rejoined. 'Then I found that Constable Burt hasn't shown. I expect there's a good reason for it but can you get young Guillam to go to Swanwich just to be sure. That's if he isn't too badly hurt. Fix him up with a horse from the livery. He can just about get there and back tonight. No need to bother me unless he returns with a serious problem. I've written some further orders for the constable that Guillam can deliver.'

While Nathan was talking he and Reg had entered the court house. Leaving the militiamen and Avery in the foyer of the building, they moved into the office and Nathan handed over the orders saying, 'Well I think that's everything, I'm sure you can manage from here Reg so this time I really will be off.'

'I can indeed, Sir,' Reg replied. 'You have a good night and don't worry about anything here.'

At last Nathan set off to catch a few moments with Madeleine. He doubted she would still be at Dr Palbrey's house but decided to pop his head in just in case. He was right, she was not there but he did see the doctor who was somewhat inebriated and more talkative than usual. They spoke of Mrs Ridley and the doctor professed some concern at the slow rate of her recovery and suggested this was aggravated by her mental state. Nathan told the doctor of the events that had occurred at Swanwich and how Jack Ridley would soon be coming to Corfe and visiting his wife. They both expressed the hope that this would help with the patients recovery and then after extensive pleasantries, Nathan was able to escape the doctor's company and resume his search for Madeleine.

He finally found her at her aunt's house. The aunt having welcomed Nathan warmly left the young couple in the lounge. After exchanging the latest turn of events they spent a relaxing evening gossiping away about all kinds of trivial matters. Eventually, propriety necessitated the Aunt's return and Nathan took his leave. The evening having progressed well into the late hours, he decided to lodge another night at the Bankes' Arms rather than to return home. He would need to be in Corfe tomorrow anyway, he reasoned.

The following day Madeleine went to visit Ayala, as she had done each day since the patient's arrival. Previously, Madeleine had visited early in the morning. Not wishing to over tax Ayala, who was still quite weak from her ordeal. She only stayed long enough to ensure all was well and to see if the patient required anything in the way of toiletries and the like. So far nothing had been needed and Molly was making a fine fist of her nursing duties, so much so that Ayala was showing clear signs of improvement on a daily basis. This day Madeleine arrived later than usual and was hopeful that the news of the Major's imminent arrival would have had a noticeable effect on her charge's condition. Feeling sure that Ayala would want to look her best for her husband, Madeleine had brought her own essential travelling companion - a cosmetic box containing all manner of powders, rouges and perfumed waters.

Mr gamble opened the door for her and she fairly flounced into the spacious hallway, where she was surprised to find Dr Palbrey and Molly in deep and serious discussion at the foot of the staircase.

The doctor broke off from this conversation and turned to greet Madeleine. 'My dear Miss Armitage,' he said. 'I am so pleased to see you, You come not a moment too soon. It is so good of you to donate so much of your time to this poor unfortunate lady. Alas all your efforts are in vain it seems for she has had something of a relapse I'm afraid. She has gone right back into her shell and doesn't even acknowledge young Molly here, who was getting on so well with her.'

'But what could have caused this?' Madeleine said. 'Hasn't she been told her husband arrives in Corfe today?' She was perplexed. The wind taken completely out of her sails.

'Molly and I were just discussing it,' the doctor said. 'Last night she was positively bubbling over with excitement. Captain Eldine informed me of the arrangements for the constable to bring Major Ridley to Corfe and that the Major, under strict parole, will be allowed to visit his wife. Well this was indeed good news, it would have to be handled carefully of course but I could see no way that such good tidings could have any but beneficial effects upon the patient. I wasted no time in passing the news on and as I say it proved to be a wonderful fillip to the lady's recovery. Until this morning, that is. The recovery was short lived, I'm afraid. All progress was undone as Mrs Ridley realised her husband was soon to be hanged!'

'What!' Madeleine, who was normally a calm and placid person, shocked both the doctor and Molly as this news prompted her violent response.

'Who on earth told her such a thing,' Madeleine said. 'As far as I am aware, there is no certainty that Major Ridley will hang. Why, he hasn't even been charged with a crime as yet. Regardless of that - that anyone would be so inconsiderate, stupid even, to tell the poor woman such a thing in her condition is absolutely disgraceful.'

'I agree my dear,' the doctor said, waving his hands in a calming motion. 'The fact is, nobody told her. Unfortunately she heard Mrs Gamble and our maid, Alice, gossiping. I have spoken to them about it and I have their assurance they will speak no more of this. Gossip is a terrible thing. Before you know it the whole town is talking and the man is as good as hanged before he has had a trial even.

'In truth I may have exaggerated things regarding the lady's condition. There is no knowing how much she heard as she does not speak of it but it was sufficient for her condition to deteriorate. It may only be temporary but for the moment she seems to have lost all her fight. It is not surprising when you think about it, her whole world has been thrown into chaos. Worse than that, it has been destroyed and at a time when she finds herself in a foreign land with no family or friends to comfort her. Then when a small light appears on the horizon, she overhears a conversation which diminishes even that small hope. I fear she may lose the will to live altogether. You can see why she will need the most attentive kindness in her nursing.'

Internally, Madeleine was still fuming with anger, the doctor may have chastised his servants for gossiping but who had told them of the latest events. It could only have been the doctor himself. Little was to be gained from loitering on this, so Madeleine controlling her ire, turned to Molly. 'This is most unfortunate as the doctor says,' she said as calmly as she could. 'We must do our best to get Mrs Ridley back on the road to recovery. Much will depend on you Molly my dear, you must behave as if nothing untoward has happened and under no circumstances must you speak of the Major's troubles.

'When he visits his wife you will need to make sure that he knows not to mention them either. I will try to get word to him to that effect but you must make sure that my warning has been delivered. In the meantime just act naturally when you are with her. Can you do that, Molly?' Madeleine spoke soothingly. She could see the girl was clearly agitated.

Molly was more than agitated she was distraught. It was when the doctor spoke of Jack and the fact that he was to hang that her mind was set racing. She was desperate to think of some way to save him. She had grasped at one glimmer of hope, when Miss Armitage had said it was not certain that he would hang but the reality of the situation overwhelmed this prospect and threw her back into the depths of despair.

Until now Molly had been coping well. She had put all thoughts of her love for Jack and their affair out of her mind and had thrown herself into her nursing duties with great enthusiasm. So much so that even Ayala had noticed, telling Molly that she did not need to clean everything quite so thoroughly nor so often.

She had then urged Molly to sit and read to her from a romantic novel borrowed from Dr Palbrey. This might have been an embarrassing ordeal, given Molly's poor reading skills, had it not been for Ayala's weak condition. As it was, the patient hardly noticed Molly's laboured efforts, for as soon as Molly started reading Ayala's eyelids would drop and she would slip in and out of sleep. So obvious was the soothing nature of the exercise that Molly soon stopped reading from the book and simply prattled away with anything that came into her head.

These activities had helped Molly come to terms with her disappointment but now talk of Jack's return and his potential hanging had brought all her wretched emotions back and she felt quite overwhelmed. It was as much as she could do to acknowledge Madeleine's instructions as she muttered between three deep gasping sobs, 'Yes, ma'am, I understand.'

Not for the first time, Dr Palbrey was surprised by her reaction. He studied the girl but was completely at a loss to fathom why she was prone to these belts of unprompted crying. He decided she must be a little simple, although he had to admit she had proved to be an excellent nurse.

Abandoning any hope of understanding, he turned to Madeleine. 'So my dear,' he said, 'now that you know the situation perhaps you would like to see the patient for yourself.'

CHAPTER 23

It is approximately fifteen miles to walk from Swanwich to Wareham. Little of it is on the flat, so a constable with prisoners in tow can take the best part of a day to accomplish it. Especially when he is partial to a stop off for a refreshing ale at several of the hostelries he passes on the way and allowing for a bite to eat at one of them. Half way through autumn the days are getting quite short so the journey must be started early and a good pace maintained if walking in the dark is to be avoided.

William Burt had made the trip many times during his career as a constable of Purbeck. The route, often referred to as The Constable's Walk, was fairly straight forward. On leaving Swanwich, the road to Langton Matravers climbed steadily, passing the village of Herston snuggling in the valley below. The path continued to rise steadily all the way to Kingston. This stretch of the route was also known as Priests Way on account of the fact that the friars from the Chapelry at Kingston used the road to visit the various villages to preach. The constable would not stop at the Ship Inn at Langton, having only just started his journey. He did stop at Kingston, however, to slake the fine thirst he had worked up on the long climb.

Normally, he would not give his prisoners a drink but would manacle them to the village pump so that they could take on some water should they wish. He would then sup his ale, sitting in the stable yard at the back of the inn, looking down on the village and ruins of Corfe Castle below. The place he chose to sit not only gave him a superb panoramic view of Purbeck and beyond but also meant that his prisoners at the pump were in clear view.

On this occasion he made an exception. He had two prisoners in tow and one of these he shackled to the pump as usual. This was Bowles, who he was taking to Wareham. Sometimes prisoners were tried at the courthouse in Corfe Castle and Squire Eldine was one of the magistrates that would officiate. These court rooms were not always in operation. They were used mainly for civil disputes, which could wait to be heard at the quarterly sessions. Unless one of these

215

sessions was imminent it was not appropriate for criminal offenders to be held over for trial. Consequently such prisoners were sent on to Wareham, where there was a resident Judge to dispense swift justice.

The other captive was Jack Ridley who was not bound and who, due to special dispensation from Captain Eldine, would be taken to Dr Palbrey's house to visit his wife. After which, he was to be held in the cells of the courtroom at Corfe, awaiting further instructions from the captain.

Until such instructions were forthcoming, Ridley was on parole. His cell door would not be locked and he could visit his wife freely provided he returned to the cell before dusk each night. The prisoner had given his word that he would not attempt an escape. Burt knew that parole given by one gentleman officer to another was considered sacrosanct and that no gentleman would ever break it. So he reasoned, If the man's word is good enough for the captain, then it's good enough for me.

Consequently, he had not manacled Ridley and they had walked side by side along the route. Bowles had trailed behind with his shackled hands attached to a leash held by the constable. Despite this favourable treatment, Ridley had remained downcast and they had spoken little.

Like all those who knew the circumstances, Burt had much sympathy for the one time soldier and decided not to leave him at the pump. Instead he invited Ridley to join him in the garden and to partake of a glass of ale. An offer Ridley gladly accepted although he insisted on paying for the beers and it was Burt's turn to happily acquiesce. They sat in silence. Ridley being a victim of his despondency, had nothing to say while Burt, normally a cheerful and garrulous individual, recognised the signs of a tortured soul and did not know what to say.

They did not sit for long. Partly because their beer attracted the attention of wasps, drowsy in the autumn sun. The constable waved these away muttering 'Damn jaspers!' More important was the fact that Burt had to get to Wareham and he still had another two prisoners to collect from the Corfe lock-up. These were the Cornish man, Avery, and a wife beater who had gone too far this time to be ignored. This was George Fancy, who Burt knew to be an unpleasant man - difficult not to offend at the best of times. The second half of his journey from Corfe Castle to Stourbridge and the across the bridge to Wareham was going to be more perilous and far less pleasant than the first.

Although he had not been present at the arrest of Avery, Burt had heard all about it from young Guillam, the militiaman sent to Swanwich with fresh orders. Those orders asked the constable to obtain a parole from Major Ridley and outlined the conditions for his treatment and subsequent detention at Corfe provided the parole was given.

It was not unusual for Burt to accompany a number of prisoners on his walk and he rarely had cause for concern. Mostly they were petty criminals who would not have the nerve to take on a constable. When really violent criminals were being escorted, he might take a deputy constable along or even a small detail of the militia. He had not considered such precautions when he left Swanwich with just Bowles and the Major. Now, as the prison party descended the hill towards Corfe Castle, he was becoming more and more apprehensive. Burt recalled Guillam's description of Avery and the desperate struggle that had led to his capture. Naturally the young militia man, who was nursing a sore arm, had exaggerated the details of the struggle in order to make his own part more heroic.

The constable gripped the handle of the truncheon that was hanging from his belt and its sturdiness raised his morale slightly. Even so, he remained a little nervous and wondered whether he would be wise to seek backing when he got to Corfe Castle. He knew from the new orders that he would now have three serious villains in tow. Bowles and Avery were undoubtedly gallows bound and desperate enough to try anything. The constable had no qualms about handling Bowles on his own. He was a slippery character but no fighter. The two of them might be a different matter and there was no knowing whose side Fancy would come down on if there was a confrontation. The wife beater was a sturdy fellow who had already spent two nights under lock and key and would no doubt be feeling much aggrieved.

Burt had intended making this journey the day before but Josh White had died in his cell at Swanwich. This meant he had lost a day, making arrangements for the disposal of the body - tidying up loose ends and preparing the necessary paper work.

217

Of course, had White not died, there would have been three detainees for Burt to take to Corfe and four on to Wareham. In that case, especially with one of them being as dangerous as White, the constable would have arranged for a deputy, at least, to accompany him. No good worrying about that now, he thought, I'll cross those bridges when I come to them.

When he arrived at the Court House, his worries dissipated as he found Nathan and the constable from Wareham waiting for him. The two constables were well acquainted, having made the next part of the journey together on numerous occasions.

'I expect you and Constable Travis here, would like some lunch before you continue,' Nathan said after the initial exchange of greetings.

'Thar be nice,' said Travis. He was of similar build to constable Burt, if a little stouter, and clearly enjoyed his food. Unlike Burt, Travis's uniform fitted him perfectly, a consequence of the fact that his wife was a fine seamstress. Even so, standing here, side by side, they looked more like a comedy duo one might see on the stage rather than a real pair of law enforcers. Nathan knew differently. He was well acquainted with both men and knew them to be extremely efficient and a lot more nimble than their physiques might belie.

'I arranged for constable Travis to come to Corfe,' Nathan explained. 'I thought you might appreciate his company, given the character of your charges, especially Avery, whom you've yet to meet. When you did not arrive, yesterday, I had no idea what had caused the delay or whether there was a serious problem behind it. Is there? I see you haven't got White with you.'

'No, Mr Eldine, sir,' Burt said. 'He died of his wounds the night before last. Sorting it all out delayed me I'm afraid, so that it was too late to set out yesterday.'

Burt stood as erect as he was able as he delivered this formal report. 'I'm sorry it meant I was not able to follow your orders, sir, but I did start out first thing today, Mr Eldine.'

'Died did he?' Nathan said in a reassuring tone. 'Well I cannot say I'm too sorry to hear that. It will save the courts and the hangman a job. I did not realise he was so badly injured. The doctor implied he would pull through and I naturally assumed that to be the case. As to my orders, I think you have carried them out perfectly, Will. Yes most efficient given the change of circumstance, I would say.'

'Thank you, Mr Eldine, sir,' Burt said. 'You are right about the doctor, he was as surprised as anyone, sir. We called him back when Whitey took a turn for the worse. The doc looked at the wound and said he couldn't understand why it was still bleeding. Said he'd done all he could and we'd just have to wait and see. Well, we didn't have to wait long. Whitey just slipped away.'

Nathan recalled Reg Gaddie's rough interrogation of Josh White but decided there was no point in mentioning it. 'Well let's lock Bowles up,' he said. 'Then I'll take the Major to his wife and you can get that bite to eat. When you're done you will find Corporal Wallace and another lad at the Bankes' Arms, I kept them back to help you and Travis here. I know you are quite capable of escorting three prisoners to Wareham but these are a pretty desperate bunch and I wasn't sure what problems you had run into. So I hope you won't feel offended?'

'No, not at all Mr Eldine, sir, the more the merrier,' Burt said. Far from being offended, he was very relieved.

Nathan considered the other two men in the courtroom who had been standing just inside the door. Bowles, heavily manacled, looked surly but said nothing. Ridley, on the other hand, free of any restraints, stood upright and alert. He did not look happy but he did look attentive.

'Well Jack, this is a sorry mess,' Nathan said sadly, 'I'm delighted the doctor did not lose you as well. I trust your wounds are healing satisfactorily but to what end I don't know. Anyway, enough of that for now. I expect you want to go and see your wife. One happy thing to do at least.'

'Yes... yes please,' Ridley replied, animated for the first time.

Nathan knew that this was the second time Ridley had incurred serious injury and yet as on the first occasion he seemed to have made a swift recovery. His demeanour was such that it was hard to imagine that he was suffering at all although in truth he must have been in great pain. Once again Nathan warmed to this man. On impulse, he put his arm around Ridley's shoulder and the two men left the room, looking for all the world like two old friends reunited.

219

CHAPTER 24

Nearly three weeks had passed since the wrecking and in that time Nathan had been all over the Purbeck peninsula as he pieced together the various episodes of this story. He had been away from his home considerably for the first fourteen nights, grabbing lodgings wherever he could. Apart from the one night he had spent at the Armitage's he had slept fitfully in strange beds, twice at Dr Palbrey's house and once at the Stockwell's. On other nights he had hunkered down in whatever hostelry was appropriate, twice sleeping rough. The first time, when he had waited for the non-existent smugglers at the cove, seemed a very long time ago. The second occasion was the night before the taking of Avery, when he had billeted down with Reg and his men in the stables at Swanwich. He had not stayed there long, however, having to leave early to fetch John Tilley from Kingston, as their guide to the caves.

He had lost count of the times he had travelled the road between the villages of Swanwich and Corfe Castle. Finally, three days ago, with the arrests made and the prisoners delivered, his travels had come to a halt and he was at last able to return to his home and a well earned rest. He had arrived at his lodge at around mid-day and after a light meal he had moped around his house, too exhausted to achieve anything useful. Supper came and went and he retired early. Despite his tiredness he did not sleep well, going over and over the events of the preceding days. The next day he had little more energy than before and spent another fruitless day. Thankfully, he had fallen into a deep sleep the following night and had woken this morning feeling much refreshed.

He knew he should get on with the business of compiling his report, which would be needed in Wareham in order that the trials of Avery and Bowles could get under way. Something was causing him to delay this report and he knew what it was. It was Jack Ridley and his part in this affair. The man had been the victim of such a terrible crime and had suffered so much horror and anguish that Nathan was having difficulty in coming to terms with punishing Ridley for the retribution he had reeked.

Nathan knew that what Ridley had done was against the law and could not be tolerated in a civilised society but was it more than any man worth his salt would have done given the circumstances? As well as this, Nathan had a powerful liking for the man. A strong bond of friendship had developed quite naturally between them.

So Nathan prevaricated.

He tried several times to make a start but the knowledge that once the report was written and despatched there was no going back, caused him to fail to put pen to paper.

Ridley had given his promise and was on parole, enjoying a few days with his wife, who, once again, was recuperating well. The report would put an end to that. Nathan might even be in trouble himself for being so lenient with the prisoner, although he gave this thought little attention. He was not the sort of person that would let his own interests interfere with his actions, he was more concerned that he did the decent thing.

He was also concerned that he did his duty to the best of his ability. Reconciling these two positions was what was troubling him. Frustrated, he decided to leave the report one more day and to enjoy this day by visiting Madeleine. I've been charging about, non-stop, for two weeks now, surely I have the right to a couple of days off, he justified.

Gloomily, he realised that visiting Madeleine meant he would almost certainly have to meet Armitage who was bound to want to hear the whole story and the content of Nathan's report. In truth, Armitage had no right to demand such knowledge but he seemed to believe that the posterity of Purbeck, if not the whole of East Dorset, was dependent upon him as his Lordship's steward. As such, Armitage considered it his right to know all the ins and outs of events within this land he governed. Nathan knew this not to be the case and was well aware of the man's self aggrandisement but he had no wish to antagonise his future father-in-law.

He decided instead to go initially to Corfe Castle, there he would check that Ridley was sticking to his word and that all was well at the Palbrey House. With luck, he reasoned, Madeleine will be visiting the patient as well, and I can spend some time with her, without going to the Manor House. If not, at the very least the ride to Corfe will give me time to reflect on the situation and maybe I will find some way of resolving these issues.

To his great delight and relief, Madeleine was at the doctor's house. She was still staying with her aunt so that she could visit Ayala on a daily basis. She had been on such a visit when Jack Ridley arrived to see his wife. According to his parole he was free to come and go as he wished provided that he returned to the cell when he was not with his wife. He had given his word on this and was unaccompanied when he arrived. Because Ayala was still weak, Dr Palbrey had recommended that these visits be no longer than two hours so as not to over excite her. As hard as it was to be apart from her now that she had been returned, Ridley was as rigid in his obedience of the doctor's orders as he was with the terms of his parole, heading straight back to his cell directly his visiting hours were over.

He might easily have dawdled back, enjoying the delightful village on his way, especially as the young squire had ensured that Ridley's actions had not been made public. Jack Ridley was not the kind of man to do that. He had given his word and that was unconditional in his mind.

When Ridley arrived Madeleine made the normal pleasantries before tactfully withdrawing as she appreciated how important this little time together must be for the couple.

This was around the same time that Nathan arrived in Corfe. He first visited the Court House, which was empty. He realised this meant that Ridley must be with his wife. Had Nathan been aware of the doctor's limit on visiting hours, he too might have respected the couple's privacy and settled down to await Ridley's return. As it was he went straight off to the doctor's house. He was received by Gamble who advised him that the Major was indeed with Mrs Ridley and asked whether the squire would care to wait for him in the parlour.

'Miss Armitage is there at the moment,' Gamble said, 'but I'm sure she will be agreeable to your company.'

'Miss Armitage, in the parlour? That's wonderful! I mean it saves me a trip out to the manor, don't you know?' Nathan was flushed, having reacted so eagerly in front of a servant.

'Quite so, sir,' Gamble said, with the slightest hint of disapproval as he directed Nathan to the appropriate door.

'Nathaniel, my dear, how lovely. I was beginning to think you were avoiding me,' Madeleine, rising from a sofa, teased Nathan as he entered the room.

'Not at all my darling, I simply needed a little time to catch up on things. Although I was not aware you would be here,' he explained. 'I was just calling in to check everything was alright before going to the Manor to see you. As it is, perhaps we can go somewhere to talk, somewhere we could get a coffee or a tea if you would prefer.'

'Tea would be nice, although we do not have to go out for it, Madeleine replied. 'Mrs Gamble will bring us a pot, I'm sure. Then we can sit here and have a nice chat. We won't be disturbed. Major Ridley is with his wife, he'll be with her for another hour at least. I suggest you leave them till then, it's the only time they have together each day. Dr Palbrey is quite adamant on that. He says too much excitement is bad for his patient. Personally, I think the Major's visits are doing her a world of good, she seems much livelier after each visit and is recovering remarkably quickly. She is a very strong and determined lady.' As she spoke, Madeleine pecked Nathan on the cheek and then walked over to a bell rope. She pulled this before returning to sit on the sofa where she encouraged Nathan to sit with her.

'The Doctor is on his rounds,' she said. 'What that means I am not sure. He goes out each day for about three hours, returning just as the Major is leaving. I had no idea there were so many sick people in the village to require so much of his time. Mind you his breath does smell of sherry when he returns, so perhaps it is not all work.' Madeleine sported an impish smile. 'Oh, and Molly is out and about too. So you see we will not be disturbed. At which point the young maid Alice knocked and entered the room.

'Was there something you wanted ma'am?' she asked.

Madeleine instructed her to fetch tea for them, then once the girl had left Nathan, picking up the conversation said 'Ah, Molly, yes I have been wondering about her. How is she bearing up?'

'Molly is fine!' Madeleine said. 'She has accepted the situation and is slowly getting over the hurt. Time will see her through. She found it hard the first time Major Ridley and his wife were together and had to leave the room to cover her emotions. Now she knows the time of his visits and she takes herself out for the duration. I think Ayala, Mrs Ridley that is, has noticed this and is aware something is amiss. She's no fool, but I do not think she has realised exactly what is behind Molly's behaviour.'

'And what of the patient?' Nathan now asked. 'You say she is recovering quickly but what does that mean? Is she up and about? How quickly will she be able to travel? And most important of all, does she know what trouble her husband is in and if so how has she taken it?'

'Dear, dear, Nathaniel! So many questions and no simple answers, I'm afraid,' Madeleine interjected. She considered all the questions carefully, before continuing. 'She is up and about as you put it, today for the first time she actually got dressed. Prior to that, she has been getting up to do her toiletries but then returning to bed. Actually for the first two days she hardly did that. Molly had to wash her down with a sponge and coax her to take care of herself in other ways. Each day has seen an improvement. When Major Ridley turned up the progress was much more rapid.'

At that there was a knock on the door and Alice entered with a tea tray which she set down on a side table next to Madeleine, who thanked her and told her she would not be needed to serve. Nathan waited patiently for Madeleine to do this and pass him a cup before he took up the conversation again.

'Got dressed did she, not in that awful black dress I found her in, I hope?' Nathan was once again negligent with the truth and his role in dressing Ayala. He was more concerned about her progress, the stronger she got the weaker his excuse for delaying Ridley's full incarceration.

Madeleine noticed a slight discomfort in his attitude when he spoke of discovering Ayala and her condition but she let it pass. 'No, no,' she said. 'Clothes are no problem, Mrs Ridley and I are quite similar in size, so I have lent her some of my things. They will do for the time being, not having to fit perfectly but, obviously, she will feel much better, when she has some clothes of her own.

'As for the situation with regard the Major, her behaviour is strange to say the least. She apparently overheard the servants talking and we thought from this that she was aware of the dire straits he is in. Her condition deteriorated a lot at the time. Now, however, she acts as if she has no such knowledge. Whether this is because she has accepted her husband's assurances that all is well or whether she is pretending for his sake, I do not know. He has told her that he only visits for two hours each day because of her condition, which is true to some extent, and she presumes he is staying in some lodgings in town. He has done nothing to dissuade her of this notion. Mainly because Dr Palbrey said it was better she did not know the truth until she had made a full recovery.'

Madeleine paused to sip some tea. After a few sips, she put her cup down, and took up her account. 'The Doctor believes that she has shut her mind to the gossip she heard. He cannot say how she would respond to the terrible news should the truth be broken to her. He says she might go into a great despondency even to the extent that she could lose her will to live. He has seen such things before, where the patient has just slipped away.'

'No wonder Jack has chosen to say nothing to her,' Nathan interposed.

'Exactly,' Madeleine said, 'but she knows all is not right, I think she feels he should have been happier at their reunion, she senses he is holding something back but she does not seem to know what it is. If she did overhear the gossip, then it seems she does not comprehend how bad things are.'

Nathan pondered all this quietly. He had to make his report soon and Ridley would have to be sent to Wareham to stand trial. He could not delay the report much longer. He could delay sending Ridley to Wareham but only briefly. Once the report was submitted, questions would be asked. If Nathan still did not hand Ridley over the authorities would send men to fetch him. It would also be seen as a blot on Nathan's record but this did not concern him. Too many

225

people had died of late and he did not want anymore innocents to do so. He was quite prepared to suffer the consequences as he thought his actions would give this woman longer to recuperate from her terrible ordeal. She would have to recover fully if she was to face the worse tribulations yet to come.

What to do? Nathan's head was reeling with confusion. Is the Doctor right? Could such news really bring about her death? Can I take that risk? If not, does that justify delaying my report? There's no doubt she will have to be told of her husband's arrest once the report is made and he is whisked off to prison. All these questions assailed Nathan but no answers presented themselves.

Madeleine looking at her lover's face saw the anguish there, her heart went out to him and she wondered what she could do to comfort him.

'Something is troubling you, darling, what is it?' she asked.

'Jack Ridley,' he replied. 'I cannot help thinking I should let him go. They say the law is an ass and I have never really paid much attention to the saying. I think we usually assume it implies the law is foolish but it is not that. I realise now that it means the law is immovable like an ass. You cannot just bend it to suit your needs or individual cases. Otherwise it becomes no law at all. You cannot say that an act performed by one man is a crime, while the same act performed by another man is not a crime because the circumstances are different. Magistrates can vary the punishment according to those circumstances but only within the boundaries as laid down by the law.

'Jack Ridley is a good man upon whom terrible deeds have been committed but in taking revenge he has broken the law. He is in fact a murderer and should come to book for it. In all my different roles it is my duty to see that he does. There is no doubt that he will be found guilty and the most lenient sentence the law would allow would be a life sentence. The trouble is I cannot accept that he deserves that. I am not sure if I would have acted any differently than he did, who would? So how can I justify ending his freedom, maybe even his life. I really don't know what to make of it.

'I have to resolve this soon or it will be taken out of my hands. As well as that, your father is pressing me for an end to this affair. He sent me a note, saying he could not understand the delay in bringing charges now that I have all the culprits under lock and key. He says such dithering is not good for the county's reputation and it does me no credit and demands that I explain myself. A damn cheek actually and if he wasn't your father and my prospective father-in-law, I'd tell him so. As it is, it's just another reason why I need to make a decision soon. Now you tell me that Jack's arrest could damage his wife's chances of recovery or even kill her. I just do not know what to do for the best.'

'You have turned a blind eye in the past, for lesser crimes I know, could you not do so again?' Madeleine asked.

'There's a world of difference between smuggling small amounts of contraband and killing half a dozen men,' he replied.

'Even so, Jack Ridley is not the only good man,' Madeleine said gently. 'You are too, and you should have faith in yourself. Trust your conscience. If it's telling you to let him go, then perhaps you should. I have every faith in you Nathaniel. I'm sure you will make the right decision and find a way to make it happen.'

Madeleine's words were well chosen, her expression of faith in him, pleased Nathan and he felt a lifting of the gloom that had ensnared him.

'Maybe you are right, at that,' he said. 'I shall have to consider carefully how I might resolve this.'

He kissed Madeleine on the cheek. 'But I must resolve it quickly,' he added. 'This matter must be put to bed before long. Then perhaps you and I can spend some more time together, free of all these worries.'

'That would be nice,' Madeleine concurred. 'However, I fear we may not have many days to enjoy ourselves if my father is right. He was at Auntie's house last night and he told us he has received disturbing news from London. It seems that the French have invaded Switzerland and Father thinks that we may be at war any day now. If that happens, considering all the responsibilities you take on, you may well be in much demand and will no doubt have little time for me,' she chided him. 'If war is to come, you may choose to take that into account when deliberating Mr Ridley's future,' she added. Without further explanation, she changed the subject. 'As for now, his visiting time is over, I heard him leaving a few minutes ago, so I will go and sit with Mrs Ridley until Molly returns, she may be making a good recovery but she still needs care and attention.'

Returning his kiss and without waiting for a reply, Madeleine left the room.

Nathan, pondered her words for a moment then smiled as comprehension dawned. 'You clever woman!' he said aloud and purposefully made his own departure.

He hurried out of the house and headed back to the courthouse. On entering he made his way to the lock-up where a young clerk of the court, who was doubling up as jailor, showed him to the cells.

The door to the small cell was open. Inside, Ridley was sitting on a bunk with his back to a wall but he stood up smartly as Nathan entered. Before he could speak the young squire ushered him to sit down and then sat on the bunk next to him.

'This is a damnable affair Jack,' Nathan said. 'You have set me a puzzle of that there is no doubt. I cannot condone what you have done, there must be law and order, and that cannot be if we allow people to settle their own disputes. The trouble is I sympathise with you and how you must have felt and I even understand what you have done. Obviously, I cannot possibly comprehend the full strength of your anguish and the force that must have driven you but, however deep that force was, it does not excuse you or your actions.'

Ridley made to speak but Nathan held up his hand to silence him.

'I could argue that you have done us a service by ridding us of this scum,' Nathan said. 'They were only fit for the hangman's noose anyway, but as a civilised society we cannot tolerate vigilante justice which means I cannot let you go unpunished. It is a dilemma. You are a good man Jack Ridley and it does not seem right that you should end up on the gallows because of these villains.

'I have been pondering this for a day or two, I thought of sending you to the colonies but now another resolution presents itself. In my soldiering days I spent much of my time in the company of non-rankers. They were a fearsome lot. Many of them being absolute villains before they joined the army. Indeed, it seems that was why many of them were actually in the army. They had been found guilty of some crime or other and the judge had given them a choice - hang or fight for your country! Well now I give you that choice.

'It appears Napoleon has broken the treaty yet again, news has arrived that he has now invaded Switzerland and I have it on good authority that we will not stand idly by this time. War, it seems, is inevitable.'

Nathan was both right and wrong in this. The annexing of Switzerland was not the trigger as he supposed. War did come but not until spring the next year.

'This being so, England will need all the best soldiers it can muster,' Nathan continued. 'If you've demonstrated one thing these last few days, it's that you are an incredibly efficient soldier. So, I have decided to offer you the chance to enlist in the army, go to war for your country and if, when the war is over, you have survived, then you will be free to return to your wife in Yorkshire. I am taking a great chance on this and I must have your word that you will not do a Napoleon and renege on me.'

Ridley who had remained silent throughout this liturgy did not answer immediately he simply stared at Nathan.

Eventually, he gave a rueful smile. 'It is you that is the good man, Nathan,' he said. 'I appreciate how difficult I have made your life these past days. I am truly sorry for that. When I thought they had killed my wife I lost all reason. All that mattered was revenge. It drove me with a coldness I have never experienced before. I had no doubts as to my actions, no remorse and no conscience.

'When you told me that Ayala was alive, I was dumbfounded, I did not know how I felt. Delighted that she was alive, of course, but disappointed that I had not killed them all. Slowly reason returned and with it despair, as I realised what my actions meant. Ayala was safe but I had lost her again as I would surely hang for my crimes.

'Now, you offer me a lifeline and I take it gladly. You have my word. I will not let you down. I have a reason for living and I will survive this war.'

'That is decided then,' Nathan said. 'My report to the County Sheriff, will say that these men killed themselves in a falling out over the division of their meagre spoils. Armitage will like that, as it will tidy it all up into one event. Less of a blot on his precious Purbeck.

Avery and Bowles will no doubt dispute this at the trial but given their terrible crimes, they will get no sympathy and will not be believed. There will be some who will know the truth but I cannot think any of them will doubt the justice of my decision. So I think we can be assured that this will be the end of the matter.

'As for you, Jack, I have friends in the military and I am sure I will be able to get you a commission at a suitable rank. It will take a few days to sort but you can leave that to me. In the meantime, you and your wife can be my guests at the lodge. It will give you a chance to sort out your affairs as well as some time together before you have to depart.'

Nathan was finally content that this dreadful episode was over and he was pleased with the outcome.

'Oh by the way,' he said. 'While I was investigating this affair I came upon some information that solved another outstanding crime. It seems it was Parkes, who killed and robbed a certain Jack Downley last year. By an amazing coincidence it was at the exact same spot that you killed Parkes.'

Unexpectedly, for the first time for a long time, Jack Ridley laughed.

'Jack! Jack Downley! That explains it. Parkes didn't know my name. When he called me Jack, he thought I was Downley's ghost!'

The end

ACKNOWLEDGEMENTS

My sincerest thanks are due to my son Matthew, and my good friends David Hart and David Peters. They all gave me great support and advice and without their encouragement this book would have remained a retirement hobby and would probably never have been finished. Particular thanks to David Peters for reading the book, more than once, in manuscript form.

AUTHOR'S NOTE

People:
This is of course a work of fiction and for the most part the characters in it are fictional although many of the surnames used are familiar in the Isle of Purbeck. There are some exceptions, however, where actual historical figures are mentioned. Mary Burt for example really did exist and did indeed walk the fifty miles or so to fetch the preacher, John Wesley. *(Source 'Mary who went for a walk'. A leaflet available from The Methodist Church in Swanage)*. I have used the same surname for my constable who of course is entirely fictitious. However, the name Burt was and remains widespread in the area. One man who rose to particular prominence in the area was George Burt (1816–1894). His father Robert was a stone and coal merchant whose business was located in Swanage around the time of this book. Initially, George worked in local quarries until in 1835 he moved to London to join his uncle John Mowlem's stone business, becoming a partner in 1844. George, like his uncle, maintained an interest in Swanage. He established gas and waterworks and lived in a large house called 'Purbeck House', now a hotel, on the main street. The Swanage suburb of Durlston was conceived and developed by him. However it was never completed, part of the land originally intended for the development is now Durlston Country Park. Many architecturally interesting buildings and monuments were scavenged as a result of the company's construction work on prestigious projects in London, and re-erected by Burt in Swanage and Durlston. The 1670 porch for the Mercers' Hall now adorns Swanage town hall, and a clock tower commemorating the Duke of Wellington which once stood at the Southwark end of London Bridge is now a feature of Swanage seafront.

The Isaac Gulliver gang known as the White Wigs were a notorious band of smugglers towards the end of the eighteenth century and the lander Roger Ridout was one them. Isaac Gulliver, himself, was known as 'the king of smugglers' as his operation was enormous. He was at one time running twenty-two tuggers off the Dorset Coast from Poole in the East to Lyme Regis in the West. Also known as 'the gentle smuggler', because he never killed a man, his career came to an end in 1782 when he accepted the King's pardon, which was offered to counter the enormous harm smuggling was doing to the economy. (My source for this is the website *'The Dorset Page'* where more information on Gulliver can be found). As far as I know there is no Peer of the Realm called Lord Aldwin, nor has anyone of that name ever owned Estates in Purbeck.

It is well documented that the stonemason and builder, Thomas Hardy (father of Thomas, the great Author and Poet) was suspected of being a lander or at best a receiver of smuggled goods, although he was never prosecuted as such. Nor is there any evidence that he knew Ridout or that either of them ever went to Swanage. As for Avery, the 'big man's' claim to have been a descendant of Henry Avery is pure story-telling. There was a great Cornish pirate called Henry Avery who operated in the Atlantic at the end of the seventeenth century and he did indeed fly the flag of a white chevron on a black background but I have no knowledge as to whether or not he had any offspring. Bonaparte, Pitt, Addington and Fox were, of course, genuine people and I am indebted to *Arthur Bryant and his history 'The Years of Endurance'* for my descriptions of their attitudes and actions as well as for the general ambience of the nation at that time.

One individual needs special mention and that is Reginald Gaddie. I based this character on the grandfather I never knew. My mother's father that is, Reginald Frederick Gaddie, who died in 1918 when his ship HMS *Raglan* was sunk in the Dardanelles by an enemy torpedo. The description of Reg in the book is based on photographs and memories of my grandmother speaking of him as a gentle unassuming hero.

Places:
I have mostly used present day place names: The exceptions being Swanage and the Isle of Wight, where I have preferred historical spellings as being more distinctive. There is an area called Holme, containing the villages of East and West Holme but both the village and Nathan's estate of Holme Matravers are fictional. I have referred to the various drinking establishments by their current names.

Although they all date back to that time, what they were called then I do not know. Nor can I say whether they resembled my description or were more like the pubs of today.

The Bankes Arms, does indeed take its name from the noble family whose ancestors held the castle against Cromwell's forces. A fact that is readily available in much of the tourist material for the area. Also well documented are the King's various visits to Dorset, the first of which was so eagerly anticipated by the Armitages.

Early maps show that there was a river mouth at Swanage and that this was navigable by barges and shallow draft vessels well in land. The maps give scant detail as to what the area was like before the Georgians and then the Victorians discovered it as a seaside retreat. Nearly all of the present day town was built well after the time of this story. The village at that time being entirely on the south side of the river. The newly built, Georgian Mansion on the sea front is still there, having been, a private residence, an hotel and, as it is today, private apartments.

The Victorians in particular brought about a great deal of change. They rechanneled the river by piping much of it underground and they built sluice gates to control the flow, which negated the need for the flood reservoir described here. They also built the present day lower road and eventually the railway. I can only surmise as to what it would have been like before this and my descriptions are as such imaginary, including Jack Mills's ferry. Parts of the original village of Swanage can still be found - little on the sea front but further to the back of town. A war memorial now stands in what was the town centre where the village pump used to be and the overnight lock-up, though no longer in use, can still be found in the yard behind the current Town Hall.

The Agglestone Rock on Godlingston Heath has collapsed somewhat now but remains an impressive sight. While the small chapel on St Aldhelm's Head has had an opposite fate. It was first restored and re-roofed in the late nineteenth century and opened in 1874 for regular weekly church services for coastguards and their families. It was further restored in the 1960s and subsequently declared a scheduled monument. Church services are now held on Sundays throughout July and August.

234

Wrecking:
It seems there is little evidence to suggest that the intentional wrecking of ships was a regular activity, if it happened at all. For the reasons discussed in the book this would have been a much too risky adventure and there was no way of forecasting the weather or the circumstances, making it virtually impossible to prepare for the event. Popular fiction writers take much of the blame for spreading this myth as it made for a good yarn. The more realistic but equally murderous activity was the taking advantage of a naturally wrecked ship by unscrupulous villains who, in order to claim the salvage rights, might ensure there were no survivors! Even this was very rare, as the vast majority of coastal dwellers would risk life and limb to aid survivors of wrecks and Dorset folk have proved to be no exception to this over the years. A tradition that is so proudly maintained today by the men and women who volunteer their services to the RNLI and the National Coastwatch Institute working in cooperation with Her Majesty's Coastguard

Printed in Great Britain
by Amazon